D0099828

Darkness
and the
Deep

OTHER BOOKS
BY VARDIS FISHER

THE VRIDAR HUNTER TETRALOGY

Comprising IN TRAGIC LIFE,

PASSIONS SPIN THE PLOT, WE ARE BETRAYED,

and NO VILLAIN NEED BE

CHILDREN OF GOD • DARK BRIDWELL

APRIL • TOILERS OF THE HILLS

NEUROTIC NIGHTINGALE

SONNETS TO AN IMAGINARY MADONNA

FORGIVE US OUR VIRTUES

CITY OF ILLUSION

DARKNESS AND THE DEEP

BY VARDIS FISHER

1 9 43

The CAXTON PRINTERS, Ltd.
CALDWELL, IDAHO
and
THE VANGUARD PRESS
NEW YORK

The DeLuxe edition of DARKNESS AND THE DEEP is limited to 100 signed and numbered copies of which this is

Number 84.

Vardis Fisher

Manufactured in the U. S. A. by H. Wolff, New York

TO INTELLIGENCE,

quite naturally,

this book that commemorates

its humble beginnings

Darkness
and the
Deep

BACKDROP

UPON the geography of space, there are no boundaries where all is infinite, nor age where time is only the measure of change within the changeless, nor death where life is the indestructible pulse of energy in the hot and the cold. There is no morning or noon or evening for what has always been and will always be. There has been no beginning and there can be no end. But there is and has been and will always be that continuous change in the appearance of things which, in the small catalog of finite perceptions, is known as birth and growth, evolution and progress, age and death.

There in the illimitable, countless millions of years ago, occurred one of those stupendous explosive births that rearrange the destinies of the suns. One of the smaller suns, a white-hot incandescent chaos, with its surface flowing away in vast streamers and tails, burst under the antagonism of its elements, and hurled upon darkness its broad sheets of flame. Mammoth scarves of white light and great wings of fire were flung out of anarchy and far into the cold deep darkness; and there journeyed in their own wild and erratic rhythms, came together and coalesced in flaming embrace, and revolved and sped down an orbit of their own. Shot too far from the parent light ever to be drawn home again, yet not far enough to escape the laws of its stellar path and its guidance, scattered fields of light came together in torn and seething spheres and swung upon irregular orbits around the star they had left.

And thus a world was born.

Not all the gaseous elements spilled from the parent came within the circumference of this world. And there were other worlds, other planets-to-be, within this system. Smaller fires also, thrown far beyond the sun and close to the worlds, and held in suspension by the pull of the two, moved down paths of their own. These millions of smaller fires were the scattered fragments of a new solar order, and most of them were to be as useless and as extravagantly wasteful as the pieces of granite chipped off by a sculptor and thrown away. After cooling, after becoming small wandering nuggets of iron and stone, most of these fragments would in time go back to the sun, or back to the earth, streaking down through the atmosphere as "falling stars"; and the largest of them, circling around the new worlds, would become their moons.

Thus a world was born, but not in a moment or in a million years. The new planets, white-hot from birth, a group of convulsed conflagrations, would spin for ages in erratic uncertainty round their orbits before coming within the poise of fixed behavior. Other suns would fling other fires into darkness, other worlds would be born, while among these planets our planet would slowly cool, would shrink from a cometlike fog to a mass of boiling stone, would change in color from white to golden, from pink to red, and would darken at last to gray as the liquid surface hardened and a sheath of hot stone enveloped the furnace of its core.

Round and round its path went this world, our world, at first a white fire with a wake of flaming tongues; and then an irregular sphere of seething elements, slowly cooling upon its journey and drawing its circumference closer to its heart. Like a rampant and distorted outlaw from chaos, it followed no charted course on the stellar ocean, but shortened its elliptic when yielding to the homeward pull of its sun, or lengthened it when, frenzied and wild and almost free, it sought to escape. For it was a delirious runaway upon the prairies of the infinite. It swayed and dipped as if the molten ballast of its equator alternately poured in a flood from pole to pole. It revolved swiftly in its journeying, with the brilliant day upon its surface, or the faintly shadowed night, fleeing with the minutes.

But all the while this headlong world was seeking the immutable laws that were to govern it; and with every turn of its body, with every cycle like a lone headlight in darkness round its solar path, it lost a little of its erratic waywardness and settled more securely to the harmonies running in its being. Because even from the moment of its explosive beginning, its waywardness was only apparent, only the flush of ecstasy in a new birth and a new morning. It was only the exuberance intrinsic in those universal laws that plant the seed of rose and nightingale in the astral fields of flame.

This new world was not lawless, and seemed to be so only in the impetuous eagerness with which it sought its laws; nor was it dead. It was a vibrantly living thing in every part of its flame. It was a thing of elements, and some of them are called iron and copper, carbon and gold; but all these were life, having been so always and destined to be so forever. In all of these was the primal pulse out of which the heart has come; in all of them were the energy and rhythms and harmonies which were their only substance, and the only substance of all things that are.

This was a living world, but a very simple world of elements in an incandescent dance; and then, after a long time, it was a quieter world in the firmer cohesion of its seething masses; and eventually it was to be much quieter still as its wild ecstasies moved in the orderly patterns of change and growth. In it, from the moment of its birth, and even beyond then to the infinite non-beginning, there had been the soul of all that it was destined to be. In it, indeed, pulsingly insentient, hungrily unaware, were all the various and undeveloped forms of its being, including the highest of them all, the man that was to come.

But this living world, so violent in its eagerness, so immeasurably swift in its dance, so superficially chaotic in its form and movement, also had deep within it the patience of time and change. A million journeys around its sun were only a finite moment in the infinite forever of its existence. A hundred million times around its path, a hundred million of those change cycles called years, found it still a white-hot pilgrim; for impatience is only a superstition of the finite. Its gaseous body was condensed to a liquid, its surface was roughly rounded across its hemispheres and poles. There was no nervous and fretful haste, there were no mutations, within the inflexible laws that swung it round its orbit, and shaped and prepared it as a birthplace of more complex forms of life.

Within the finite, where birth and death, youth and age, are words used to denote changes in the appearance of things, this world was a new world; but within the infinite it was neither new nor old. Its energy had always been. In times without number it had changed its form. It had been a part of other suns, of other worlds; it had been a part of the cradles of sentient life and the homes of civilizations, and it had also been a part of the graveyards of these. Nothing had been destroyed and nothing had been lost. If, in the universal cycles of change, there is stored in the heritage of what has been the germ of nobler things to be, then this new planet was flung upon a greater destiny than any it had lived before; but if progress is only a conjecture of human vanity and hope, if it is only a mirage of light in the inscrutable darkness that houses the mind, then this planet was thrown out only to fulfill another cycle that is meaningless to human thought. It may be that all the changes through which it had come, this sphere of gas, this shining new world, had endowed and enriched it and made it potentially the home of a more complex life; or it may be that there was no evolution in its dance from change to change, but only the endless manifestations of its energy upon the illimitable and the changeless.

If that is so, this story will chronicle only a part of another cycle that is essentially no different from countless cycles that have gone before. If, on the other hand, the conjecture of hope is also an intuitive and unerring reach toward certainty, then this is the story of a change that was built upon former changes; that brought from those changes its own heritage of beauty and intelligence; and that, in turn, when its cycle is done, will add something precious, even though very small, to another civilization on another world.

The insatiable hunger of human striving would have it so. The price we have paid for a little beauty and a little good will would have it so. The long pilgrimage out of darkness toward light, out of slime toward the cathedrals of the soul, declares not only that nothing is lost but that something is gained from each cycle of sensate things through birth and age and sleep. Being what we are by no will of our own, by no wisdom or no ignorance that is ours, in that feeble hope we must find our meaning and our destiny, or there must be only the folly and futility of creatures driven by universal laws to seek, and denied by those laws the eventual goal.

If we are only the blind driven down to the seas, it would be a senseless pain to look back upon the dark and bloody trail which we have followed. If beyond our perishing in our present form, when our earth shall have finished its cycle, and shall have had its cold stone drawn back to the incandescent womb —if, then, all that was best in us shall become part of another world in another time, using not the pettiness of our personality but the stuff of our dreams, we can believe that nothing we have suffered has been in vain. If this is so, then a look backward upon our path becomes an adventure in self-discovery which the intelligence of man owes to his spirit, and the dark and brutal past becomes a searchlight that we can turn upon the future.

This is the story of this, our world, and of us, its tenants, journeying through darkness and the deep.

Time is the finite measurement of change. For a longer time than we have power to grasp, the new world fled around its sun and changed only from a gas to a liquid with a hardening crust. Under the crust its elements boiled in intense heat and from time to time erupted, blowing enormous segments of crust away and spouting great volcanoes out of the red fires within. After another long while, the new world was clothed with a dense atmosphere of hot fog and rain; and hot rain continuously fell upon the blanket of cloud; and no sunlight broke through to touch the surface. The rotation of the earth caused extremes of density in the atmosphere, and mighty winds, in consequence, plowed through the fog-blanket and opened deep valleys in the clouds. Great winds, far up, cooled the water vapors, and rain poured in a deluge; but it was vaporized again before reaching the hot earth and rolled upward in oceans of steam. These were the terrible primeval winds within which our wildest tornado would be only a fitful breath.

There, too, were the primeval storms, with thunder like the crashing of planets in the engulfing fogs, and with lightning bursting in immense white sheets that covered hemispheres. The steaming blanket enveloping the earth was a thin ocean from pole to pole; because there was suspended, between the world and its sky, the major part of all the water that was eventually to make the seas. On the tumultuous upper masses sunlight fell; but under the blinding surface there was utter darkness, the hot thick darkness of a new world's envelope. When a fragment of the earth's surface was blown away, and a red vomit of boiling stone ascended, then the heavy fog was permeated with golden fire and the vapors rolled upon themselves in seething tides. When thunder broke like the sound of continents exploding, and lightning spread its stupendous white waste, then deep in the atmosphere pale valleys opened, with foglike drenched mountains on their borders. For a very long time, this was the overwhelming spectacle of our seething world, lost within its vaporized and enveloping ocean.

It would have seemed to be, to an intelligence such as ours, a thing of incalculable fury and violence, of monstrous and purposeless anarchy; but there was neither anger nor lawlessness in the bellowing of its thunder or in the vast prairies of its light. It was only a virile and immeasurable energy making a home for its seed. In the dancing harmonies of its heat, there was in it then, as there had always been, every flower and tree, every creature from worm to man, and every thought and dream that were to be its meaning and destiny in the future of its time. Man, the hero of this story, was already there in the boiling inferno under the blanket of fog. Because this was a living, not a dead, world; every particle of it was alive and vibrant in its own rhythm. The whole of it was a great pulse, a throbbing heart, indestructible and eternal; and all that it was, all that it could ever be as a separate planet upon its own path, was a cycle of changes, the simple or complex variants of its own energy, within the fixed periphery of its soul.

After the temperature of the crust dropped below the boiling point of water, the atmosphere fell in huge drops and did not vaporize, but danced on the hot stone surface and formed tiny pools. These filled the depressions and overflowed and came together; and after another long time the earth was covered with water. It was completely clothed with a hot freshwater ocean, and as the atmosphere steadily poured down in torrential rains, the ocean became deep in the great depressions of the earth. The atmosphere was still so dense that no sunlight came through. It was a heavy wet atmosphere, an enveloping cloak of cloud-steam and poisonous gases; but little by little, very slowly, through the crawling millenniums of time, most of the water in the sky settled to the breast of the seas. Here and there, the buried surface of the earth sank in gigantic downwarping abysses, and floods of water poured into the yawning chasms and boiled far down where it touched the white-hot stone of the floor. Here and there, too, the buried surface rose in a mighty convulsive thrust of stone, and above the ocean's level there stood a barren and jagged peak.

If the dense atmosphere had been swept away and there had been eyes to look across the expanse of the world, they would have seen, in this time, only a rounded and steaming body of water, only a rolling desolation around the equator and from pole to pole; but if the eyes had waited and watched, they would have seen upon the lonely surface a great shoulder of rock emerging like a beast from the seas; and, still later, they would have seen the barren headland sink slowly, or vanish in a breath-taking moment as the convulsed earth shuddered under its watery cloak and drew its solitary island again into the deep. They would have seen the ocean lifted under the strong muscle of the winds into waves that looked like marching mountains and broke and fell into steaming reefs; or they would have seen upon the gray heaving breast the sudden belch of a volcano, hurling up from the depths a column of poisonous gases and liquid stone.

Eyes, if they had been there to see, would have beheld only a primeval waste of rolling waters; and ears, as delicate as a seismograph, listening at the ocean's surface, would have heard prodigious movements underneath, as if gargantuan muscles alternately flexed and relaxed. They would have heard the deep rumblings of earthquakes, the folding, under enormous pressure, of continental floors, the opening of abysses into which the seas spilled, and the sound of deep fires. They would have heard the sudden explosion of flame driven upward with such force that it rolled the ocean back, or the sinking of a platform so swiftly that a part of the sea dropped with it in a maelstrom that swirled round and round its great funnel until it looked like a circular and speeding tableland of granite.

And all the while, everywhere, in the earth enveloped by its ocean, in its water and air, were the active forces which, alive in themselves, had the latent power in union to produce a higher life; to produce the organism which would have a personal identity, a meaning, and a world of its own, separate, yet related to all that is, having within it the urge to seek and grow and develop, to move, to feed, to reproduce its kind, and add one by one the faculties necessary to preserve and protect it.

All this was a womb in which pulsing energy was reaching toward sunlight and intelligence. Each organism to come would possess in itself a priceless heritage of change, of adaptation, of sloughing the useless and the outgrown, of making more complex and eager the simple movements of its first being, and of feeding its environment into the stomach of its needs. From simple movement out of darkness into light, out of the artless dance of energy into the purposeful stir of growth, each would bring with it, as a treasure invisibly stored in its tiny cell, its own latent and imperishable granary of progress that would enlarge and enrich and reproduce it and people continents with its kind.

But also, within this womb of energy, there was now, and there was always to be, the struggle of form against form to make its own kind supreme. There was the need to be and to grow, and this need would devour or destroy the weak and the ill-adapted; for in this time of coming to more complex birth, there was no pity, no mercy, no charity, all these being, upon their appearance later, either a distortion of the cosmic harmonies or a higher manifestation of their inscrutable will. In this primordial and purging flame, in this convulsed struggle to build an atmosphere for wings and a floor for feet, there was provision not of sanctuaries but of graveyards for the forms of less eagerness and less strength.

It was to be a vast and ruthless and unpitying war in the eras ahead. It was to be, not a stingy birth of a few species, granted a planet of security and privileges, but an incalculably prolific spawning, as if a cosmic intention, ignorant of what was best or most worthy, designed the new world as an experimental laboratory and battleground wherein every possible kind of life would be given a chance to establish itself and endure. The fecundity of the intention, and not a beneficent guardianship, would seem to have been its only demonstrable purpose; and ability to survive, or the engulfing oblivion of extermination, has been, if not its primary, at least its most obvious law.

Toward all this, with theatrical explosiveness but with leisurely preparation, the new world moved. As the crust cooled, there emerged from the shoreless ocean headlands that were twisted lava sheets; and though most of these sank again and disappeared, some of them kept their desolate rock above the water and enlarged their areas and slowly built the platforms of continents to be. Mephitic vapors rose from the fires below, issuing from fissures in the stone, and poisons mingled with black clouds and made a pall of the sky. Now and then the dense atmosphere rolled back and opened valleys between the fog banks; and down these deep sky ravines came sunlight to lay its golden heat on the headlands. But for a long while these avenues of light from sun to earth were infrequent and brief; the clouds, bellying downward, heavy with rain, and riding constantly upon the wild winds, would come together in tumultuous coalescing; and the valleys of light were swallowed and there was darkness again on the promontories of stone. There was darkness save round the vents and crevices where tongues of flame shot up from the furnaces far underneath.

If a wanderer could have journeyed across this world, he would have found it a strange and a terrible thing. He would have moved under a ceiling as deep as night, wild and wind-driven, with thunder and lightning of cosmic magnitude roaring and flaming above him; and upon the ocean he would have been tossed from wave to wave that rolled like high black mountains. On gaining a headland, he would have clung there, with superhuman strength, while dark waters lashed the bleak outcropping of rock, poured up its sides and broke in mighty downrushing floods, and vaporized on its hot flanks in clouds of hissing steam. He would have wandered over the hot, torn surface to peer into awful chasms of red fire or into cauldrons of boiling lava or into crevices where gases smoked in their own deadly poison. If he had gone over the whole earth, around its equator and around its poles, he would have found upon the vast expanse of wild ocean only these rocky monuments, thrust out of depth.

After another long time, after countless millions of years, he would have seen a heart-warming change. The emerging continents were larger now. Some of them were so large that upon them were fresh-water lakes, and small valleys in the platforms of stone. Though the surface was still hot, there were no flames leaping upward like strange bonfires in the darkness; but the rock was still utterly barren. They were swept day and night by terrific winds that were sculpturing a new world.

If, seeking evidence of change where everything seemed fixed in the changeless, the wanderer had examined the stone at his feet, he would have found the more sheltered pockets floored with sand. He would have learned that the winds, sweeping as great abrasives over the headlands, were wearing the rock away and scattering it upon the waters where it sank to the ocean's floor. Emerging lava sheets, twisted, fire-pocked, and jutting in spires and pinnacles, were eroded to the smoothness of marble slabs. As mountains of virgin stone thrust up from the sea, the winds bore down upon them, having in their keeping one of the mightiest tasks of all. Before the world could come into its fruitful heritage, the stone would have to be disintegrated into soil; the oceans would have to be floored with mud and the continents with sand. The atmosphere, too, as the earth cooled, would deposit on the seas much of the water it carried; and golden sunlight would mix its chemistry with that of water and wind.

But a very long time was still to pass before the new planet would be habitable for higher forms of life. Huge mountains, faulted and warped, and presenting terrifying aspects, would rise from the oceans like backbones or like solitary shoulders; and the winds, aided by the intense cold of night and the intense heat of day, would slowly level them to featureless plains. As if to hasten its work, the wind gathered the sand of its erosion, and, using the grains of stone as chisels, it first sculptured the crags, eating away the softer masses, and then attacked the grotesque skeletons of granite and carried them grain by grain back to the sea. Heavy rains poured with the winds and washed the surfaces clean. Hot lava poured out and congealed and interbedded with land erosions, and these also were worn smooth.

The cosmic intelligence working here, knowing that the higher forms of life would first arise in the sea, was preparing a nest for the things to come. It was using emerging continents to floor the ocean. It was laying vast beds of sediment in inland lakes. The time would come, after these tasks were finished, when upon the barren plains it would lay the soil of life.

The sea was the first cradle; and as soon as sun and wind and cold had covered the rock floor of it with mud, the alchemy of change brought the simple patterns there into more complex movement. The magic of dancing energies formed the complex unions of microscopic molecules; and in their bath of dust and moisture and warmth these built the harmony of a single cell. That cell was no more alive than the rhythms that united to make it; it was only more complex and various in its dance of life. It was an orchestrated waltzing family of former duets; and inherent in it, potentially the soul of it, was the capacity to make its dancing increasingly complex until the wedding of energies would flower eventually in the intelligence of man.

In its lowly simplicity, without vision or mind, it nevertheless was richly endowed with tendencies of reaction and response to its environment, and had the power to move up or down in the water, to seek holes or crevices for its protection, and to place itself more happily in regard to heat, cold, and light. It could move by a kind of rolling of its tiny mass; it could thrust downward with a tentacle into which a part of it flowed, thereupon changing its position; or it could thrust out or downward with invisible leglike extensions, and so turn itself as if on rotating spokes. In eating it could flow around a smaller object and engulf it; and it could seek protection by affixing itself to any body larger than its own mass.

Life, in protozoa or in man, is much the same kind of activity. The former, in this long-ago time, became able, as it developed, to swim forward or backward by means of its microscopic hairs; it could ingest as food nearly anything small enough; and in all its behavior it was marvelously plastic and adaptive. After a long period of time it evolved into a hunting creature with more power of selection and movement; it could swallow an object ten times its size and seem to be only a film over its dinner; and it could maneuver with astonishing skill when threatened by danger. These creatures in the sea, so admirably various in their movements, so adaptive in their responses, were so small that thousands of them could swim in a drop of water; but innate in them was all the abundance of the life to come. They were the experimental patterns of response in the struggle to survive and grow; and in their blind gropings, their hit-or-miss impulses, was the laboratory of the instincts to be. In the thrust of an invisible hairlike appendage was the future blow of hoof or hand. In the immeasurably small rollings away from cold or toward heat was the lowly beginnings of the migration of beast and bird. Much would be found useful and would be used; much would be found purposeless and would be discarded; but everything to be on this planet was already there, feeling its way out of the dark and the blind.

In the new ocean was not the beginning but only a very humble form of the hero of this story. We shall not say that he has come to birth. We shall say that out of darkness and the deep he has moved within the range of our obtuse perceptions; and now, in his long journey up from the slime, we shall follow him and watch him grow and change, and possibly come to a little better understanding of what he is, and of what in the future he can aspire to be.

These single-celled invisible organisms multiplied into many cells and grew into colonies, and the colonies in time became masses of seaweed. Without root or anchor or self-willed power of movement, they drifted in apparent helplessness with the tides; but stored in them was an urge, sleepless, constant, and working in its own sorcerous way, toward a life more various and abundant and self-determined. There was an urge to sink roots, to become more than the buffeted flotsam of the sea. There was, indeed, in this simple primitive urge, this feeling, this inheritance from time and darkness, the will toward legs that would walk and wings that would fly; because everything that was to be upon this earth was stored there in the algae drifting by the ocean's shores.

There was the impulse to become animals that would look, at first, like a handful of floating moss or a fragment of drifting stone. Intelligence could not have said in this time, when a higher life was coming to birth, that a drifting island of bacteria was either animal or plant. It was either or both. It was the parent of those forms that would stand upon roots or legs, but now the roots and the legs were one. They were a feeling in the organism that reached toward an extension of its purpose and activities. If some of its offspring were to become plants, with legs fixed in the soil, and others to become animals, with legs designed to move about, that was only because environment acted upon and shaped and directed the complexities stored in the seed. In this time plant and animal were one until sunlight and water, and the inscrutable mysteries hidden in themselves, impelled them to diverge and reach out to their separate kingdoms.

This divergence was so very slow that for a long while the two were almost identical. A stone-lily, or a floating wormlike stem, was hardly different from the algae; and the algae, indeed, were so close to the rock from which they had come that in perishing they built reefs of pebbles and lime. So close to stone were the first animals that they were little more than hard shells. These living things were born of rock, decomposed by water and wind, and upon finishing their brief life span they became rock again. Of the skeletons of animal and plant, enormous beds were laid on the ocean floor and these were often several miles in depth. Upon the margins of lagoons were coral-like masses of algae and long reefs of limestone; and upon rocks at low tide were patches of seaweed, red and green and brown.

Then the day came when this higher form of life, obeying its deepest urge, took a firmer foothold in its world of stone and water. A withdrawing tide stranded a sprig of seaweed in a sheltered cove where winds had laid a thin soil, and it clung there, not with roots, but with the simple wish to feel itself rooted and anchored. A deluge of rain carried it back to the sea. Other weeds clung there in a later time and were borne outward on the floods, and after them came other weeds, year upon year and age upon age; for the will to leave the sea and grow upon land was stronger than the might of rain and wind. And eventually a plant did remain on thin soil, triumphantly removed from the vagaries of ocean tides. It was without roots and its kind was to be so for ages to come, but the urge to sink roots and make itself secure among the tantrums of its environment was an invincible part of its being.

For millions of years, however, it was water that offered a more friendly environment to the evolving life. There it was protected not only from wind and rain but also from the extreme heat of the day and the bitter cold of the night. Colonies of cells, drifting helplessly with the tides, ate and breathed and reproduced, and reacted to the great bath in which they floated; for there was latent in them an impulse to develop higher faculties for their use. There was an urge to hear, to feel, and to see. Even more strongly, during this time, there was an urge toward integrity of structure that would enable them to resist the tides instead of drifting with them to be stranded on barren islands or buried in the sediment of the deep. Out of their need they would develop spines to make them firm in the rolling waters, fins and tails to control their movements, and eyes to see their food and their enemies.

But countless ages would pass before a drifting handful of moss would become, through successive and imperceptible changes, the mighty rulers of the seas. There would first be flowerlike animals, or animal-like plants; strange hollow sponges whose passageways were lined with hairlike tendrils which, by constant rhythmic motion, produced water currents toward the cavities of its stomach; tubelike creatures with a ring of tentacles round the vent that was becoming a mouth;

and jellylike masses that were free-swimming, propelling themselves not with fins but with a convulsive movement of the whole organism. There would be innumerable creatures resembling uprooted plants, having at the end of a long stalk a bundle of flattened tubes through which they breathed. There would be enormous colonies with rounded branches, thin leaflike foliage, and lacy fronds; but they would have an alimentary canal, a nervous system, and sensitive tentacles round the mouth through which they breathed.

The ocean teemed with life like a vast and experimental laboratory, indifferent alike to its waste of species or to anomalous development of structure that must soon perish. Nature then, even more than now, was prolific and extravagant, and depended not on the careful nurture of a chosen seed but on the experimental planting of everything in her womb. She would produce both motes and monsters, the gentle and the savage, the seeing and the blind; and among themselves all these could fight it out to the triumph of the few and the extermination of the many. Among the millions of freaks, among all the eccentric and aberrant destinies of the luckless and the doomed, there would be a few endowed with the precious heritage of survival. And from the laboratories of the sea and the land, one beast eventually would emerge to rule the planet and break all other creatures to his will.

That time was far hence; and meanwhile the waters of the ocean and the continents standing upon its floor were to be soaked with the blood of the struggle.

This is a law of life: to feel the need of an organ or a faculty is to evolve it if the urge is constant and prolonged. Among the creatures of the sea, some were strongly endowed with an urge to master their environment; but in others this urge was not a constant and fierce lusting, and they fell back upon the need to protect themselves against the strong. The one developed the trait of aggressive seeking, the other of protective coloring or armor, or of flight. Once set upon either of these paths, there was no turning aside; the trait persisted and became fixed. The one perfected its dreadful power to kill, the other to hide or to flee.

The killer, being far more aggressive and determined, evolved more rapidly; because the will to conquer and destroy has sired and brought to their highest development the talents that are potential in the seed. One of these is intelligence, and in the murderer it was to come to its highest fruition. Those creatures, on the other hand, that were impelled to a gentler way of life, were content to be sluggish and stupid, feeling no urge within their heavy protective armor to develop claws and fangs. They would often be only a torpid jellylike mass, walled in by their limestone shells. They would become snails, having a mouth, eyes, ears, and tentacles, as well as a broad clumsy foot with which to crawl awkwardly across the ocean's bottom. They would feed on inoffensive plants, as the weaker beasts have always done; or they would be the lazy scavengers of disease and death. Too sluggish to feel an urge to leave their stone houses, too irresolute and stagnant to evolve backbones, they dwelt in primeval torpor, excreting stone and adding chamber by chamber to their impregnable prisons. With some, the foot became a funnel-shaped swimming organ through which water was ejected to propel the creature backward or sideways. Some, heavily armored, developed legs with which to crawl or swim, and long tentacles with which to sense the presence of food or enemies.

Taken all in all, however, these animals were little more than stone sluggards on the ocean's floor. They were the idiots, half beast and half rock, in Nature's amazing family; she smiled on them with ironic indulgence and allowed them to specialize until they were practically sealed up and lost within their stone dungeons. During this era of time, as well as in all the eras to follow, these weird monsters would crawl about in darkness, thrusting witless heads out of their stone prisons. A million or a hundred million years would pass over them and leave them practically unchanged. Peace they would have, but Nature abhors peace. An invulnerable refuge against enemies they would have; and as the price of it they were sentenced to eternal stupor.

Nature, deep in her inscrutable heart, reserved for the most savage killers the award of intelligence. Consistently, from the earliest experiments in her vast laboratories, fearlessness has been the highest of all virtues; and if members of her family were allowed to withdraw from struggle into their armored homes, perhaps that was only to prove that safety weds with ignorance. Because the chronicle of this story, its achievements, its progress, and all its slow and terrible emergence from darkness into light, have been recorded in murder. If all the creatures of the ocean had developed armor and fed on seaweeds, there would today be only a world of snails and turtles, a blind and insensible paralysis without passion or daring or hope.

The heritage in the germ, the urge that has reached steadily toward the mind, has always been in the keeping of the ruthless beast, indifferent to all the protective devices of color and armor. The omnipresent sense of danger, the threat of foes, has impelled him to develop active weapons of protection. Instead of a shell, he hungered for great teeth, speed of movement, keener vision, and invincible strength. No sluggard of jelly in a stone fortress, he wandered in the depths, with his sleek flesh vulnerable to fangs and with a moment of inattentiveness as the price of his life. He was the bold adventurer in this drama, asking for no quarter and giving none. The greatest weapon in his arsenal would eventually be intelligence, and all his murderous hungers contributed to the evolution of a mind.

Long before his time, it is true, some of his cousins had perished in armor. King of them had been a gigantic monster with a great plate of stone above its head that could slide backward as a sheath to protect its body. Without teeth, it had two enormous jaws, two crushing shears of bone; and for a long while it was the tyrannical overlord in the ocean's depths. Propelled by a huge tail, rolling like a thing with shifting ballast, and with its jaws wide open, it moved awkwardly and with no apparent purpose, a dull and overgrown beast that fed into its stomach everything that entered its mouth. Without intelligence or more than the feeblest vision, it prowled like a dredging machine; and its gaping jaws closed on everything they touched. They closed on coral reefs and on limestone crags. They closed on unwary fish, too, or on small armored creatures that were crushed and swallowed, armor and all. Now and then they closed on a projecting neb of cooled lava; and the mindless monster, unable to crush the rock, and too dull to distinguish between food and stone, would lie suspended as if anchored, with its mighty jaws set on lava like a steel trap. After a while the tide would float it away; and again, with gaping mouth, it would go with the current, its tail slowly moving like a rudder to right or left. Sometimes, when swimming into a buried ledge, it would respond with a thick-skulled tremor of fear; and then the heavy armor of its head would slide backward and the monster would wait for an enemy to strike. Whereupon, moved not by a will of its own but by a simple reflex, the skull would slide forward, the jaws would open again to their widest reach, and the king of the ocean would thrust with its great tail and move off.

Now and then these lumbering beasts would swim, mouths agape, head-on into one another, and their powerful shears would close on the thick plate of one another's skulls. Thus for hours or days they would remain interlocked, drifting with the tides; and when at last they were freed from the vises that held them, it was only because their muscles relaxed a little and their jaws fell away. When an unprotected part of the body of one drifted into the mouth of another it was instantly crushed, and the captured creature threshed with its tail and slid its useless skull cap back and forth.

Hungering for thicker armor and more bulk, instead of for speed and daring, these beasts became slower and more awkward and of vaster size. They sank more and more to the ocean's bottom and lay there like stranded hulks. As the price of being armored and gigantic and secure, they perished as all creatures must that overspecialize. From all danger they withdrew into their fortresses and sank in the depths and were buried by the sediment of wind and wave. Instead of the frontiers of struggle, they chose the refuge of the reluctant, and the ocean floored itself with their graveyards.

While they were moving away from danger, their cousins were moving toward it. These sought neither armor nor vast size, but teeth and speed and audacity. The new overlord of the seas would not be a bone-plated and sluggish hulk; he would be a swift and streamlined killer. At first he was a small fellow, this ancient sire of the sharks, this long-ago forbear of the tiger and the man; but he had teeth as sharp as needle points, and a speed and grace of movement that made him master of his home. He had the kind of daring that looked upon the entire ocean as his frontier, and on all other creatures as his prey.

He also was driven by an urge to greater size, and through the ages the fathers in one species bequeathed to their sons a little more bulk, until at last this tyrant of the seas became the most formidable killer that has ever lived on this planet. As large, eventually, as the biggest whales of a later time, he was not, like them, an awkward and slow-moving monster. He was a long swift torpedo of flesh, and almost with the speed of a torpedo he moved through the depths, propelled by a broad rudder and gigantic fins. His dreadful jaws, which he could open to a width of ten feet, were set with four rows of six-inch teeth; and when these gleaming bone chisels snapped together, they could crush a victim weighing tons.

Along with size and speed, this tyrant of the seas developed an appetite which in voracity has been without parallel. His lifetime was spent in devouring and digesting, as if Nature had fashioned and equipped him to exterminate all other creatures; but so abundant were the other beasts of the ocean that for a million years he fed with insatiable gluttony and found the supply equal to his ravenous lust.

We shall follow the marauder in one of his journeys.

Gorged with flesh and blood and bone, and a little sleepy, he has been lying idly in shallow waters off the barren coast of an emerging Asia. He has not been asleep. He has merely been suspended in drowsy content while his incomparably perfect digestive system assimilated into his blood and muscle the glut of his dinner. His eyes, alert, and shining like two huge black marbles, have been watching small fish drift by him or a clumsy lizard shoal toward the bank. In them he has no interest. When surfeited and digesting, he does not mind if other creatures come close to him; for in his mote of a brain, entombed in a great skull, there is only dim awareness of their presence. He has no enemies that dare attack; and if this huge murderer, idly digesting in sunlit shallows, had had the power of reflection, he might have foretold his end in the completeness of his triumph. He might have known that Nature eventually levels to the graveyard those beasts whose might makes them secure from all enemies. For in struggle alone is there the will to survive.

This stupendous shark was absolute master of the deep. There were other monstrous carnivora but none with the speed and power of this king. There was none to dispute his control and urge him to further development; and in consequence he had reached that terrible haven wherein he could devour and digest and degenerate.

Among his distant cousins, much smaller than he, and surrounded on all sides by enemies, there was constant groping toward faculties which they did not have. Their mind was only a mote, too, but it was growing. They were swimmers in the sea, but dimly, sleeplessly, they were reaching toward a life on land. They devoured, but they were also eaten; and in the menace of their environment lay their promise of a higher life.

That was not so of the king tyrant whom a jesting experiment had made invincible. And now, having digested his gorge and felt pangs of hunger, he gives a thrust with his mighty rudder and swings, and under the powerful winging of his fins he shoots out into deep water, a mammoth sea-raider who is little more than teeth and stomach. Overtaking a school of cuttlefish, he spreads his jaws wide and snaps them together, and swallows a dozen creatures whole. The two hundred chisels in his mouth are only for capturing and crushing. Next he comes upon a slothful turtle-like beast the size of an ox; and between the jaws, closing like pile-drivers, the creature's thick armor breaks into a thousand fragments. He overtakes and swallows a few of his small cousins, but his eyes all the while are seeking his favorite victim.

This is a great monster with the head of a lizard, the teeth of a crocodile, and the body of a serpent. It is a gluttonous killer, too, but it is only helpless prey in the grasp of the king-shark. Moving through the sea at high speed, and as soundlessly as a piston in a bath of oil, the shark sees the monster swimming near the surface, drawing its long paddles up and forward and thrusting them backward. Its long neck is above the water; and turning on it to scan the ocean are two small eyes in a flattened skull. Coming up swiftly like the long dark torpedo that he is, the shark circles his prey. Sometimes, in attacking this beast, he closes his jaws on the paddles and tears them from the belly. Sometimes, with a deflecting stroke of his tail, he comes up in a flashing arc of power; and wide-open jaws break the surface, and teeth gleam like double rows of ivory chisels, and water is a spilling pool deep in the mouth and throat. Then he closes on the tall slender neck and snaps it off. But today, after circling like a long curved darkness, he clamps his mighty vise on the tapering hulk of the tail.

The captured beast, taken unawares, rears with all its strength, its four fin-paddles climbing with the might of broad oars beating upon the water. Its mouth, hinged back against its throat like a reptile's, opens wide, and its rows of teeth are bright and dreadful in the sunlight. Its long neck writhes like the body of a snake. In the first upward thrust toward escape, its front paddles come above water and strike the surface like the flat slap of huge palms. Then all four paddles churn the calm sea until it rolls backward in foaming reefs or opens downward in sucking maelstroms.

The tyrant killer still has his jaws set on the tail. The juicy hulk of it is crushed in his mouth, and while the monster threshes vainly, the shark is content for a little while to drink the blood. Then, in an effort to tear the huge tail off and swallow it, he thrusts with his rudder and smites with his fins; but now, as in so many times before, he succeeds only in dragging his prey under the surface. Releasing his clutch he shoots backward and moves in for a more deadly attack. With jaws agape to their fullest span, and bloody water boiling across his open throat as he comes, he sets his vise on the underbelly and his chisels meet in the soft mass of guts. Turning on his enemy, the captured monster bends his neck backward in a long curve and bites into the shark's back; but the killer does not mind that. He has a deathhold, and death is relaxing the jaws of his victim. After drinking the warm living fluids that gush out of the belly and flood his throat, he devours the carcass; and marking the place of his banquet is a red patch on the sea. Glutted, he moves back to shallow water and drowses lazily until pangs of hunger move him again.

For hundreds of centuries his clan would devour and procreate and lie in idle peace where the sun warmed the waters. Undisputed master of all creatures in the deep, there was nothing else to do and no need to be more than they were. For they were perfect in the environment of their time. They had no need of greater speed or longer teeth because no beast ever approached them except those who mistook an idle tyrant for a submerged ledge or reef. The ocean was their garden and orchard of good things. Nature had been kind to them. Nature had made of them flawless engines of destruction without competitors, without foes, and without ambition.

But Nature, when she errs in achieving perfection, is wise enough to see the folly of it and ingenious enough to plot its death. In her laboratory, perhaps she now and then achieves perfection because she is curious; and if she destroys the perfect thing, that is doubtless because she abhors it. Because perfection begets a lazy indifference to growth and change. It mates with peace—and Nature also abhors peace. In all the long and brilliant history of her experiments, she has given the pith of her scorn and her most devastating rebuke to perfection and peace, having perceived in both the complacent degeneracy of the changeless.

Upon this planet, her first perfect creature, and perhaps the most remarkable in its perfection, was the shark-killer that ruled the seas. He was also her first child of great promise. As long as he was driven to seek speed and size and courage, his evolution was steady and exciting; but when he became king of all the beasts, he was content to feed his hunger and to accept the world as his special province. Having no need of faculties which he did not possess, he felt no urge to acquire them, and so spent his time in idleness and gluttony. At the height of his glory, his own unparalleled and invincible position sentenced him to death.

Other creatures, meanwhile, whom he ate and terrorized, were not satisfied. In the killer's tyranny lay their strength. Danger fostered their urge to growth; and Nature, observing the folly of her first favorite, left him to degenerate and perish, and gave her interest to the wide-awake strivings of his prey.

During all this long time, convulsive physicking had continued under the hot floor of the ocean, and land had slowly emerged. Most of present-day Asia stood above water, but it was only a featureless and barren waste of rock. There were no mountains upon it, no verdant valleys, no cool clear streams. Across the desolation of stone swept the great winds, busily eroding day and night and carrying sand back to the seas. Beds of gypsum and salt were laid down, and the ocean floor was covered with sediment, often miles in depth.

Southward was another continent, vast and bleak, comprising what is today Australia and much of Africa and a part of Asia; and between the two continents lay the huge Tethys Sea across what was to become North America, the Atlantic Ocean, and a part of Europe. Upon both continents there were only torrential rains and the winds gathering the sands.

The floors of the oceans were slowly sinking and shifting and warping. Now and then part of a sea-bed was thrust up in the form of craggy reef or peak, and rain and wind eroded it into soil. Still later, there were stupendous upheavals, both from the ocean's floor and the continental platforms; and mountains were pushed into the sky. In crevices, in sheltered coves, and here and there along protected beaches, sand fell from the herding winds; and thus was begun the task of converting stone continents into gardens and forests.

It was a task that would take millions of years; and meanwhile, as if impatient, the first land plants, migrating from the seas, made use of a soil that was only coarse sand. It is little wonder, then, that these first land plants were so strange in appearance, and seemed to be, as in large part they were, mere vegetation of stone. Green, red, and brown algae, leaving the sea and standing on thin rocky beaches, were almost encased with lime. Some of them looked like greenish lime-encrusted toadstools, or like clumps of coral or patches of stone seaweed. Others, sheathed with lime, resembled the outspread feathers of a cock's tail. All of them were stone plants out of a stone world; and, after completing their simple life span, they fell over and formed beds of limestone.

But these, like the creatures in the sea, were "dreaming on things to come." That clump of brown seaweed, standing behind a coral reef and looking like queer foliage of rock, had in it the seed of the pine and oak, the lily and the rose. In the ocean, this dullard, creeping blindly with an appendage thrust from its stone house, is cousin of the plant on the shore. If shattered by a blow, there would be little left of either except a pile of stone fragments; yet they were the lowly parents of two great kingdoms.

On the shore of an inland lake, formed by a withdrawing sea, the rising sun one morning shone upon this landscape. A few miles in the background was a row of mountains, each bleak hulk looking as if a sculptor of phenomenal size and strength had completed his first chiselings. Utterly naked, each peak, like an inverted cone, stood in monumental loneliness; and below them, the flanks were terraced to the lake shore. Upon the lake's surface were several steaming vents; if human ears could have bowed low to them, they would have heard deep in the earth the gurgling of liquid stone and the hissing of steam. The volcanic action under the lake floor was constantly boiling upward and overflowing; and as the spilling stone cooled, it formed inverted funnels, with the mouth of each set on the lake bottom and the apex serving as a vent for escaping gases.

On the shore opposite the mountains was a forest. Chiefly it was funguslike plants, left there by a withdrawing ocean; and the largest of these plants had reached the size of a tree. They looked like weird hybrids of wood and stone. Among them was a creeping swampland plant with hairs instead of roots, and a forked stem clothed with spines. There was also a kind of frond, tufted at the top, but with leafless branches.

A hundred thousand years later, the sun rose on a scene that had changed little. The fumaroles of volcanoes were still smoking. Along the south shore had been piled huge dunes of sand. The water of the lake was a uniform green except small patches where decaying vegetation had turned it brown. The leafless trees, still no more than straight hard shoots rising from underground stems, looked like spires eroded and sculptured by the wind-borne sands. Among them now the swamp was carpeted with a slender rushlike plant, and at a distance it looked lovely and green. But neither in this forest nor in any of the others like it was there sound of insect or bird or of any living thing. There was only the sound of volcanoes and of water and wind.

After another long time there is a more noticeable change. Most of the spinous leafless plants, with their archaic features, have disappeared. They have evolved into fernlike fronds with veined leaflets and various organs. The largest of them vaguely resembled the Joshua tree of today; smaller ones, straight of shaft, were crowned with an umbrella-like canopy of branches and leaves; and under them were the ferns. The fumaroles have stopped smoking, having been buried under sediment carried down by wind and mountain stream. The lake has shrunk to half its original size, and the great dunes on its southern shore have been scattered into thousands of tiny ravines and coves. But still far and wide upon the land surface of the new world there was no living animal.

There was sentient life only in the seas; because it was there for countless millions of years that Nature made her laboratory, and there she brought more species into being than she was ever to produce again except in the insects. In size and in shape, in ferocity and in shyness, in alertness and in torpor she experimented in the vast bath of water, begetting every conceivable form adapted to an ocean home. Most of these creatures were content to float lazily in their deep and fluid cradle, having no ears and needing none, and no hands to stimulate and develop their minds; and yet in them there was, perhaps even from the beginning, an urge to resist the luxurious haven of water and move toward the violent temperatures and hazards of a land life.

Some of these beasts, drifting into shallow places or tossed upon beaches by the tides, looked with feeble eyes upon another world. They had no minds, no power of thought, but in them, nevertheless, as a part of their heritage, as a part of their inscrutable will to seek and grow, was an urge to leave the ocean. It was the kind of blind and irresistible urge that moves fish upstream to their spawning grounds and drives them even to death before they will yield; the kind of will that wings in the migration of birds; the kind of guidance that leads the winds and the tides. From the deep these sluggards, both great and small, moved toward a home on land, and their efforts wrote one of the mightiest chapters in the history of persistence and courage. By the thousands, by the millions, they perished, and their bones were buried deep in the sands where they died. For they had gills, yet strove to breathe the pure and intoxicating air of earth. They had paddles and fins but they tried to walk.

What a beast wills with inflexible purpose, its far-distant progeny may achieve. These creatures thrust heads from water and looked around them; they were stricken by a burning inrush of oxygen and withdrew. On shallow bottoms they waddled on paddles, and darkly, patiently felt the need of legs and feet. Stranded on shores by retreating tides, they died there; and they died when, threshing like seals from water to land, they suffocated for want of air in a world of air which they could not use. But their will was unwavering, and they had infinite time.

Century after century and age after age this magnificent

struggle continued—this exodus of the sea-born and the sea-living from the sea to the land. Life in the ocean was seeking a home in the forests. Creatures with gills and paddles were striving for lungs and feet. It was the most spectacular of all struggles that have been upon this earth; and in its waste of life and its slow, dumb, and invincible seeking it is the greatest saga in all the long journey from crinoid to man. Nature cared little if it cost a thousand million lives to achieve one barely perceptible change in the evolution of gills into lungs. The vast oceans were her womb and her nursery, and there was no limit to the numbers she could throw into this uphill fight. And in regard to time she had an eternity if an eternity were needed.

And so for millions of years this struggle went on. Huge reefs were made of the bones of those that perished; islands rose from the graveyards of the dead. After a very long time, some of the creatures were able to waddle to muddy banks and lie there until forced to return to water to breathe; but they came out again, and the generations after them, and each added a little to adaptation and change. Their fins became things they could crawl with among the rushes and the canes; and all the while, too, they were developing ears and the power to hear, and a brain that was more than a mote. In form they at first resembled lizards, frogs, and salamanders, and for ages these dull flesh-eaters lived along the banks of streams or in bogs and swamps, feeding on fish and worms and the weaker members of their own kind. Some, less valiant, were content to remain in the swamps, and eventually became the river pirates of the crocodile clan. Others, looking like ferocious scorpions three or four feet long, moved away from the seas and the swamps, but for a long time they had to return to the ocean or the rivers to give birth to their young. And the young lived there in the water, developing in a little while the lungs that had cost their ancestors millions of years of effort.

Some of the emerging beasts lost their aquatic armor, some brought it with them to land; but they were all the amphibians, sons and daughters of the fish, born from the laboratory of the sea. Whether armored or not, they were monsters all, even the tiniest of them; but they were more intelligent than the fish and more victorious, and in their land-breathing, ferocious, and ungainly bodies they bore triumphantly to the mountains and the forests the image and the soul of the man to be.

During that very long period while some of the fishes were becoming amphibians and evolving lungs from gills and legs from fins, Nature was preparing a home for them; because plants, too, moved in a worldwide urge toward growth and change. Rootless and naked trees, set like monuments of stone on barren headlands, had been seeking roots and foliage and flowers; and during those millions of years they became softer and lovelier and a few of them became fragrant. There were dense dank junglelands of fern that ranged through six thousand species, and in size from small delicate plants to tropical trees fifty feet tall. Some wore crowns of large beautiful leaves, some unrolled in huge bouquetlike fronds, and many were dainty climbers that built a tangled undergrowth. There were magnificent scale trees a hundred feet in height, standing in groves carpeted by club mosses and creeping vines; and there were vast jungles of horsetails, their trunks sheathed with whorls of narrow leaves that made each tree resemble a tall staff growing out of a cylindrical vineyard. And there were strange-looking conifers, the parent of today's pine and fir.

But not at once, not for a long time, did the beasts emerging from the sea take to the forests. They were an in-between clan of monsters, sea-born but land-driven; as cold-blooded as the killers who still swam in the ocean and were content to remain there; and so stupid that they could only waddle around in the mud flats and try to devour everything that moved. Most of them could smell a little, some of them could faintly hear the most violent sounds, and nearly all of them had flat teeth to crush or long curved chisels to seize and hold. They were not of great size yet but many of them would be; because Nature, moving her principal laboratory from the sea to the land, turned her creatures free, giving them only the law of their urge and their hunger. As if appalled by the stultifying luxuries of an ocean cradle, where her beasts had been content to roll with the current and eat and propagate and die, she fetched a part of them to land where they would develop their minds or perish. From a lazy bath of water, she gave them to changing temperatures, stinging winds, and a burning sun.

And on land, as in the seas, some of the creatures sought the protection of size and armor. They became stupendous bone-plated machines that were controlled only or almost entirely by a few lower reflexes. In Nature all intelligence is supposed to rest; but a backward look at her experiments and fumblings suggests that she had no certain knowledge or foresight, but moved by trial and error, sensing only that among her vast and clumsy and murderous progeny there was a man coming to birth.

The most the ocean had been able to produce was the killer-shark who had perished in his perfection. Now Nature had two new mediums, the land and the air. Instead of swimming, beasts had to learn to walk or fly; but above all else, the ability to grow and change was the price of the lease to live and endure. Of fish she had spawned thousands of species, wastefully, extravagantly, until the oceans were choked with the kinds; and from those millions of years of experiment there had evolved the great urge to migrate from water to land. That was the one priceless heritage in the cold-blooded sluggards that wallowed like boars in the slime and caught faintly the stench of their own brothers rotting on the beaches.

In her second laboratory Nature was to be more prodigal than in her first—as if hoping among a million seeds to find one that could build a kingdom. In form, in size, in appearance her creatures now moved to every possible extreme. From the amphibian horse, with flat head and wide mouth, came active lizardlike beasts that developed their legs; ugly brutes that specialized in armor and bulk; and hopping monsters that strove for batlike wings. All these, in turn, divided and subdivided into innumerable species, until land and air were alive with them and the stage was set for the mammal to come.

But the air, like the sea, is a medium that encourages slothfulness and arrested growth. Insects multiplied until after a while there were more than a thousand kinds. There were beetles as large as sparrows, cockroaches four inches long, and dragonflies with a wingspread of thirty inches. These flies, upon whom Nature must have smiled in their early history, became another of her odiously perfect beings; because after having with speed and voracity made themselves secure, they were content, like the killer of the seas, to be changeless. It was out of the bloody struggle of creatures that crawled and then walked that intelligence was to be born; but among these, too, all those species which sought and achieved safety were sentenced to death.

The past of this planet is, in considerable part, an enormous graveyard of those creatures that chose physical safety instead of intelligence; and the largest of those cemeteries has been filled with the reptiles. The amphibian became in turn the cold-blooded lizard and the snake, and the first of these was for a long time the undisputed lord of earth. His clan multiplied into many species. A few of these returned to the waters to prey on fishes, a few were content to be ungainly hulks feeding in swampy places, and others developed agile legs for swift running; but one of them, who in time was to have many cousins, strove for size and armor and became the invincible tyrant of them all.

As if sardonically curious to learn what sort of menagerie of grotesque monsters the world could be, Nature gave to the reptiles millions of years in time, a favorable climate, and lush plants and hordes of smaller beasts on which to feed; and the result was a marvel of awkward, ill-shaped, and purposeless ugliness. Never before or since has she been so lavish in the production of stupidity on a colossal scale. Never have such extravagant hulks of muscle and bone housed such small and feeble brains or eaten gluttonously to such little purpose or evolved such amazing variety of form only to floor lakes and valleys with the carcasses of their tribe. It may be that Nature was again intent on defining and declaring the folly of perfection; because these beasts became perfect, each in his own way, and were sentenced to extinction. In the great dank forests of this time, and upon the prairies and plains, these beasts could have been counted by the millions; but all their brains combined in one could hardly have served the need and purpose of a solitary ant.

Yonder, on a hill, stands one of these formidable machines, measuring nearly a hundred feet in length. Upon four huge legs, his trunk resembles that of an elephant; and from the trunk behind extends a forty-foot cylinder of useless tail that drags on the earth when he walks. His neck, more than half as long as the tail, and looking much like it, supports a small head, a head so absurdly small that it appears to be only the end of another tail, set with eyes and teeth. This beast lives chiefly on plant life and insects, and his neck, therefore, serves a purpose in reaching to foliage; but his tail, dragging like a great calloused palm over the stones, is only several tons of useless flesh.

Across the valley from him is a herd of his enemies. One of them resembles him in shape, though the hind legs are more massive, the long tail is armored and looks like a monstrous javelin, and the head, set with huge flesh-rending teeth, is a plated engine of destruction. The front legs, though much smaller than the rear ones, are taloned; but another monster, not far away, has lost all use of his front legs. They hang from his breast, ridiculous vestiges from ancestors that walked on four feet. Nevertheless, this beast is the king of them all. Standing twenty feet in height and fifty feet in length, he has an armored skull as large as a grown ox set with broad powerful teeth half a foot long. The curved claws on his feet are a little longer than his teeth. Half-sitting on his tail, he can rear on the pillars of his legs and look far over the landscape; and then his terrible head is thirty feet from the earth. He feeds on anything he can kill and tear apart.

Around him are beasts whom he cannot destroy. One of them is even more frightening of aspect—a monster resembling an overgrown hippopotamus. He lives solely on vegetation, and to protect himself he has evolved an armor unbelievably perfect. Backward from his skull, and curving upward, is an enormous bone shield nine or ten feet long and almost as wide; and growing out of the front of it are two huge horn-sheathed spears. On his broad nose is a snout, another sharp horn-spear, but it is not so deadly a weapon as the two javelins projecting four feet from the skull plate.

Among the many other monsters is an awkward ungainly brute about twenty feet long and half as high; it has an absurdly small head close to the ground, and an arched back, rising in a great curve from its neck to its rump and continuing in a downward arc to the end of its tail. Upon the entire length of this arc, from head to tail, are two rows of pear-shaped plates of bone, looking from some distance like enormous petals growing out of the spine. Below them, the tail, dragged on the earth, is fitted with four sharp spears, curved upward and parallel like the tines of a fork. The thick legs are encased with armor, and imbedded in the tough hide are plates of bone. This beast is secure from all enemies, but is so weighted down with armor that it can barely move. Among creatures sacrificing everything to safety, and perishing as the price of it, Nature has never achieved a more formidable and horrifying instance of perfection.

Over the earth during this time life was a spectacle of continuous and bloody slaughter. The king tyrant, like the killer-shark, fed on everything he could kill—and when hungry he attacked all objects that moved, including members of his own clan. He was a machine of reflexes and appetites, destroying, gluttonous, and perfect. Too powerful to feel fear, too dull-witted to distinguish between friend and foe, and impelled to stir only when pangs of hunger goaded him, he fixed his stupid gaze on anything moving across the landscape and moved toward it, walking on his two mighty legs and balancing himself with his tail. The herb-eating monsters, with long tails and necks, and with no bone plate on them anywhere, he found easy prey; with his awful teeth he could crush or gut them or tear their heads off, but when he attacked the armored vegetarians his chisels closed vainly on bone.

A great male, seeking a ton of dinner, has espied one of the two-horned monsters and is lumbering toward it; and with the amused indulgence of Nature, we may as well watch the fight. Spanning ten feet at a stride, the tyrant comes; and the beaked one, sensing danger, turns to face him. He turns toward him his stupendous plated head and gleaming horns. Braced on four short pillars, as well as by the heavy trunk of his tail, he stands foursquare, a leviathan of prodigious strength; but like his enemy he has almost no brain at all. There is no intelligence in either beast. One is moved by voracious hunger, the other by fear.

As the tyrant approaches, barely able to distinguish between a hulk of living flesh and a ledge of stone, he opens his mouth into a wide cavern of teeth and wet throat. Under the roof of his upper jaw a small child could have stood. He comes up, with the earth trembling under his taloned feet, and reaches down over his prey to close his vise; but at this moment the horned monster lifts his head suddenly and drives the two sharp spears into the tyrant's breast. He drives them a foot deep into the flesh, and while he waits, the other, towering above him, stands impaled. Then the tyrant closes his jaws on the broad curved shield and bone rakes bone. Six-inch chisels rake scars across the shield but they do not crush it or bite through it; and all the while the two spears stand in the killer's breast. There is very little pain. These giants of the ancient world felt little pain even in violent death; they were only torpid mountains of bone and meat with the sluggish and cold-blooded nervous system of the reptile. The tyrant moves backward and the horns withdraw from gaping wounds; he turns to sink jaws into the body, but the beaked monster swings, too, and faces him again with shield and horns and the great bone-nub of his snout. There are no bellows of rage. There is no sound at all save that of heavy feet and breath and of bone on bone. There is no agile feinting, no maneuvering, no cunning attack. Two hulks are deadlocked, the one trying to devour the other; and presently, with the dumb patience of water that hesitates and turns aside from an obstacle, the tyrant strides off. He comes to one of the defenseless beasts with the long neck and tail and makes his feast.

And so it was for millions of years upon the earth. These were only a few of the many species of dragon that lived on the ground. Meanwhile, smaller dragons had taken to the air, flying on wings like those of the bat; and in appearance they were even more dreadful than those that walked on feet. Some of them had the wingspread of a small airplane. The hairy weblike wings had grown to their arms and legs, and the creatures when flying looked naked and spread-eagled, with talons at the elbows of their wings, and talons hanging from their rear where wings had grown fast to ankles. They had the cold bleak eyes of vultures. They had beaks two or three feet long, set with rows of teeth. Bird-hipped and bird-footed, these were the reptiles of the air and the ungainly parents of the birds to come.

It was a world a brief glimpse of which would turn our blood cold; but it was Nature's marvelous laboratory, and among the dreadful flying vampires were the lark and the nightingale to be, and among the monsters on the ground was the father of man. He was not the huge reptile, laying eggs a foot thick in the sands. He was among the smaller beasts that were becoming mammals and carrying their young in wombs. He was, very anciently, in the beast-toothed theriodont, a reptile too in the beginning, a blood brother of the tyrant himself; but this beast developed, not size and armor, but longer legs and greater speed. To speed and precision the nervous system responded; the body rose in temperature; the metabolism became more complex; and while the monstrous reptiles, of both land and air, stagnated in their protective devices, the lowlier beasts forged ahead and entered another and a nobler kingdom.

Nature's experimenting in dreadful killers came, as before, to a sudden and dramatic end. The dragons that had ruled for millions of years perished in a few centuries. Overspecialized, unable to adapt to climatic changes, too sluggish to migrate and too long supreme to sense approaching peril, they froze to death by the tens of thousands; and hastening their exodus to the graveyards were small alert mammals about the size of rats. These ate their huge eggs or gathered in flocks to chew at their helpless feet. More and more, too, the dragons devoured their own kind, having come to be little more than insatiable appetites. They had been a mighty and invulnerable clan, but time moved a glacial epoch down upon them and floored continents with their bones. Indulgent for a long while, but bored at last, Nature turned them under and sent them back to the stone beds out of which they had come.

And the voracious reptiles of the air, those grotesque appendages attached to a pair of enormous wings, she also destroyed. They had ruled the atmosphere, eating anything they could find, including one another; but they were helpless against a wind. It overturned them and sent them in gawky sprawling defeat to the earth. Above all, however, these creatures, gliding on leathery wings and spending most of their time in gluttonous feeding like vultures, were content to be what they were. The largest of them Nature sent after the earth-dragons; for her interest and her laboratory were now to be given to another kind of beast.

Almost for the first time in the history of the planet, the creatures to which she gave sympathy and care were creatures of fear. From the day of their birth to the day of their death they were terrified. It was as if, having experimented recklessly and with incalculable extravagance, Nature perceived at last that neither security for life nor perfection of machine-like form was the goal she sought. During millions of years, fear had been a casual and unimportant thing. The killer-sharks and the tyrant lizards had been her favorites, and there had been no fear in them; but now she turned to the beasts who were born with terror in their souls and lived in dread.

Dragons of land and air she destroyed, as well as most of those in the seas; and as if to prepare the earth for a new and a greater experiment, she softened and beautified the formidable earth, covering the mountains with forests and scattering gardens of wild flowers over the hills. The valleys teemed with butterflies and singing birds. To the morning and the evening she gave the lights and shadows which we know today.

The mammals had come, including the milk-givers. They housed the unborn in their bodies and gave them care after their birth. Love had entered the world. But it was not, by any means, everywhere the gentle dawn of a gentler era. Among the mammals there were savage beasts, the cat and all its kin—the saber-toothed tiger, the bear-dog, the great wolf. There were the giant hogs and the mammoths. There were flesh-eaters of many kinds; because in this new experiment of intelligence evolving out of fear, there was need of those who killed, of the murderer as well as his prey. The world was to be a kindergarten of the terrible and the terrified, but there would no longer be, except in survivors of an ancient time, the security afforded by thick armor and monstrous size. Even the great cats were to be haunted by fear, too; but instead of a bone-plated fortress they were to seek speed and agility and courage. Speed and cunning were needed now, but above all else, in the mighty struggle to survive, intelligence was needed; and to urge intelligence to rapid growth, every creature in the sea and upon the land and in the air was given its enemies, and in every living heart fear became the vigilant and vivid lighthouse of the mind.

Into two great clans all the earth's people were divided. There were the predaceous killers who ate only flesh and spent most of their waking hours in stalking and trapping their prey; and there were the timid beasts that fed on the plants. From one of these clans, Man was to come. It is the origin of intelligence, and its forgotten glory, that it came from the leaf-eaters who daily fled for their lives. It came from beasts who trembled in terror in the jungles and forests and upon the prairies and hills. It came from the ancient cousins of the rabbit and deer and gazelle.

But as the cats were an extreme on one hand, becoming arrested by their very ferocity, so was the forbear of the gazelle an extreme on the other hand, making of terror almost its sole meaning, and a shy and timorous path its way to defeat. Between these two somewhere, with courage and fear mating and assisting one another, was the golden mean which Nature sought. Neither brutal slaughter nor wild flight could fill the house of the skull. And so on one side were the fangs and talons, and on the other were nimble feet or wings; and between them, feeling both, and uniting them in purpose and plan, were the animals who took the middle road into the modern world. Courage they had because without it they would have been gazelles; and fear they had because without it they would have been chiefly fangs and claws. They were creatures of muscular strength, but strength alone was not enough. Over the whole earth, and in the waters if they ventured there, were beasts waiting to tear them limb from limb. In the jungles were huge serpents and deadly insects; upon the prairies were the gaunt wolves hunting in packs. There was no spot on earth where the ancestor of man could safely lay his head, and if he had not taken to the trees he might have perished long ago.

In the high ceiling of the forest he made his home, and practice there gave him such amazing agility that he was able to swing from branch to branch with surpassing grace and ease. For ages he was an arboreal tenant, rarely venturing to the ground; for he drank water from the leaves and he ate the foliage and he made his bed in a tree crotch. After a long while he came to the earth more frequently and loped along on four feet, but at the sight of an enemy he ascended with astonishing speed. In his high leafy temples he could scold to his heart's content and survey, with brown alert eyes, the spectacle of endless slaughter below him. If he had been willing to remain in the trees he would never have been more than the monkey that his distant cousins still are.

He was not willing to remain there, nor, upon coming to the ground, was he willing forever to walk on four feet. He attempted to stand up on his hind legs and look around him; and though he fell awkwardly because of a curved spine and lack of balance, he tried again and again, generation after generation, until the day came when he stood upright on short bowed legs and walked erect. He discovered then that his hands were freed to other uses; and this, the greatest of all discoveries in our long dark past, made of the creature a man. When his front legs became arms and his front feet became hands, his mind was freed to a path of development that lay in full sunshine ahead. He was, or he soon would be, the king of the earth. He had fallen, not by chance, but by persistent trial and effort, upon a pattern of behavior that set him free; and never again could his supremacy be threatened, or his enemies be more than his slaves.

Now we shall give to him this early chapter in his long journey out of darkness and the deep.

Part One

I

THROUGH dense growth and into deeper jungle, seeking a dark and tangled fastness for the night, went a group of thirteen in single file, with Ho-wha, the mighty lord and guardian of the family, leading the way, and Ka-ka, the oldest of the women, bringing up the rear. The time was late spring. After a winter of hungry and nomadic prowling, they had come in their wanderings upon a broad and succulent thicket; and for many days they had fed gluttonously and put on weight. Their bellies this evening were stuffed with good things, and they were all content except Ghak, an old and sick and petulant man who was always driven from the juiciest patch of foliage and fruit and had to feed where he could.

Their hunger was appeased and they were sleepy, but they were watchfully alert. Never for a moment did they dare to relax their vigilance in a land where deadly enemies skulked in the undergrowth and vultures soared overhead. Ho-wha now and then paused to smell out the scents of the jungle or to listen; and Ka-ka often turned to look behind her, or stopped, tense and expectant, if she heard a sudden sound. A great bird, unexpectedly taking off in flight, or a small ground animal, scurrying in the dusk, could fetch them all to a rigid attitude of listening and lift for a moment in fear and anger the stiff thick hair on Ho-wha's crown.

But there were no enemies around them tonight. For half a mile they marched in single column; whereupon, perceiving that they were in dense growth, with materials for beds all around them, Ka-ka busied herself in choosing the most favored spot as her own. In this they all deferred to her wish. She was not only the oldest and the chief of Ho-wha's women; she was also far advanced in pregnancy and needed a soft bed on which to lie. After her, the preference was given to Who-ah, the second wife, to whose back clung a suckling only a week old. There was no social equality among these persons. From the queen-mother down to the lowliest, from Ka-ka to the second wife and the third, and from them to the children, the old woman, the old man, the dwarfed waif, and the ugly female with the sickly skin and thin hair, the rank was fixed. They all knew their place and they all kept it except when Ho-wha fell into deep sleep.

Now they were all making their beds. Each sought a thick clump of pliable vines and shrubs. Standing within it, he bent them all toward the center and interlaced them until he had formed a kind of vine hammock on which he could lie. It was an excellent bed when properly made. Sometimes the older children fashioned a vine mattress in the crotch of a huge tree and slept securely above the earth; and more rarely the women did likewise when they could find a tree to their taste. The men never left the earth. Above all else, Ho-wha was guardian of the group, and he would never have thought of placing himself wholly beyond danger. Like all the family guardians of this time, he slept when he could with his back toward a stone ledge or a very dense thicket; but he always faced the area from which attack would most likely come. Too, he chose the most unsheltered and approachable of the sleeping places, giving to the women and children the more protected spots.

The children tonight were not ready for sleep. Gah, the oldest girl, was a roguish and mischievous and curious lass who loved to frolic about; and now, after going a little way from the group, she found some juicy fig leaves and began to smack her lips over them, looking meanwhile at her half sister Murah. Murah watched her with sober interest for a long moment and then went over to join her; and presently the two of them began a game of hide-and-seek in the tall grass. With cries of gleeful challenge, Gah darted away and into a tangle of liana and then dropped into the grass and was still; and Murah ran after her, chattering excitedly, and pausing again and again to part clumps of fern and peer for her sister. When she found Gah she threw herself on her and the two girls rolled squealing and clawing among the grasses; but after a little while Gah drew the younger girl to her in a tight embrace and held her and thrust her tongue against the back of Murah's neck. Murah liked the caress. She yielded, happily expectant, though she was not, like her sister, budding in young womanhood and she did not feel Gah's erotic bliss. She liked to be fondled, but when Gah stopped caressing with her tongue and began to examine her, Murah drew away. She was only eight, and Gah was ten.

For many weeks now, Gah had been looked upon with covetous eyes by Wuh, a strange young man who had joined the group. He was an interloper who remained apart from the others because Ho-wha turned upon him with scowling anger and threatened him if he came near. While the girls played, Wuh sat in his bed and looked round him. He had built it, as he always did, at some distance from Ho-wha and the women, but his aloofness did not mean that he was content to live apart from them. Sly and cunning, like all the people of this time, and resentful of the overlord's monopoly of the females, he lived and slept on the margin of their lives and awaited his time. If he had dared, he would have gone to Gah to roll in the grass and embrace her. That she was ripe and approachable he had known since the day he joined the group, when, standing apart and looking in turn at the females, he fixed his lustful interest on her.

He was not the only young man here with such knowledge and lusting in his mind. Hwah, Ho-wha's own son, a huge fellow of sixteen, also coveted Gah; and the fact that she was his sister was not one of his recognitions. These people knew nothing about kinship. A man took a mate when and where he could—and he took his own mother if the father was slain in battle or if the son could drive him out. Dull-witted, and less cunning and eager than Wuh, Hwah had curled up in his bed to sleep; and if he had been able to express his dim thoughts, he might have said that he expected soon to be driven from the group, as was the custom with his people. He would be driven forth, as Wuh had been, and would, like him, join another family elsewhere.

Wuh, sitting in his bed and listening to the shrill excitement of Gah, was troubled by the invisible boundary which he dared not cross. Ho-wha was a selfish and tyrannical lord. Insatiable in his lust and absolute in his despotism, he forced his women to yield at the most unlikely moments, and ignored, as an obdurate tyrant is privileged to, the greedy and angry watchfulness of the other men. Not always, Wuh reflected in his small dark mind, would life in the group be as it was now. If he could not slyly seize a mate and run off with her, then the day must come when he would attack Ho-wha and try to kill him.

An unexpected sound drew his attention away from the girls. Ho-wha had summoned his youngest woman to his bed; and she now went over, like the obedient slave she was, to scratch his back. With strong fingernails she curried the heavy dark hair on his broad shoulders, and he grunted with pleasure. Wuh wanted a mate to do these little things for him; because he itched, too, sometimes with almost intolerable impatience. He wanted a mate who would search his scalp for bugs that housed themselves there, who would fill him with bliss as she dug sharp nails along his spine, and who, when he was well fed and vain and indulgent, would fondle him and examine him with little cries of pleasure. He wanted, in this moment, to grunt out of deep delight as Ho-wha was grunting now.

On Who-ah's back clung her infant who looked curiously round him, and presently he decided to explore as much of the dark jungle world as lay within reach. Venturing downward, and grasping his mother's hair as he descended, as if letting himself down from a tree, he at last freed his clutch on her and squatted on the vine hammock, still looking brightly about him. Who-ah now divided her attention between her mate and her son. She raked the broad dirty back and then paused and turned to see what mischief her son was up to; and when he moved to crawl away on hands and knees, intent on exploring the leafy depths around him, she reached down and gave him a smart slap on his pate that knocked him over. He whimpered but he did not return to his perch. Ho-wha spoke in a rumbling growl of warning, and at once she resumed her scratching, but her eyes and ears were still on her son. When he made another move to escape, she seized him by a leg and dragged him back and cuffed him, and thereupon he was content to sit by her and stare with dark brown eyes at the dank gloom.

Wuh had been watching this family idyl and thinking of it with all the mind he had. Two months had passed since his father had attacked him with awful fury and driven him out into the world. It was always that way with these people. When a son reached manhood he was forced to leave the group and seek a life of his own; but the daughters remained in the group and became sexual mates of their father. Sometimes, though, a son grew to such strength and courage that he stood his ground and fought it out with his sire. If he won in the duel of ferocity and might, he took over the family as his own and the father became a solitary and lonely wanderer.

There was Ghak. He did not belong to this group. He was an old man who had been chased out by his own son or by the son of another; but instead of leading a solitary life, as most of the old men did, he was trying to attach himself to Ho-wha's clan. He had never been, even in his prime, a mighty man like Ho-wha. From a scrawny and undersized tantrum child he had grown into a neurotic adult, subject to stormy moods and glottal cramp attacks; and he had been, in consequence, an easy victim for any more aggressive and more powerful man. He was, indeed, and had always been, full of self-pity and mean vengeful trickeries, and now in old age he hated and feared every living thing.

Wuh was not that kind of man, nor did he have Ho-wha's sullen and wrathful temperament. By nature he was sanguine and gay, full of fun and optimism and hope, and inclined to plot for what he wanted rather than to fight for it. He was by far the most intelligent man in the group. Never for a moment, save when feeling foolhardy and frustrated, did he intend to have a physical showdown with Ho-wha. He was afraid of him; and besides, Wuh was a very cunning fellow with the makings in him of a smooth and practiced knave. Most men took by force what they wanted; but some, like Wuh, sat around with sly faces and infinite patience and bided their time.

Watching Who-ah curry her lord's back, Wuh was content to wait. Sharply intuitive, and quite alert in reading feminine whims and fancies, he had perceived from the first that Who-ah was bored with her mate. Or perhaps that is not the right word. She resented him and his moody and unexpected hungers and his insatiable wish for little attentions when she was sleepy and tired. Of the three, she was his favorite woman, but favoritism in Ho-wha placed on the unlucky one not greater kindness but greater burdens. Kuoh he ignored completely, and not in many evenings had he summoned Ka-ka to search his scalp or awaken ecstasies along his itching spine.

All these things Wuh intuitively perceived, no matter how dimly. They were not facts that he counted off one by one, relating each to its cause and motives. They were matters which he sensed as he sensed the approach of morning or evening or the invisible presence of a leopard or the erotic hunger of Gah.

His plotting, too—such as he was capable of—though far beyond in its subtlety and sagacity anything Ho-wha could have understood, was not the pattern of a clear and calculating mind. It was very simple because its materials were simple things. He felt, for instance, that if he ever caught Gah safely out of sight of the tyrant he could quickly approach and embrace her. Perhaps Ho-wha knew that much also—because he never let her out of his sight. Wuh realized, too, with an emotion akin to despair, that Gah would soon be drawn into Ho-wha's group of women, and that Murah, in time, would follow her. He knew these things as clearly as he knew the use of bananas or the covering of the oil palm or the leaves of the Christmas tree. He thought and worried about them and plotted meanwhile to wrest authority from Ho-wha and drive him out. If he had been a little more intelligent than he was, he would have fashioned some kind of snare for the man and choked him to death.

Murder was not a crime among these people. By discovering new uses for their hands, and thereby releasing their minds to curiosity and growth, they had lifted themselves far above the level of beasts; but they had no notions of right and wrong. Selfish, greedy, sly, covetous, and vain, their chief task was to survive, to outwit their enemies, to find an abundance of good things to eat, and to spend their sexual hunger in lustful mating. The men took women when and where they could and kept them as long as they were physically able; and as they grew old and feeble they lost them to younger men. A part of their lives and their energy was spent in ferocious brawls over women. Toward their fierce feuds and fighting the women were indifferent, going obediently with the lord who in any moment proved to be their master. The men were jealous, and often murderously so, but the women were not. They were content to be protected and to bear their young and to be guided to the lushest feeding grounds.

After Who-ah returned to her bed, with the infant again riding her shoulders, Ho-wha lay in his big vine hammock, with his face on a hairy arm, and fell asleep. In another bed, Gah and Murah, the two girls, were asleep, too, lying in one another's arms and almost mouth to mouth. A small lad shared his mother's bed; Ka-ka slept alone. Hwah, the big morose son, slept alone, too, as did Kuoh, the old and unloved and barren wife. Ghoo, the horribly ugly woman, slept near the only one in the group who was kind to her, Kughh, the dwarf.

Wuh looked round him at the deep jungle night but he was still thinking of the females and particularly of Gah. In his mind was the dark and obscure notion of going quietly to her bed and dragging her off to his hammock. Perhaps, indeed, he could flee with her while all the others slept; but also in his mind was fear of Ho-wha who often awakened during the night to peer about him and see if all was well. He was a dreadful brute when aroused to fury; and nothing called forth his wrath like an attempt on the part of another male to steal one of his women. But also, during this long-ago time, there was nothing that could goad a man to such foolhardy daring and dangerous risks as his lusting for a mate. That is why Wuh sat on his bed, sleepless, resentful, baffled, and considered his loneliness. He was helpless between his fear of Ho-wha and his hunger for the girl.

Sometimes, when placed in such a predicament, bachelors less timid or less discreet challenged the lord of a family and fought it out with him; and then the jungle roared with the desperate struggle. They fought with powerful hands and strong teeth, and the women and children stood back, trembling, and waited. Usually the vanquished one was driven out, lacerated and bloody and defeated; now and then he was slain. More rarely the two fought until they were both killed or later died of their wounds.

Almost from birth until he was driven out, Wuh had seen his father put to flight or destroy the bold men who invaded his domain; and because he was an uncommonly thoughtful child he had decided that discretion was of more worth than valor. That was a tremendous decision to come to. Perhaps he was not the first among men to perceive that sly plotting could often accomplish more than frank and unabashed warfare, but he was one of the first to stick to this social philosophy, even in the face of the most provocative temptation to fight. This new perspective was to become his great advantage over less intelligent competitors. Obscurely related to it was another fact which Wuh had observed. He had no concept of old age, but he knew, perhaps intuitively, that the time must come when the boss of any family would be overthrown by a rival.

That had happened to Ghak. That had happened to many old fellows, now gray and solitary, whom Wuh had seen during his wanderings. They had been driven out to spend their last years in solitude and to die alone. Some of them, possibly all of them, were eventually slain by their enemies, by the great snakes or the leopard or by other beasts of forest or plain. These old men, enfeebled, crippled by old scars, and full of inflammation and pains, became more and more defenseless; and at last the beasts and the vultures closed in.

But Wuh was not thinking of that. All that, it may be, was a dimly realized part of his knowledge and of his feelings about himself and his people; but when a man was young and vital he did not think about the old or care what they did. Age and death were not a part of his consciousness or his interests. He was solely concerned about females and food and safety from his foes. It never occurred to him, or to any other young person of his time, that some day he would be old and abandoned, diseased and sick, and haunted not by the fears of youth but by the loneliness and dread of age.

Wuh stirred on his bed of vines. Across a distance of forty yards, he could hear Ho-wha's deep and rumbling snores, and in the beds around Ho-wha he could see the dark bodies of the women and children. Discretion told him to curl up in his bed and sleep, but the hunger in him was a persistent and throbbing unhappiness that beat as an invigorating and wakeful pulse in his whole being. It was an almost irresistible impulse to reach out with his arms and clasp and embrace. It was a hot and anguished wish to explore with his hands and eyes and tongue. And it was an unrelenting compulsion that made him sit up in his bed, rigidly attentive, his eyes staring with hypnotic earnestness into the darkness where Gah slept.

At last, moved by the aching hunger in him that was as

deep as life, he rose softly, stealthily, and stood erect. His breathing was as loud and labored as that of a beast in pain. After staring for a long moment over at the black shadow of Ho-wha and listening for the sound of his sleep, Wuh stepped, with extreme caution, out of his bed, and went as noiselessly as if his feet had been sheathed with fur. Without snapping a twig or rustling a vine he reached Gah's bed and dropped softly to his hands and peered at her sleeping face. She and Murah were lying on their sides, with arms thrown across one another. As soon as he felt the warmth of them, Wuh almost yielded to an impulse to examine the girls. He wanted to pull Gah toward him and turn her over and over and with all his senses inspect her from head to feet, feeling and smelling her, biting her gently, exploring her with his tongue, and discovering everything about her that made her a woman and not a man. He wanted her to examine him, too, and play with him; to slap and cuff him about with excited interest; to awaken all the lust in him and bring it into sharp focus and then to assume a sexual posture and reach round with a hand and draw him to her. Never had he known the embrace of a female, and his instinctive behavior was a little inhibited and confused. Besides, all the while, like a dark threat of teeth and hands in his mind, there was his realization of Ho-wha, snoring in slumber a few feet away.

Without touching the girls, Wuh sat by their bed and continued to look at them. He stared at their faces as if expecting to find there a response to his desire. Presently he had to fight against another impulse. He wanted to crouch forward and lick Gah's neck and cheeks with his tongue; and he did move a little toward her, very gently, but instead of touching her he began to play with himself.

A few minutes later, without having touched or disturbed the girls, he slunk back to his bed. He felt more at peace now, but it was a shoddy and unmanly peace that gave no homage to his ego. It was a softening of the wild and lusting pain that had driven him, against his fear and judgment, to risk Ho-wha's wrath. He felt like one returned from the leopard's path to the rabbit's den; and he felt, too, the gall of his plight, as if his feast of ecstasy had been tinctured with bitter juices. He felt no shame, no guilt, no disgust, but in him was the obscure unhappiness, the frustration, the outrage of his manhood that would eventually, in the ages to come, father and foster a concept of sin.

He stretched out on his bed under the black canopy of the jungle but he did not sleep for a long while.

2

When morning came Ho-wha was the first to bestir himself. He awoke and yawned and stood up to look round him, and then gave a thunderous yell to arouse the group. One by one they stirred and rose, including Wuh who had been dreaming simple dreams of eating and lusting. The women and all the children, except the morose and sullen Hwah, gathered around their lord. Hwah and Wuh and Ghak, the embittered old man, remained at a respectful distance.

It was barely daylight; the jungle was still full of the sleepy dusk of night. Ho-wha, still standing in his bed and looking round him, was wondering in which direction grew the juiciest plants and fruits. His hunger for food, like that of all people of this time, was ravenous, and especially upon waking in the morning. He felt as if his great protuberant paunch had been empty for a long while. Shouting again, as if the sound of his voice gave him a sense of dominance and power, he left his bed and set off through the leafy and interlaced walls of vine and fern, with the women and children eagerly trailing him and the other men falling in behind.

He fed a little as he went, pausing to gather a handful of leaves or to break a stalk and examine its heart; and humbly the others paused behind him, waiting on his will. He was seeking a plantain thicket, and after a half-hour of wandering he came to one in which nobody had eaten during this season. It was a rich and abundant breakfast, close by a garden of fragrant bloom. Taking as his own the choicest spot, Ho-wha began to eat, and he ate with the zestful gusto of the tiger or the wolf, feeding his huge mouth with both hands and acting as if he intended to draw the whole forest into his stomach. He liked the fruit of the plantain but preferred the succulent heart of the stalk. The stalk he tore open and twisted until the heart fell free in his hands. The fruit, a red pod filled with bitter seeds and soft pulp, was a favorite with the children; but Ho-wha found it a little too caustic in the first ravenous hunger of morning. He had more relish for it after his belly was nearly full.

While he ate, indifferent to all hungers but his own, Who-ah nursed her baby. The infant seized with both hands a dark pendulous breast and sucked for all he was worth; and his mother caressed him and stared at him with affectionate wonder that was comically solemn. Ghoo, the ugly one, was bending stalks down for Kughh, the dwarf, to reach and rend; and with that maternal tenderness which was her most dominant trait, she denied her own hunger while feeding the hideously malformed idiot whom she had adopted as her own. Ka-ka was feeding with the girls close by her.

At some distance from all these were the other men.

Hwah, a greedy and selfish lout, born in the image of his father, paid no attention to anyone. Ghak, the old man, full of self-pity and tantrums, half-screened himself with a vine tangle, but he divided his attention between food and Ho-wha, whom he constantly watched. During most of the time his fear of Ho-wha almost paralyzed his will. When that giant looked at him he began to tremble and stood as if hypnotized; and the instant Ho-wha took his scowling gaze away, Ghak hastily withdrew to a safer distance. He lived on the margin of the group life and never dared venture close to any of them. Even when overcome by insane rage that made him hop up and down and scream and beat his knuckles on the earth, he kept himself ready for instant flight.

Wuh was also feeding apart and alone, with one eye on Ho-wha and the other on the women. He was eating, and staring with a kind of meditative lustfulness at Gah, when Ghak, for no reason at all, began to work up a dreadful fury. Perhaps a thorn had pricked him or the fruit had been too bitter on his tongue; or perhaps, and more plausibly, it was only because he felt abandoned and useless and wanted the others to be compassionately aware of him. In any case, he suddenly gave a fearful yell and then beat his breast while uttering a dismally plaintive "Ohhh!" that dropped a note in pitch and ended in a long-drawn whine. Nobody paid any attention to that; whereupon, as if he had only been announcing himself, Ghak began to leap up and down and tear madly at the vines and howl as if he were being butchered. If his rage at first was simulated, it became, nevertheless, very real—so real, indeed, that it churned him in its violence until his mouth slobbered and his eyes bulged. His cries now started off with a long doleful bleat and then burst explosively as if set off with powder and poured out of him in choking howls. He tore at his hair, at his limbs, at the brush around him. He gouged at the earth with his long nails or attacked a tree and ripped scars down its bark. He beat the tree with his hands, hopping up and down meanwhile, and then hurled himself to the ground and tumbled over and over, hissing and writhing as if in the throes of a deadly poison.

Ho-wha had stopped feeding. It was not that he cared anything about Ghak or what the petulant old fool did. It was only because violent sounds and extremes of frenzy invaded his breakfasting calm and demanded attention. He looked over at Ghak as he might have stared at any trivial madness, but he did not move. He was mildly, quietly annoyed because this unpredictable lunatic was making such an uproar that feeding for the moment was out of the question.

Others, too, were looking at Ghak, but only one of them moved toward him. Ghoo, the ugly one, the warden of the dwarf, was sympathetic, but she went experimentally, as if her legs responded step by step to the uncertainty in her mind. Upon approaching within a few feet of Ghak she paused and looked at him, her large brown eyes full of compassionate inquiry. But she made no move to touch or restrain the self-pitying simpleton who was now sitting on the earth and hammering it and venting his sickness of soul in chilling wails. Ghoo stood where she was because she was baffled. She had seen him in a tantrum before but his behavior was a riddle to her, as it was to all the other people here. Tantrum children she had seen and in a mother's way she had understood them;

but there seemed no reason why an old man should behave as if he sat helplessly on a nest of thorns.

Ho-wha resumed his eating. A lot of things interrupted and angered him a little as this old man did. There was the loud racket of jungle birds or the gibbering of monkeys. They often beat upon the morning calm, but they were not dangerous and Ho-wha strove to ignore them. Ghak was the same kind of harmless nuisance. If Ho-wha had ever felt deep anger because of the old fellow's tantrums, he would have slain him long ago.

Ghak had worked himself into an attack of cramps that had silenced his voice and almost paralyzed his body; and now he lay on the earth, suffering intense pain and looking beseechingly at Ghoo. She was the only one who paid any attention to him after his outcry ceased. Wuh had been slyly watching and eating. The sounds of physical agony in one of their fellows was deeply disturbing to all people except infants; but their response to suffering was wholly emotional and beyond their will, a part of their heritage, a matter that quickly touched their sense of their own personal welfare. Perhaps it was instinctive with them. Even Who-ah's baby had cried out as if in pain, and the other young children had moved in close to their mothers.

Wuh had been excited, too, by Ghak's dreadful yelling, but he was more intelligent than the others and had dim notions of a few relationships and values. He knew, or at least he felt, that Ghak was only acting a part; but nevertheless his scalp had begun to tingle and the hair had risen on his head, and over his body he had a creeping gooseflesh alarm. He had made an irrational response and vaguely he knew it and that is why he had tried to ignore

Ghak. He wondered, meanwhile, if Ho-wha would march over to slap the old fellow down. If he did, then, Wuh perceived, there would be a chance for him, in the confusion of the moment, to seize Gah and drag her off into hiding.

But Ho-wha did nothing of the kind. After a long moment of sullen contemplation of the old man, he had resumed his eating, and he did not pause again until his belly was full. The women and children also ate again, being largely guided in all but their instinctive acts by what their master did. The baby stopped crying. The other children moved away from their mothers.

After Ho-wha had crammed into his bulging stomach all the plantain hearts it would hold he was thirsty, and when he wanted a thing he never consulted any wish but his own. With a roar to advise them that he was on the march again, he set off in search of water, and obediently the others fell in behind him. Ghak was the last one to go. Either very sick or pretending to be, he paid no heed to them until Ka-ka had passed out of sight; whereupon, with a howl of dismay and terror, he leapt up, as nimble as any other, and rushed after the column.

Ho-wha took a devious course, sniffing the jungle air for scent of water or pausing now and then to lick a spoonful of dew from cupped leaves. When he came to a fresh-water lake he shouted again as if to point out to them what they could all plainly see. Many generations before, their ancestors had drunk by kneeling to a stream and lapping in the manner of wolves; but these people had learned to drink from their cupped palms. Sometimes the children preferred to lie on their bellies and drink. Like all the other people of the earth they were afraid of water and none of them was able to swim. When, in their nomadic wanderings, they came to a deep river or lake, they made no attempt to cross it but accepted it as one of the boundaries of their domain. Deep water for them was a terrible thing like lightning and thunder and fire. A storm on a lake or the sea, plunging in great waves and roaring toward them in a foaming tide, could almost paralyze them with dread and make the boldest man whimper like a child. Moving water seemed to them to be an angry and destroying thing.

Having slaked his thirst, Ho-wha marched back into the jungle, followed by the others. He wanted an open spot where he could stretch his huge body at ease and feel the warm sun upon it. This area of wilderness pleased him. Food was abundant, and he had seen no sign of his most deadly enemies, the skulking leopard and the coiled and waiting snakes. He was a lazy, a complacently indolent, man who was content to feed and mate and sleep. If all people had been like him, there could have been no progress, but only the cycle, endlessly repeated, of birth and vigilant idleness and death. It was restless and frustrated men like Wuh and women like Who-ah who added a little, generation by generation, to the heritage of their race.

Finding a big tree in full sunlight, Ho-wha sat with his back against it and relaxed. His long hairy arms lay idly at his sides. His chin sank to the thick growth on his chest. He was sluggish with digestion and peace but his dark brown eyes, showing no iris, and set with small pupils that were like points of light, missed nothing that went on around him. Every member of his family, as well as the interloping bachelor and the silly old Ghak, he kept within the circumference of a watchful distrust.

Ka-ka, the pregnant one, was resting not far from her lord. By a drooping wall of vegetable ropes and mosses and parasitic creepers, Murah was playing with a half brother, a lad of four. They were busy inspecting one another and picking insects out of their hair. At some distance from them sat Ghoo, gazing fondly at the stupid and misshapen and almost speechless Kughh, whom she had adopted to care for and cherish. Ghoo was so repulsive that Ho-wha had never shown her any favors. Ugliness was not a recognition among these people unless it was so extreme as to be horrifying. Ghoo was so pathologically thin of hair that she looked naked. She looked as if she had been caught in a sandstorm that had sheared her and pimpled her flesh with tiny chronic sores; for her skin seemed to be abraded and yellow and ripe with disease. The natural body odor of these people, when glowing with health, was a strong musk smell; but about Ghoo there was an awful stench. None of them could endure the smell of her except the dwarf about whom there was a strong unnatural odor. Ghoo's face was as hideous as her skin. Her grotesquely long upper lip was completely hairless and looked leprous; and her overhanging brow ridges were barren and yellow. But in her face was a gentleness to be seen in no other face here—the kindly inoffensiveness of one in whom all the native savagery had been chastened and subdued by social ostracism. Timid, submissive, and denied children of her own, she kept out of everybody's way, asking only the privilege of devoting herself to the idiot who had been abandoned by his own family.

Once or twice she had made a friendly gesture toward Ghak, the old man imprisoned in his tantrums; but even Ghak spurned her. He had nobody, not even a dwarf, to call his own, but he did not want this unsightly and ill-smelling female. In his foolish old heart he wanted Gah, and he often sat and looked at her, perceiving no good reason why an old and worn-out man like himself should not have a young girl. He did not actively strive to possess her. He was too lost in self-pitying darkness to do more than to stare at her with rheumy old eyes that were full of chronic lusting and an outcast's loneliness. He hated Ho-wha with all the strength left in his senile mind, and if he had had the power of prayer in him, he would have prayed for Ho-wha's death.

Ho-wha sensed none of all that. He suffered the old man's presence because he did not recognize in him a rival; nor did he, for that matter, see a rival worth bothering with in Wuh. To understand why, it is necessary to see Ho-wha in all his bulk and brawn. Considerably above the average man of his time in size, he weighed more than three hundred pounds and stood close to six feet in height. Never had he faced a rival who had been a match for him. More than one bold bachelor had invaded his small kingdom to dispute with him over his women. All but one of them had fled with the marks of Ho-wha's teeth in their flesh and the memory of choking hands on their throats. One of them Ho-wha had slain.

He did not like the presence of Wuh, but as long as that man minded his business, the lazy and complacent Ho-wha was content to let him remain. If he had been more intelligent, if he had observed and understood what was going on around him, he would have been worried by Hwah, his oldest son. Ghak eyed the giant with petulant resentment, Wuh with sly distaste, but Hwah looked at him with thoughts of murder maturing in his heart. And Hwah, not fully grown yet, gave promise of being as mighty a man as his sire.

The morning drew to noon and the lord of the clan still sunned himself; but another hunger was beginning to suffuse him with its warmth. He looked at the women—at Ka-ka first, who, lying on the ground, seemed to be nothing much except a great belly to which were attached arms and legs and a head. He looked at Who-ah, who was nursing her infant. The babe had grasped a brown dug with both hands and was vigorously drawing milk from a nipple. For a long moment Ho-wha stared at the child. These people never mated during the period of lactation; and Ho-wha, therefore, had had for more than two weeks only a pregnant wife to ease his lust. He was weary of her and more morose than was his habit. Ka-ka did not feel well. She resented his despotic demands; and besides, she was a large and powerful woman and sometimes when he laid his hands on her she snarled at him and bit or struck him. In the end, of course, she always yielded, not because she wished to but because he was stronger.

After looking at Who-ah and sensing that the child made her unapproachable, Ho-wha turned again to Ka-ka; and as if the sight of her had been enough to release his will, he grunted and rose to his short hairy legs. When he rose, every person in the group except the baby stiffened with uncertainty and suspense. They did not know what was in his mind, but whatever it was, they knew they would not like it.

While Ho-wha stood by the tree, staring at Ka-ka, and intending in a moment to go over and seize her and force her to mate with him, his attention was caught by his oldest daughter. Gah had been rolling in the grass and playing erotically with Murah. Ho-wha sensed in her a lustful excitement, and instead of striding toward Ka-ka he turned toward her.

A strange thing happened that would be difficult to explain. Perhaps Gah was frightened by his abrupt advance or perhaps she was only coy in the way of her kind and fled an approaching male because it is in the nature of the female to flee. In any case, she leapt up and ran, and Ho-wha paused in astonished wrath to stare after her. She ran to the leafy wall and vanished into it and then turned to peer out; and for a long moment Ho-wha, baffled and angry, looked at the spot where she had disappeared, and the other persons looked at him.

The people of this age had not learned to express their joy or their malicious triumph in laughter. If they had been able to shout with glee, Wuh would have shouted now. He was as maliciously pleased as a primitive man could be. At first he thought of dashing into the thicket to seize Gah and make off with her; but on second thought his ardor was cooled by the threatening hulk of an angry man. So Wuh sat where he was and waited to see what Ho-wha would do.

Ho-wha struck his breast a great blow and roared—and the roar was a command to Gah to be done with her girlish foolishness and come to him. If he had had the power of speech he would have scolded and abused her; but because he was only a dull-witted man he started toward her in baffled rage, and in the same instant Gah's face completely vanished.

When she withdrew her face, Wuh moved swiftly toward the thicket, but a roar of anger that could have been heard for miles stopped him in his tracks. Ho-wha had read the man's intention. His annoyance with Gah had been nothing at all in comparison with the rage he felt now. He started toward Wuh, but that sly fellow, who depended more on his cunning than on his teeth, promptly fled away from the thicket and threw himself to the earth and cowered abjectly. Ho-wha paused. He looked at the wall where Gah was hiding and then at Wuh; and after turning from one to the other as if caught helplessly between two urges of equal strength, he swung suddenly and laid his big hands on Ka-ka. He shook her with such violence that she screamed.

All of them, including the baby, now watched him with intent eyes. Gah was peering out to watch him too. Shaking more with fury than with lust, Ho-wha rolled his woman over and over as if she were a barrel and then lifted her and set her down on her rump. After staring at her a moment, he reached long arms around her and set her on hands and feet, making it as plain as he could that she was to assume a sexual posture. But Ka-ka was an angry and an outraged woman. She bit his arm, an indiscretion that fetched from him a dreadful bellow of wrath; she tore at him with long sharp nails; she slapped him with the calloused heels of her palms. If she had persisted in the struggle he probably would have killed her.

The excitement of the moment, the vision of a huge despotic fellow mauling a female, threw Ghak into one of his tantrums. He began to howl as if covered with leeches. Grasping a shrub, he uprooted it and struck wildly about him, and then dropped it and smote his breast. His eyes all the while were fixed on Ho-wha mating with his woman. The sight of it was almost more than he could endure. Thrusting his long lips out in a monstrous pucker, he drooled with rage and fear and drummed with both palms on his distended cheeks. He was so excited and terrified that he fouled himself with his own excrement.

Wuh's anguish was just as extreme but he gave no sign of it. His face had turned a brownish yellow and his loose lips quivered, but he did not move because he was the prisoner of fear. It was Hwah, the oldest son, who was the most dreadful one to look at. He stood on his feet, his body tense, the hair erect on his scalp, and his eyes shining like windows upon the murder in his mind.

3

A FORTNIGHT later, Ka-ka knew that birth of a child was imminent. For many days she had been sullen and silent, dreading the ordeal ahead of her; because birth among these primitive people was not the easy and casual thing it was among the beasts. Parturition often took an hour or more and sometimes the mother's agony was severe and prolonged. Sometimes, indeed, the child was born dead, choked by the cord or suffocated in the delivery; and now and then a mother, especially if very young, forfeited her own life. Childbirth was one of the most harrowing of all the experiences common to these people, and none of them, during the delivery of the young, was unaffected by the mother's struggle and her cries of pain.

When, therefore, Ka-ka took great care one evening in the making of her bed, they all sensed that a crisis was at hand. Adding to their apprehension was the ominous rumbling of a dark and distant storm. A wind made whips of the tree tops and the jungle roof lashed like frenzied arms. Lightning awoke on the night sky in broad dim fields. There was a smell of rain. There was a shuddering and inexplicable power in the forest and the earth.

Unaided, but with the whole group watchful and sympathetic, Ka-ka bent many supple vines toward a common center and united them in a soft and cushioned tangle; and then she gathered huge green leaves and spread them over the hammock. For an hour or more she labored, fastidious and thorough and silent. She wanted a deep lush bed on which with ease she could assume the crouched position of birth-giving.

These people had not learned to build shelters. Under the wildest storms or in the bitterest weather they were unprotected except by their hair. When drenched by a sudden deluge they sat around like shivering half-drowned things, waiting for the storm to pass. In unusually cold weather they sometimes drew vines and big leaves over their bodies, but a thunderstorm was a wet and roaring terror which they fearfully and patiently endured.

Ka-ka looked up through jungle ceiling at a patch of sky, sensing that in this night a wild storm would be roaring above the trees and loosing upon her the spit of its anger. She was afraid of it, and she was trembling when she entered her bed.

Ho-wha felt as tender and solicitous as a man of his dull and savage nature had power to feel. Only two things in life, a mother giving birth and a helpless infant, could soften him to gentleness. This in him was not, of course, a reasoning and purposeful behavior; it was only his heritage, the instinctive duty of the guardian male. After a child was old enough to care for itself he paid no attention to it unless he saw it in danger; nor did mothers have maternal interest in their offspring after they were grown.

The affection of father and mother, the latter's much stronger and more enduring, was chiefly a watchful custody of the child during the years when it was easy prey.

Ho-wha was anxious tonight. He sensed that another child, a tiny creature, naked and helpless, and dependent on him, would soon join the group. Until the ordeal was over there would be no sleep for him. There was need to stand guard against his enemies, the tiger and the leopard, who, smelling the blood of birth or hearing the cries of a mother in pain, might press in from darkness, eager to kill. At thought of them he felt the hair stand erect on his skull and down his spine. While Ka-ka smoothed her bed and took a crouching position, he marched round and round her, now and then giving a warning cry that roared with the thunder or rushing toward the jungle wall when he thought something was moving there; and after she began to shake in her bed and moan he doubled his vigilance. If one of the other males had ventured near her he would have leapt upon him and tried to tear him limb from limb. In a time like this he did not distinguish between enemy and friend. The path he made around her bed was the boundary against all invasion; and the others, more in dread of him than of the storm, had withdrawn to a considerable distance.

They had been silenced by Ho-wha's thundering roars. After making and entering their beds they were disturbed and unhappy; for they were only a small group of people in a vast world, in a dark and terrible world that was full of pain and struggle and death. Their dread of it, of the unknown and the unforeseen, was always with them, was in their minds a troubled wonder and a constant anxiety even in their most carefree moments. When feeding or mating or playing their games there was about them the nervous apprehension of the hunted. Their fear of death was an instinctive and desperate struggle against it. Of what it was or why it must be they had no notion; but it was for them one of the certainties; and in opposition to the destroying power of it they had set the wonder of birth. Birth, too, they did not understand at all, but in their simple way they thought about it, and they had begun, no matter how obscurely, to invest it with mystery and to regard it with superstitious awe. Now and then a new life issued from one of them. That much they knew. They did not know that their sexual matings had anything to do with the miracle of a new life. Periodically, mysteriously, it came; and after a while it ceased to be.

There was no natural death among them. When young they sometimes died of wounds or more infrequently of disease, and when old they were slain by their enemies. This was so not only of the males who were driven out to a solitary life, but also of the females who, becoming enfeebled, fell more and more behind the wandering groups. Birth, therefore, was a precious thing for them, and their eager welcome of a babe was as characteristic of them as their indifference to the old. They learned early to rest their faith in the womb instead of the graveyard.

It could not be said of Ghak or Wuh, or indeed of Ho-wha himself, that they had any affection for the baby now coming or would ever have; but they wished, nevertheless, to have another child among them. In numbers, in the mysterious fecund power of the mothers, was their principal assurance of survival. This in them was an intuitive recognition born of their instincts; and when twins came their delight was extreme.

So they all waited, hushed and anxious and expectant, while Ka-ka delivered a child. Crouching on hands and knees in her bed she clutched the vines and repeated endlessly a low plaintive whine of pain; and above her, thunder shook the world, and lightning opened white valleys in the black sky. Ho-wha stood alone, a silent sentinel in the rain. Now and then he bellowed if he heard a sound or he went close to peer at her and learn if the new one had come. Rain was falling on the jungle. Rain hung in big drops to his hair and with a finger he would touch the drops and lick moisture from his hands. After a while he looked like a wet and gleaming monster in the darkness. When lightning flashed he lowered his shaggy head and trembled, and when thunder crashed close by he bellowed with sudden anger and fear. This invisible voice out of the deep he hated because it came from nothing that he could see or attack. The lion sometimes roared, too, but he had seen the lion, as well as the saber-toothed tiger and the howling jackals and wolves; but the angry bellowing above him and the terrifying illuminations in the dead of night came from some gigantic enemy whom he had never seen. He answered challenge with challenge, and when the thunder became louder and more threatening he worked himself into a dreadful fury. Then there was a lull in the clamor overhead and a steady rain fell.

It was past midnight when Ho-wha peered at his woman and saw that the baby had come. Ka-ka was holding the infant in her lap and was very busy with it. The umbilical cord had not been severed but there would be time enough for that after she had made the child breathe. Babies were sometimes born dead; nearly always they were born breathless and would have died soon if the mothers had not known what to do. For a few moments Ka-ka blew breath into the infant's mouth. When that did not arouse it she slapped it vigorously and jounced it up and down. The child gave a barely audible gasp; whereupon, with startling abruptness, like one who knew there was no time to be lost, Ka-ka clutched it to her breast and put her mouth to its mouth and blew again. With her belly heaving like a deep bellows, she breathed into the babe, alternately forcing air to its throat and sucking the air out. Failing in this she shook it again and slapped its back and belly with hard blows; and suddenly, with a strangled gurgle, the infant gulped air and filled its lungs. Ka-ka held it up and looked at it and listened. Perceiving that it was breathing naturally and steadily, she laid it across her lap and began to dry it.

With rough palms she rubbed the moisture of rain and birth from its body, and with her tongue she licked moisture from its face. During all this while she made low sounds of joy. The sound she made was a repeated cry, plaintive and monotonous and faintly tuneful. Some of the others, hearing the cry as they lay in their beds, sat up and listened; and there was joy in their faces. There was joy in Ho-wha's big brutal face as he stood by Ka-ka and watched.

Next, she severed the cord. Holding the baby up and resting it on upturned palms, she chewed the cord in two close to the navel; and then she grasped the placenta and moved it away from her bed. In an earlier time the mothers had eaten the placenta, and some of them did still, but Ka-ka had always thrown hers away. She now wanted to dry the child and make it warm. A heavy rain was falling and the babe was wet and chilled and whimpering. Weighing only about four pounds, and absolutely hairless except for the heavy growth on its skull, it was a helpless and shivering creature; and Ka-ka was so eager to protect it that she reached out and broke off some leaves and spread them over it. But the leaves were wet and only added to the babe's dismal whimpering. Perceiving this, Ka-ka brushed the leaves away and tucked the child close against her belly and bent forward to shelter it; and in this position, holding it to the warmth of her body and keeping it dry, she spent the remainder of the night.

When daylight came she inspected the babe. He was nothing much but a tiny paunch to which were attached two short and crooked and unfleshed legs, two powerful little arms as long as his legs, and a head covered with coarse black hair. His face was so seamed with wrinkles that it looked very old. His feet, with toes spread and grasping and with the large toe far removed from the others, were much like his hands. His eyes were tightly closed as if, having once looked at the world and found it frightening, he was resolved never to look again.

The first thing Ka-ka did was to open his eyes. With a finger she thrust against an upper lid and turned it back until she could see part of an eye; but the instant she removed her finger the lid closed again and the wrinkled face puckered as if repressing a sneeze. Patiently and in turn she thrust the lids back and after a little while the babe began to blink in the strong light. The small eyes, a dark smoky brown, and with pupils so tiny they were barely visible, stared for a moment at his mother's hairy belly and closed again.

Ka-ka's next urge was to feed her child. She held him cradled in her left arm and with her right hand pressed his face to her breast. At once, with eyes still tightly shut, he began to root about in search of a nipple; and upon finding it he sucked with strong lusty hunger. His hands meanwhile explored and clung to her, and his feet also; because his power of grasping with his feet almost equaled that of his hands. After he had nursed a few moments at one breast she put a palm to his face and thrust his head back and guided his seeking mouth to the other nipple. While he filled his belly and clutched her hair with both feet and both hands, she bent over him, striving to caress his homely little face with her tongue. Her effort to reach down dislodged the nipple from his mouth, and with an impatient wheeze followed by a shrill bleat of anger, he tried to climb her frame; but she shoved him down, allowing him to sit now on the shelf of her paunch, and gave him the nipple again.

After his hunger was satisfied she held him up and gazed at him long and earnestly. She was not looking for birthmarks or malformed bones; and yet in her simple way she was searching him to see if he was all right. He was so small that her hands completely encased his body, leaving only his head and feet visible. Next she laid him across her lap and turned him over and over, carefully and patiently examining every inch of him. She inspected his feet, his legs, his genitals, and the wound at his navel; she peered into his ears, she opened his big mouth and stared gravely at his throat, she searched the thatch on his skull for bugs, and she unclenched his hands and licked his palms. After looking him all over, she held him up again, her big strong hands embracing him, and stared at his face. He was a hideously naked little monster of bony angles and wrinkles and brown skin; but not for her. Deciding that he was all right, she fondled him against her breast and murmured over him.

The others had been eating their breakfast. They had spent an anxious night, alarmed by Ka-ka's cries of pain and frightened by thunder, but the morning was cool and calm, with enough water on the plants to satisfy their thirst. They were talking in the way they had. Symbolic language they had not learned, but they made many sounds which they all understood, sounds of joy, of questing, of friendliness, of excitement, of anger, of concern. Now they were chattering happily because the crisis with Ka-ka had passed and their dreadful enemy in the sky had killed none of them. It was a ripe morning, full of fragrance and peace.

Ho-wha was feeding alone when he heard a shriek from Ka-ka's bed and quickly he marched over to see what the trouble was. But there was no cause for alarm. Unwittingly the mother had tickled her child and he had let off a howl of pleasure; and now she was looking at him as if bewildered, and the babe was grunting and rooting at her because he wanted her to tickle him again. The hair on her arms had brushed the tender soles of his feet and he had liked the tingling sensation that flushed his nerves. Of his own will he moved his feet about and when at last he succeeded in tickling himself he puckered his face and gave another howl of joy. Ka-ka held him up to look at him. Ho-wha, too, stared at the babe. He bent forward, comically grave, and wondered if the cry had been one of pain. But the infant—whom we may as well call Kooloo because it means man of the woods—was only coming to life, now that his belly was full, and beginning a curious and insatiable exploration of a strange world. He had discovered that there was pleasure in it, and he was to be greedy, almost from the hour of birth, for all the pleasure he could find.

Ho-wha's grunt as he turned again to his breakfast seemed to be one of disgust.

After the others had eaten they gathered round Ka-ka to stare at the newcomer. A baby just arrived was always for them a strange and inexplicable object, not only because it was so small and hairless and helpless, but also, and perhaps chiefly, because they had no understanding of how it came to be. Birth was the darkest of all mysteries. A babe, they knew, came from its mother's body, but they had no notion of how it got there; and they were always a little astonished to see one. They had a wish to take it in their hands and carefully inspect it from head to feet, as if by curious examination they might discover the secret of its origin.

Because birth was a mystery, the people of this age had begun to feel for the mothers a vague reverence and awe. This was especially true of the males. They produced no young, and, so far as they knew, they played no part in the miracle. They had come to expect, almost to demand, infants from the females, and when one of them, like the unfortunate Kuoh, turned out to be barren, they resented and distrusted her. Often, in former times, Ho-wha had solemnly examined Kuoh's genitals as if to learn why there was no baby in her. More recently he had tolerated but had felt no friendliness for her, and he cared little enough when she died.

Now, after gathering round Ka-ka, they divided their attention between her and the child. Comically polite and reserved, thev did not presume to touch either of them; and all the men, of course, except Ho-wha, remained discreetly in the background. Who-ah pressed forward, with her own child riding her shoulders and clutching her hair, and with her went Kuoh, the barren one, Ghoo, the ugly one, and the girls. While they peered at the child and talked out of excited wonder, Who-ah's baby, perceiving the hideous little fellow lying in Ka-ka's lap, decided to come down from his perch. He descended as if from a tree, with feet and hands clutching his mother's hair or skin, and moved to crawl toward Kooloo; but his mother cuffed him a vigorous blow that knocked him over. That so angered and frightened him that he gave a terrible squeal. Then Who-ah seized him and shook him and set him again on her shoulders, and he stood on her back, grasping the hair of her skull, and peered over and down at his half brother.

Ho-wha, meanwhile, had been standing apart, a scowling sentinel who uttered warning growls and kept his eyes on the other men. They, in turn, cautiously watched him while trying to look past the women at the child. To all this curious interest Ka-ka gave no heed. She licked her child or held him against her body to warm him or now and then with sudden interest she parted his coarse mop to look for bugs. If she glanced up, in the quick nervous way they all had, there was something tense and expectant in the way brown eyes looked into brown eyes.

After a few minutes Ho-wha's growl was almost a roar. He meant that the time for gawking was done and they should all scatter and mind their business. The other men moved away. Soon they all withdrew except Kuoh, the barren one. Sitting close by Ka-ka, she remained, her gaze fixed intently and hungrily on Kooloo; and when Ho-wha gave another guttural warning she did not seem to hear. More than she wanted life, this social outcast wished to take the babe in her arms and fondle it. She wanted to warm him and press his face to her empty brown dugs. When Ho-wha roared at her and came forward to strike, she did not look at him or move.

Such disobedience frightened the others. It was a law among them that when the lord of the group spoke, the others must obey. As a matter of fact, every member of the group bossed, or, except Ho-wha, was bossed by somebody. There was no equality of privileges and rights. Only a person out of her mind could sit as Kuoh sat and dare the wrath of the tyrant. He growled again as he came toward her and when she did not leap up and run he struck her with a flat hand on the side of her skull and almost knocked her senseless. She lay sprawled and quivering by Ka-ka's bed. When Ho-wha reached down to strike again, Hwah, his big morose son, stopped him with a thunderous cry.

For a long moment there was the silence of death.

Why Hwah shouted a warning at his father it would be difficult to say. He cared nothing about Kuoh. Perhaps it was only because he hated the brute; more likely it was because people were awakened to instant and almost uncontrollable fury when they saw one of their kind in grave danger. It was the most violent of all the blind and murderous rages which they had power to feel. After Hwah shouted his warning, Who-ah screamed, and Ghak hopped up and down in shrill defiance.

Instead of striking a second blow Ho-wha stood erect and looked across a distance of thirty yards at his son. The struggle between the two that was inevitably to come might have come now if Ghak had not made such an infernal uproar. He acted as if he were the one who had been abused. His insane behavior distracted Ho-wha's attention and calmed his wrath.

Kuoh, meanwhile, had crawled away.

4

THE people of this long-ago age were sometimes happy but they never lived happily together. In Ho-wha's group or in other groups hunting through the wilderness there were old enmities, petty feuds, jealousies, and the constant struggle for dominance and power. It could not have been otherwise among persons so restless and curious and energetic who had so little besides eating and sleeping to keep them busy. All of them except the meek ones like Ghoo or the stupid ones like Kughh were arrogant and overbearing egoists who wanted others to wait on them and defer to them and obey their will.

When in the presence of enemies they swiftly united, of course, and forgot in the moment of danger their dislikes and grievances; but when sheltered and secure they turned on one another. This was as true of the children as of the adults. Gah and Murah often played together, but Gah was the boss and often slapped her sister down. Who-ah's older son, a husky youngster, was a tyrant with his younger brother and sometimes would have beaten him soundly if others had not intervened. From birth to death, nearly all of them tried to boss those who were younger or smaller. They seemed to find their chief meaning, their sense of personal worth, in domination, and the more tyrannical it was, the better they liked it. If they had been more intelligent, the stronger ones would have tried to enslave the weaker ones and hold them in serfdom.

They were not yet civilized enough to perceive any advantages in that. Nevertheless, Ho-wha now and then seemed to have a vague inkling, and Wuh an almost definite notion, of what a more ruthless and resourceful tyranny might achieve. The former, for instance, not only delighted in summoning his women to scratch his back or search his hair; he also would sit at ease, as if labor were unworthy of him, and try to command the others to bring him food. If he usually bestirred himself at feeding time, that was only because he had a selfish desire to seize for his own use the best of everything in sight.

The children faithfully imitated him. Observing one evening that Ho-wha sat by a tree, clamoring for attention, Who-ah's older son resolved to do likewise; and he chose a tree and sat by it, assuming, as well as he was able, the posture and the ferocious aspect of his sire. Then he yelled angrily at his small brother, trying to make him understand that he wanted whatever it was that Ho-wha desired. But the younger lad would have none of that. On the contrary, he sat by a tree, too, and barked at his sisters. He looked over to observe how his brother was sitting, and the brother in turn alertly watched the father; and so the three of them, arrogant and impatient, sat there by trees and yelled at the women and girls.

It was during such family scenes that Wuh came close

to a sense of humor. He did not actually smile, but he did narrow his eyes and thrust his long upper lip out and down. Perhaps, though, the joy he felt was malicious and always more intense when Ho-wha was thwarted; because Wuh, too, wanted females who would wait on him, and children who would jump and tremble when he yelled. He did not realize that frustration was developing his mind and leading it to notions that otherwise he would never have perceived; or that Ho-wha, on the other hand, was seduced by his arrogant power into being content with what he was.

For many days after the birth of Kooloo their lives were uneventfully lazy. Each day they ate in a new spot and each night they slept in fresh beds. In all but Wuh there was little incentive to seek more than they had or to wish to be more than they were. Wuh, the plotter, the sly bachelor, the fawning and two-faced interloper who had been kicked out of another clan, impatiently watched and waited. One evening the discretion in him almost gave way to foolhardy courage.

Since Kooloo came, Ho-wha had been a continent and a very sullen man. Each day had added to his moroseness and his wrath. One of his women was old and barren, another was ugly and sick, and Who-ah and Ka-ka were nursing babies. Each evening after eating his supper and making his bed he had growled in gloomy discontent because nobody now scratched his broad and dirty back or picked thorns out of his flesh; but chiefly he growled because he was an erotically frustrated man. He would glare at his two favorite women, sitting in their beds and caring for their infants, and when neither of them paid any attention to him he would bellow with rage. Because the older children and the other men had daily become more afraid of him, they made their beds half-screened from his sight. What Ho-wha could not see he was unable to be aware of. He would look round him as if searching for the other men and then fix his terrible gaze on the women; and after growling and roaring and making everybody anxious he would fall asleep.

One evening while shaking himself in a tantrum of anger and self-pity he espied Gah. At once he fell silent and looked at her as if wondering where she had been all the while and why he had not summoned her long ago; and Wuh, slyly watching, knew that the hour had come. After staring at the girl and making up his dull mind, Ho-wha called to her. It was the cry of the male to the female. Gah understood it and turned to flee, but a furious bellow stopped her short. She understood that, too. Trembling with fear she looked over at him and Ho-wha looked at her; and then he called again.

It was a tense and dreadful moment. As usual, when he saw a younger man lusting for a woman, and was thereby reminded of his own senile loneliness, Ghak began to talk in hysterical gibberish. None of the others made a sound. Hwah softly rose in his bed and looked across at his sire. Wuh sat half-concealed and peered at Gah. She was still transfixed between fear of disobedience and a desire to flee.

It was a trait of women to be both attracted and repelled by their men. As if born to rape, yet resenting its brutal indignities, they were coy and timid and felt an urge to flight; but at the same time they were fascinated and allured by the male's imperious strength and will. This was especially true of them when young. But even in the older women, even in the grandmothers, a shy and timorous modesty sometimes made them behave like virginal girls. They, too, were both fascinated and terrified by the candid lustfulness of their master.

And so it was with Gah now. She was so frightened by the big shaggy monster calling to her that she trembled all over; but she was also thrilled by the fiercely lustful way in which he looked at her. One desire urged her to flight. The other desire was almost a wild compulsion to run over and throw herself at his feet and grovel before him. She wanted his big rough hands to seize and examine her. She wanted him to take her and force her to mate with him and then thrust her from his bed after his will was done. With an emotion no less intense she feared and hated him and wished to run into the jungle and hide. Caught and held by the ambivalence of her heritage, she was unable to move.

Ho-wha left his bed and went toward her. She began to cry. She cowered and raised both arms as if to protect herself from blows. Her cry of fear and distress was a whimpering wail, and after a moment her sister Murah echoed it as if she, too, had been chosen for a dreadful mating. She leapt up and ran to Gah and threw her arms around her, and the two girls shivered and wailed together and waited for Ho-wha to strike.

But he only seized both of them and dragged them to his bed. Presently Murah broke free and ran. Hwah, with his jealous rage beyond control, now advanced a few steps, smiting his breast and shouting a warning; and Wuh, forgetting his customary discretion, also left his bed. The two men, standing almost side by side, set up a fearful outcry. They were telling Ho-wha not to ravish the girl.

But Ho-wha paid no attention. Like one who had found a treasure that completely engrossed his interest, he was examining Gah as if to learn how ripely female she was. He handled her with powerful ease, turning her over, laying her on her back, or setting her on hands and feet, and grunting all the while as if deeply pleased by what he saw. He did not look at the two enraged men who threatened and challenged him and drew nearer step by step.

Gah had been helpless between fear and a wish to surrender. They were helpless between fear and rage. Hwah, the braver of the two, advanced again, leaving Wuh standing alone. He was still beating his breast and shouting a wild challenge. Wuh had cooled off a bit. A moment ago he had lost his head and had almost attacked a man twice as powerful as himself; but now, recovering a little of his poise and remembering that he was not one who with hands and teeth took what he wanted, he fell silent, content to let Hwah do all the shouting. He even withdrew a few steps and looked calmly around him.

The women were paying no heed to all this uproar. When a male took a female, it was no affair of theirs. All their lives they had seen males, both man and beast, fight over the females, and Gah's cries now they understood only too well. Years before, when young, they had cried aloud, too, when possessed against their will. Slaves to the passions of men and the chattels of their lust, they had learned that surrender and obedience were their lot in life. Ka-ka and Who-ah were holding their babies in sleep. Ghoo was lying in a bed with the dwarf, and Kuoh, the old one, was alone. Not a one of them stirred or looked over at the son who was crying murder at his father.

If Murah had not been so young, Wuh would have

tried to abduct her while Ho-wha was busy. Perceiving that she was only a child, he looked at the women, but they were old or ugly or burdened with infants. He returned to his bed, this man who had in him the simple rudiments of a philosopher, and Hwah was left alone.

Hwah was still howling with furious indecision. If he had been capable of so fine a judgment, he would have told himself that the tyrant could examine Gah as long as he did no more than that, and he would have been content merely to threaten and restrain him. As it was, he thought he could frighten Ho-wha and make him run. Men always strove to frighten their enemies, attacking only, but by no means always, after their breast-beating and shouting proved unavailing. Hwah did not say to himself, "I'll make a fearful racket and if that does not scare him away I'll attack." Nevertheless, that is what he had vaguely in mind.

Ho-wha seemed to be in no hurry. He behaved as if he were prolonging a blissful expectancy; because never would he have examined an older woman with such deliberate and lustful thoroughness. Gah had stopped crying. As a matter of fact, Ho-wha's hands were now so gentle and his manhandling of her was so exciting that she had lost most of her fear and was content to let him have his will. Hwah perceived the change in her. Her submissive and almost cooing behavior mixed lust with his rage, and he advanced to kill.

He reached the bed before Ho-wha became aware of him. Leaping up, and giving a roar that would have stopped a lion, Ho-wha's mighty hands reached for his son, and in this moment Hwah's courage deserted him. If his spine and all his other bones had suddenly been withdrawn from his body he could not have felt more limp and helpless. Strong hands seized him, and strong teeth sank and came together in the flesh of his shoulder. For Hwah that was more than enough. There came to him, like a nightmare, memory of all the years when he had lived, as they all had lived, in terror of this man. He wrested his body free and loped off, howling with pain and dismay. He vanished headlong into a thicket but after a little while he came slinking out and found his bed; and there, looking toward Ho-wha but unable to see him, he shook with the sickness of a castrated thing.

Wuh, more philosophic, and quite serene now, looked over at Hwah and thought of this dark matter as well as he was able. Ho-wha had completed his seduction. After lustful dallying he had mated with Gah and thrust her from him. Wuh had seen her steal through the darkness and a few moments later he had heard her murmurous wonder as she lay at Murah's side. The tyrant had taken another woman and now he had five. When she was old enough, he would take Murah also, and then he would have six. Wuh could count to that number and beyond it; and now, sitting in his bed, he thought of Ho-wha's women. He thought of Ho-wha, too, and for the first time there came to the mind of a man the idea that perhaps a rival could be killed while he slept.

It was not a notion that came to him suddenly like a light out of darkness. It was a long time in coming out of the desperate thinking of an unhappy man. First he was dwelling on the realization that Ho-wha slept. He had taken a woman and now he lay in his bed asleep. That was the first thought. The second thought, growing naturally out of it, was a question: could he, Wuh, steal over to

Gah's bed and embrace her? On that prospect he dwelt with the threatening presence of Ho-wha enveloping it. His problem was a desire opposed by an obstacle. It was a very simple problem, but he found it baffling and exasperating, and his thought shuttled back and forth. There was Ho-wha and there was Gah. He considered one and then the other, or with almost frantic desperation he tried to consider both at once and understand the relationship between the two. Then his thoughts would slip away to Gah and he would feel only her nearness and his wish to be with her, and his eagerness would impel him to make a move toward her; but in the next moment he would be inhibited by fear. He would pause and sink back to his bed, and his thoughts would turn to Ho-wha.

The instant thought returned to his enemy, his obstacle, the erotic longing in him was obscured and dulled, and in despair, in anger, he would give his whole mind to the hulking despot who was dimly visible to him across the darkness. Then again, as before, would come the realization that Ho-wha was asleep. In this recognition there was instant relief. It was the relief, however, of temporary security and not of the understanding that in sleep an enemy was helpless and unaware. That is the thought Wuh was trying to come to. It was as if, in an effort to solve his problem, he moved round and round Ho-wha, looking at him and wondering what to do about him. A man's thoughts at this time were fickle and erratic and danced about in confusion. They tired him easily. Wuh's dim and vagrant reflections, for instance, were constantly interrupted by his physical needs or an itching back or the sound of a night bird. Always, when he seemed about to reach a conclusion and see a way out, a sudden emotion would fetch him up and darken his mind; and then everything was blotted out except the steady and burning hunger that was his only reason for thinking. Then his thoughts would dwell lustfully on the presence of Gah until an impulsive move toward her would remind him of Ho-wha.

Like a creature endlessly threading a maze he would begin all over again. He would return to the simple recognition of Ho-wha's presence, and Ho-wha would again absorb his entire interest. With futile and despairing effort, wasted by its own intensity, blinded by anger, and interrupted by his physical sensations, he would again think of Ho-wha and come, as before, to the realization that the man was asleep. As before, too, there was joy, there was a sense of security, in this recognition. But not for a long while did Wuh's mind reach beyond this point. As soon as he felt secure, the moment his angry apprehensiveness was lulled, his thought returned to Gah; and so for a long while he moved between the two poles of lust and fear.

His effort, however, was not entirely futile. In turn he thought of his desire and of the obstacle which stood in his way; and both of these he saw clearly in spite of the strong emotion that clothed them. He perceived the relationship of the two as a problem vital to himself. But how to restrain Ho-wha while embracing the woman he was unable to figure out. New thoughts, new ways of doing things, new modes of behavior came only rarely to these people, and then only to the genius among them who was more resourceful and more intelligent. Necessity was also at this time the mother of invention. And Wuh was a genius. His problem was one that no man before him had been able to solve, and that very few, indeed, had thought about. If a man did not have the strength to take a mate, he went without one; and those like Wuh who were physically weaker and whose boldness was tempered with sly discretion never mated save now and then in a chance moment when the lord of the clan was caught off guard.

Wuh did not intend to make all his years wait on the lucky chance. He had resolved to possess Gah and to keep her; and perseverance, which is the soul of resourcefulness, he had in abundance. Nevertheless, he was a baffled and unhappy man tonight. He was consumed not only by jealousy but also by the lust of the weakling male to murder his stronger rival; but when at last he left his bed, going softly in the grass, there was no thought in his conscious mind of killing. He was not moved by any conscious purpose. He left his bed because hours of unprofitable thinking had bewildered and emboldened him. Deeper than all that, however, was the fact that his unconscious mind had been harvesting the materials for a tremendous conclusion.

He went noiselessly to Ho-wha and looked at the big fellow. He was sleeping on one side with his head on an arm and with the other arm lying along his body and reaching below his knees. Resting gently on hands and feet like an animal ready to spring, Wuh leaned forward and peered at the slumbering giant, his nervous eyes marking the size of him. And suddenly in this moment there came to him the harvest of hours of thought. There came to him an idea that no man before him had ever had. It was the thought that perhaps he could kill Ho-wha while the man slept.

If Wuh had been the man now that he was to become,

Ho-wha would have died this night. A blow from a club or a stone would have crushed his skull. But men had not learned the use of weapons; and Wuh, looking at the hulk before him, never thought of a club or a stone. He was able only to think of his strength and of the power of his hands on a waking giant's throat; and he knew it was not enough. For several minutes, nevertheless, he stared at Ho-wha, thinking of him and of himself and wondering what to do. At last, like one who had walked in his sleep, he was startled to find himself so near his dreadful enemy; and he turned, shivering and dismayed, and slunk back to his bed.

Fear has been the parent of hatred, and hatred Wuh now felt with all the strength he had. Hatred made an idiot of him, a helpless and tortured idiot who sat in his bed like a Kughh, looking at nothing and focusing all the intensity of his hunger and frustration in stuporous despair. If he had been anesthetized he could not have been more unlike the man of an hour ago. Then his mind had been alert, even though confused, with all his senses framing it like a bright constellation. Now he had the dull and witless mien of a Kuoh.

But out of such excesses of alternate hope and despair have come the small and precious additions to patterns of behavior. The complacent fellows like Ho-wha, possessing all that they had power to dream of, added nothing to the race's heritage. It was the Wuhs who had come down from the trees, who had first stood erect, who had learned to walk. It was the Wuhs who, physically less dominant than the overlords, and goaded by thwarted desires, were to seek with their wits what they were unable to take with their hands.

In the centuries preceding this time, it had been chiefly mother love that had impelled one of the beasts to become a man. Among the thousands of species of reptile that had ruled the earth, not more than a half-dozen had given any care to their young. Among the birds and mammals, none paid any heed to their offspring or even recognized them after the brief period of nesting or nursing was over. It was the mother of the species destined to be human who prolonged the custodianship of her baby and perceived that it was still a part of her after it left her breast.

But now it was to be the frustrated ones, the unhappy and underprivileged ones, who would insure the steady progress of their race. In them survival would come to rest less and less on the strength in their hands and teeth and more and more on the alertness of their minds. It was intelligence they needed, and in such furious unhappiness as Wuh's, intelligence germinated and grew. Tonight, in realizing that an enemy could be slain while it slept, he had marked another milestone in human progress. He was just a little wiser than he had been before.

5

GAH became one of Ho-wha's women and his chief vassal. Two or three times a day he embraced her, and each evening after his belly was full he summoned her to him. He made it known to her that he wished to be inspected and petted and curried; but once in a while, feeling lazily tender, he would caress her, moving his tongue across her neck or cheeks or turning her over and over in blissful examination. To his love-making she yielded with delight and gave little cries of joy. After fondling her he would try to make her understand that he wished to be petted. He would grunt and act a part for her and then wait, gravely expectant; and if she did not respond he would slap or bite her or take her hands and move them over him.

Gah was an apt lover. She soon learned to do as he wished, though often, when caressing her, he bit too hard and then she yelped and strove to escape. In such moments he seemed to regard her with solemn wonder. Grasping her, he would stare at her gravely for a long moment, his eyes questioning her; and Gah, a little angry and frightened, would passively submit and wait.

Wuh missed none of their doings. He was a wiser but he was still a completely baffled man. Ever since the night when Ho-wha first possessed the girl he had made his bed where his view of them would be unobstructed; and each evening he soberly watched their love-making. Everything that Ho-wha did he wanted to do and would have done if he had had a chance. There are other things that he would have done. Because he was a more intelligent man he would have been a more resourceful lover. He was a nimble dancer, for instance, and in a simple way he had learned the use of ornaments. Ho-wha never danced to arouse his or his woman's lust and he never adorned himself.

It was with dancing and ornament that Wuh strove at last, not with deliberate but with intuitive cunning, to win Gah's interest.

One evening the group came upon an unusually lush supper and ate and made their beds long before dusk. To Wuh the moment seemed opportune and with unwonted boldness he resolved to dance. He chose a spot where dry clay had been laid upon a peat bed and was, in consequence, of such resonant quality that it intensified any sounds made upon it. On this floor of clay Wuh danced. He hopped about with rhythmic movements, beating all the while on the clay with his feet, beating on his body with his hands, and keeping time with mournful cries. The clay drum under him took up the sound and amplified it until it was a deep booming as of muffled underground thunder. The sound of his palms striking his breast were like the sharper overtones of a second drum; and above both drums was the eerie music of his cries.

Almost at once every member of the group was interested. Some watched him with sober delight and some with mild astonishment. Never had they seen anything dance as Wuh was dancing now. Presently, as if intoxicated by the sounds he made and by the rhythms of his body, he redoubled his effort, hopping and smiting in a kind of jig-time; but all the while he was watching Gah. Human eyes at this time could eloquently speak the language of love. Wuh's warm brown eyes, fixed on the girl, strove to tell her of his hunger and his loneliness. He was watching Ho-wha too.

That lazy tyrant was interested but he was not alarmed. When younger he had tried to dance, but awkwardly, as if his body were too heavy for his legs. He had seen others dance. He sensed that Wuh's dancing was an appeal to the women but he felt too secure in his lordship to care. Sitting by his bed and grunting in time to the music, he was too slothful to move, and too stupid to envy a younger man's grace.

The other men were less indifferent. Hwah stood up as if impelled to act but too confused to know what he should do; and Ghak, the foolish old one, began to leap and tumble as if contriving an impromptu dance of his own. It was the women, however, and especially the younger ones, who gave the most eager and delighted response. If Gah had dared, she would have gone to Wuh and danced, too.

Murah dared. After all, she was only a plump girl who had not entered womanhood and nobody moved to restrain her. Dancing was an inherited behavior in her as in all people. In the manner to which she was born, she found a small clearing and began to dance, whirling round and round in a circle. She acted as if she were drunk with Wuh's music. With her arms, legs, and hands she kept time, jumping up and down and leaping and spinning, and all the while vocalizing her ecstasy with a strange cry.

The dancing of either male or female was deeply exciting to the other sex. Wuh's dancing did not stir the nursing mothers, and the excitement it aroused in their infants was not sexual. These alert youngsters, with mouths agape and eyes shining, started to crawl away from their beds and were seized and dragged back. Thereupon they beat themselves in an angry tantrum and began to howl. But it was Kughh, the idiot dwarf, who behaved most strangely of all. He was a deformed monster who could not walk erect but shuffled along, bent over, with his hands almost touching the earth. In such a manner he now strove to dance; and if there had been among these people a sense of the ridiculous, they would have been convulsed with laughter or moved to pity. Because Kughh danced as if he were in a great fury. He barked. He rushed at trees and tried to tear them from the ground. He fell on his face and rolled over, his hands threshing about him and his voice barking as if he scented prey and was rooting along on the trail of it.

But nobody paid any attention to Kughh. Not even Ghoo, the ugly woman, watched the antics of her adopted ward. Like Kuoh, the old one, and Gah, the young one, she had eyes only for the lustful pantomime of Wuh. The men and boys, on the other hand, were watching Murah. The sexually immature children were delighted. Their response was imitative, but that of Hwah was savagely erotic. Sexual passion seems to be related to, and in part fed by, a sadistic lusting that sometimes appears to be deliberately cruel. If Wuh had continued his dancing, Hwah would probably have thrown himself on Murah and tried to destroy her. He did, indeed, move toward the girl, but an ominous growl from Ho-wha stopped him. That growl for Wuh was enough.

As if doused with cold water, he suddenly stopped. Looking round him, as if abashed by his own daring, he saw Ho-wha rising from his bed, and at once he withdrew. Murah, left alone, and almost exhausted, ceased dancing, too, and went over to her sister. Ghak alone remained on the scene and he was trying only to draw attention to himself.

In Wuh's mind there had been no plan to dance himself into passionate union with a female. His impulse had been much simpler than that. Dancing with these people, as with many of the beasts and birds, was a part of their innate behavior. It was a prelude to copulation. There was in it very little tenderness and gentleness, if indeed there was any at all. Sometimes a man danced himself into such a frenzied lust that he tried not to embrace his woman but to slay her. He was moved by an urge to bite and choke and rend.

Wuh had danced because his hunger had been stronger than his fear. If he had not been a sly fellow, with a weather eye for danger even in times of orgiastic release, he would have kept on dancing or he would have thrown himself on Murah. As it was, discretion had again intervened, showing that in him, if not in the others, mind was becoming the warden of emotion. After entering his bed, he forgot his reckless ecstasy and strove again to consider his problems.

The next day in feeding, the group came upon a thicket of lovely jungle orchids. Wuh adorned himself with flowers. Between sex and adornment there was at this time no relationship—or if there was, it was not conscious or deliberate. The men, and very rarely the women, thrust flowers into their scalp lock or set them on their heads or shoulders; or sometimes they used large leaves or bright stones or pieces of wood. They were probably moved only by a wish to draw attention to themselves. They were all of them vain, selfish, and strutting egoists whose greatest delight was in being the cock of the walk.

But also, to be sure, their five senses were well developed. They were attracted by large colorful flowers and by everything gaudy and glittering. Fragrance they all liked, and some of them were very fond of it. Wuh was such a man. He was continually thrusting his face against an odorous bower to breathe and smell of it; and he had, in comparison with the others, such cleanliness in his personal habits that he had learned the use of simple tools in removing accumulations of dirt from his nails and skin and hair. His delight in fragrance was sensuous. His delight in adornment grew from a vain wish to draw attention to himself.

Now he set a flower on either shoulder and thrust another into the hair on his skull and walked about as if he were sole lord of the earth. The older children, quick to imitate the behavior of adults, and especially that of the more resourceful Wuh, ran in haste to gather blooms; and presently they were all strutting in orchidaceous glory. Even Hwah, the big morose son, set a flower on his shoulder; but because he was a stupid fellow with no perception of degrees in magnificence he was content with one solitary little bloom. Soon it fell off him but he continued to march about like one enviably adorned. Wuh, indeed, was the only one of the men with enough intelligence to perceive that several flowers were more showy than one. If he had been a little more imaginative he would have carried a bouquet. More than three he had never adorned himself with; none of the others had ever used more than one.

These people were vain but their interests were fickle. In one moment they were pleased with themselves and in the next they were bored. Observing that others did as he did, Wuh lost interest in the flowers and allowed them to fall. He looked dejected. He looked as if it were hardly worthy of his talents to behave in a manner that his inferiors could emulate. What he wanted—but this he realized only dimly if at all—was a personal distinction unapproachably apart from all other living things. Orchids were nice, but always when he used them other members of the group did likewise and abashed him with their arrogant clamor for attention. If he sheltered himself from the sun with a huge palm leaf, he had only to look around to see that others were copying him. If, instead of lying on his belly to drink, he sucked from his cupped palms, the children barked with delight and drank from their hands. They observed how he made his bed and they imitated him in that. When, spurning pineapple leaves, which Ho-wha and the women ate with gluttonous relish, he turned to the fruit of the oil palm, the children gathered round him to eat nothing but fruit. If he found a nest of eggs and sat by a tree to eat them, the children squatted about and stared at him with hungry brown eyes, behaving as if eggs, above all other delicacies, were what they wished for.

Wuh was imitated because he was more resourceful. The imitation was a powerful stimulus to the development of his mind, but he was not aware of that. He did not know that he was constantly striving to behave in a way that others could not copy. In his simple soul, he wanted to be distinguished and unique. As a matter of fact, there was in him, because of Ho-wha's tyranny and his own sterile bachelorhood, an obscure and perplexed feeling of inferiority. He did not think of himself as physically an inferior one—such a recognition would be a long time in coming to men; but he did know, vaguely and unhappily, that he was not all that he wished to be.

When in these people their innate impulses were thwarted, or their desires, born of simple thinking, were frustrated, the women became patiently submissive creatures, but the men became ugly malcontents. In this group there were four frustrated ones. If an unfortunate woman was denied children of her own, she tried to mother any helpless thing she could find. If she did not, like Ghoo, find a dwarfed outcast, she strove to adopt a sick animal or a wounded bird. She would draw within the shelter of her arms any friendless thing and lavish on it that mother love which was almost the whole meaning of her life.

But in the men parental love was very feeble. Ho-wha would stand guard at birth, not because he felt any affectionate gentleness for babies but because he had learned, like most of the animals of the earth, that there was security and strength in numbers. The sentiment of love was unknown to men of his time. They found their egoistic fulfillment in sexual embrace, in acquisition and possession, in dominating other males, and in slaying their foes.

When a man like Ghak, who in his youth had known all those, was driven out of a group, he was so completely frustrated, and at the same time so old and impotent and helpless, that he could declare himself only in self-pitying tantrums. Nothing was left to him but the contempt of his fellows, and old age and death. With the young men, the Hwahs and Wuhs, it was another matter. They were neither an ugly sick woman nor an old and querulous man. Vigorous and lustful and in the full flush of their hungers, they found their frustration more intolerable and blighting than that of a Ghak or a Ghoo. Day and night they had no moment of peace. They lived constantly around one who had a generous share of everything that a man wanted. Ho-wha had women whom he possessed and bossed and growled at. He was the undisputed lord of all the men within sight. And when enemies appeared, either human or beast, he made a terrible racket and frightened them away.

The other men knew that he had these things, these possessions and privileges, and they hated him. They would have murdered him with intense joy if they could have found a way. In the hatred and despair of two of them, there was no contribution to their growth. Ghak would never be more than a howling spitfire of frantic grief. Hwah was too dull to do more than sulk and scowl and imprison himself in a small unprofitable world of dark thoughts. And even Wuh's maneuverings were hit-or-miss experiments rather than cunning design.

When, for instance, he danced or adorned himself, he did not have any definite purpose in mind. Dancing and adornment were, like scratching himself or making a bed, a part of his heritage. Nevertheless, in these, and in many other things that he did, he was impelled in a fumbling way toward discoveries and answers. He danced because instinctive lust for a little while was stronger than fear; and he set flowers on his body because they made him feel more important. Dark and groping behavior, prompted by desires, has been the mother of learning. It was restless and curious seeking that pitched a man, now and then, beyond the periphery of his bondage and set him on a new path. Of unhappy and impatient curiosity, Wuh had more than his share, and it kept him busy.

A few days after adorning himself with flowers, he did something that no man before him had ever done. He had climbed a tree to eat bananas; and while sitting on a limb with his back to the trunk, and eating fruit, skins and all, Ghak presented himself below. He wanted to share the fruit. He first vocalized his wish, chattering and scolding while he peered up at Wuh. Wuh ignored him. Then with pantomime Ghak made his desire known. He went through the motions of plucking bananas and eating them, all the while watching Wuh to see if he understood. Wuh understood but he was annoyed. Men did not wait on other men. He looked down at Ghak and scolded him for his presumption; and Ghak, who was too feeble to climb, embraced the trunk and strove to shake the fruit down. Or perhaps he was trying to dislodge Wuh from his perch. He scolded again, his voice shrill and angry, and indicated with frantic gestures that he was hungry and wished to eat.

Wuh meanwhile fed himself and looked down at the old man. When Ghak again tried to shake the tree, Wuh flew into a rage. He seized a banana and hurled it at Ghak and struck him in the face with it. Pleased with the old man's howl of dismay, he pelted him with a second banana and a third; and then, as if to test the efficacy of such a method of attack, he grasped a cluster of the fruit and hurled it at Ghak and almost knocked him down.

This was the first time a man ever used anything as a weapon to strike another. If Wuh's behavior had been more calculating and less impulsive, he might have sensed now that he had made a tremendous discovery. As it was, he calmly resumed his eating; and Ghak, unhurt, and happy for the deluge of fruit, gathered the bananas and went off to be alone in possession of them. Wuh watched him go, but there was no triumphant realization in his mind. He was conscious only of having driven a pest away. In his subconscious mind, however, there was to be troubled memory of this experience; and in the months ahead, the meaning of it would be busy there, germinating and coming to birth. It would grow there like a seed and slowly push its way into consciousness, until at last it would stand bright and certain in Wuh's mind like something forgotten but always known.

6

PEOPLE of this time were not migratory but they were nomadic and they wandered throughout the year, confined only by the natural boundaries of each group's domain. No matter what lush feeding grounds they came to or what haven of safety, they were constantly and restlessly on the move, never spending more than one or two nights in a spot. This nomadism, a part of their heritage, had grown out of fear.

For several weeks Ho-wha had seen no enemies but never for a moment had he relaxed his vigilance. Like other men, he had neither foolhardy courage nor craven cowardice; but every hour of his life was anxious, even in sleep. His dreams were mild nightmares of terror and struggle. His dread was of the leopard and tiger and lion and the venomous or devouring snakes. There were other unfriendly creatures, including the crocodile, the wild boar, and certain great flesh-eating birds, but he was less afraid of them. The boars never attacked when unmolested, and the birds were cowards who preyed on the diseased and crippled and old.

Ho-wha had led his group into jungle so dense that the sun was visible only through the canopy windows, and full noon was no more than twilight. It was a damp odorous wilderness of huge trees cloaked with the tangled ropes of parasitic vines. Monkeys and birds screamed in the high ceiling where flowers bloomed in sunlight, and mighty storms moved up there; but the forest floor was so quiet that nothing stirred. Ho-wha was alarmed to find himself in a dank gloomy prison of spiders and bats and wasps and the smell of old decaying leaf-depth; and day after day, in an effort to find his way out, he plunged through the trackless world, roofed and strangled by its lush excess.

The ferocious cats did not prowl here, but lying in wait, Ho-wha well knew, were the great snakes. The dark brown python was here. He was often indistinguishable from the foliage he coiled and waited in, though on his body there were bluish iridescent markings; and these in the dark jungle sometimes shone like a terrible and fantastic fire. Here also, especially near water, was the anaconda, a gigantic greenish-yellow murderer marked with rows of large black spots. More dreaded than either of those by Ho-wha and his people was the king cobra, the most terrible in size and deadliness of all the poisonous serpents. The python could swallow a full-grown deer; the cobra with one thrust of his fangs could paralyze an elephant.

Ho-wha knew that he had invaded the home of these mighty killers. He knew that up in the trees, with thirty feet of sinuous body coiled around trunk and limbs, the anaconda waited in silence as deep as night. He knew that in wilderness dark the cobra was always ready to spit his poison and bury his fangs. But Ho-wha had been born of the jungles, too. For countless centuries they had been the home of his people; and in their blood and emotions was this deep and lost and terrible world of wet and perpetual gloom. When he wandered out on the unclothed plains he felt more anxious and defenseless than when prowling under the tangled roof where poisonous insect and venomous snake made their home. Nevertheless, he had not intended to penetrate to the deepest heart of it, and he was alarmed.

It was Kuoh one morning who screamed in the sudden crushing embrace of a python. Old and feeble, she had fallen behind the others; and while she was passing under a big tree, the monster dropped as soundlessly as oiled rope. His great writhing body went swiftly, softly around her; and while she screamed, he coiled again and again until only her head was visible above the smooth gleaming folds. Her arms were imprisoned at her sides. She lay shoulder deep in a cylinder of snake.

Her first scream of terror lifted Ho-wha's scalp lock and chilled him to his bones. When one of his own kind gave a cry like that, he knew that a deadly enemy had struck; but from where he was he could not see Kuoh and he did not know what had happened. His bellow of fright and rage rolled away through the jungle and struck a wall of stone and broke in deep echoes. Hwah roared next, and almost at once Wuh and Ghak took up the cry; and the four voices filled miles of forest with a dreadful clamor.

Ho-wha's face was awful to look at. The cool brown of his eyes had turned a yellowish black around small pupils that shone like points of flame. He had opened his mouth in a wide snarl, with the lower lip drawn far down, and the upper lip, edged with stiff coarse hair, twitched so violently that the spasms in it pulled at his cheeks. The hair on his head and down his back stood up like black wire. Fear and fury poured like lightning along his nerves.

He struck his breast with blows that rocked him, and he continued to bellow with all the power of his lungs; but he had not moved a single step since Kuoh screamed. Following her first cry there had come another, and then a third that sounded weak and choked. It was the third cry that told Ho-wha where she was. With a wild rush that would have made a lion pause, he plowed through the jungle toward her, and after him went the other men. The women and children had gathered in a group. The babies were whimpering but their mothers were as furious as the men. Ka-ka, the dominant one, was ready to fight any foe in the world in defense of her child. A woman protecting her baby was, indeed, more reckless and savage than any male, and would throw herself at an enemy while the men stood by and roared.

Ho-wha was standing by and roaring now. His first mad rush had brought him within sight of Kuoh and the python, but he did not leap forward and attack. The vision of the monster chilled his blood and his wrath. Between dread that was in him like an engulfing nightmare and rage so overwhelming that it darkened his senses, he stood transfixed. Upon the earth the python was a pile of shining flesh, and embraced by the mound, with only her head showing, was Kuoh, so nearly crushed that she could no longer make a sound. The serpent lifted its head as if resting on elbows and looked at Ho-wha.

It was the strategy of a man to try to frighten an enemy

which he feared. That is what Ho-wha did now. With terror like an electrical storm in his scalp and back, he rushed toward the python, bellowing and smiting himself and tearing at shrubs as he went. After a savage rush of a few feet he stopped short and roared, and the ledges roundabout hurled back his challenge in thunderous applause. The other men were roaring, too, but they were not so brave as Ho-wha. Ghak was out of his mind in a tantrum; he rushed about at a safe distance and seized trees as if determined to uproot the forest. Hwah stood behind his father and echoed him, challenge for challenge; but Wuh, whose mind had not been wholly obscured by anger, barked for a few moments and then was quiet as if lost in thought.

Ho-wha rushed at the serpent and then paused to strike the earth with his feet and roar and smite his chest. As motionless as a dead thing, the python looked at him, its gaze unwavering. Ho-wha took another step or two forward and again stopped. He could not distinguish between vipers that squirted poison or struck with fangs and this monster which seemed to him ready to strike the moment he came within reach. For Ho-wha they were all lethal at five yards. In another wild rush he approached within twenty feet, and then with all the rage in him he screamed a challenge and jumped up and down; but the python never faltered in its steady hypnotic stare. With eyes as cold as death in the gaze of a dead thing, it looked at Ho-wha and waited. There was no sign of life in Kuoh now. Embraced with the huge rings, with only the top of her head showing where brown gleaming belly sank around her skull to meet belly, she was probably crushed and smothered; but Ho-wha never thought of that. He could see her skull and he knew she was there. It was his simple way to believe that a person lived until he knew beyond doubt that the person was dead. As a matter of fact, he was not thinking at all. He was depending wholly on instinctive rage and trying to frighten an enemy that could be alarmed not by clamor but only by enormous size. If Wuh had remembered his experience with the bananas and learned from it the lesson that he was eventually to learn, he would have hurled things at the python and driven it off. But all three men were maddened by rage and restrained by fear; and after roaring until nearly exhausted, they all withdrew to the women as if to seek advice or encouragement. Instead of bellowing like demented creatures, they uttered low plaintive cries.

The python uncoiled and made ready to engorge its victim. If Kuoh was not dead she was at least senseless, and she did not stir when the serpent began to swallow her headfirst. Its mouth, looking small when closed, now opened so wide that its head seemed to be only the hinged wings of a gaping cavern. Its throat dilated. Its eyes were expressionless and cold. Swallowing a prey the size of Kuoh took patience and time. The mouth closed over her head, almost enveloping it, and throat muscles sucked at her, pulsing like a bellows. Very slowly but steadily the head was drawn into the chamber of the throat and was a huge bulge there just back of the jaw hinges. Engulfing the big hairy shoulders was more difficult and took more time. If a person had been watching, he would have seen a hairy woman lying there with her head in a python's throat, and five or ten minutes later he would have observed no change; but after an hour he would have seen that the shoulders were vanishing. He would have seen that the throat had distended to unbelievable size, and that the broad shoulders lay crosswise between the gaping jaws. The monster looked more like a creature giving birth than one swallowing its dinner. The skull had been thrust so far upward that a blow on its snout could have broken it backward on its hinge and laid it helpless along the neck. In the eyes there was still no change.

Ho-wha, meanwhile, had not fled with his group. He had been growling in terror and behaving like one who had been flogged. The babes, whimpering, clung to their mothers, knowing that something dreadful had happened. Nobody expected Ho-wha to attack and slay the enemy. They expected nothing and hoped for nothing. In moments like this, when a snake or a big cat struck at one of them, they were overwhelmed by dread of the vast dark world in which they lived. Leopards and tigers and lions the men could usually frighten away, but no outcry they were capable of could drive off the python and king cobra. That is why fury in Ho-wha had turned to despair.

He had not forgotten that Kuoh was out there in an enemy's clutch. He knew that a coiled python was not far from him, cold and deadly and invincible. This encounter with the monster had been like all his other encounters. He had tried to frighten the thing away and had failed, and then he had been overcome by dread of it.

Today, after growling for an hour and recovering a part of his courage, he began to be angry again. The rage in him had been like a sheltered fire that needed only a little fanning. It fed on movement, and as soon as he began to walk about, a lust to kill flushed him with its heat. Suddenly his roar was thunder again in the jungle. Again rage and fear made the black hair stand up like stiff grass on his head and down his back, and blood poured fresh and hungering strength into his great muscles. The ledges echoed his call, and Hwah and Wuh took up the cry. The three of them screamed with renewed power, and then, as if bent on overturning worlds, they rushed in the direction of the python.

And as before, they fetched up in an attitude of frenzied indecision. There lay the serpent like thirty feet of enormous brown cable, with Kuoh's legs thrusting from its mouth. Its throat was a monstrous bulge. Its eyes were still coldly watchful. Ho-wha shouted and dashed toward it and stopped. There was not the slightest movement in the python. He did not know that the creature was helpless and that without danger to himself he could have seized the ugly flat head and torn it off. Wuh advanced and looked at the snake as if thoughtfully considering it, but he did not perceive that it was helpless. Dread of the creature stood in the way of recognitions.

Then, unexpectedly, the python began to move. As noiselessly as a thing in oil it crawled away. Ho-wha roared at it and rushed after it but he did not venture within twenty feet of the vanishing tail. He felt that he had frightened the creature, and as it disappeared, his fear gave way to fury and he howled like a madman. He rushed back and forth, making a frightful clamor, even after the python had completely vanished. Out of sight with Ho-wha was out of mind, and when, in looking round him, he could see no sign of the enemy, he became calm. Like one who had acquitted himself well, he returned to his family, and they knew by his behavior that the enemy had been slain or driven away. They did not think, "Kuoh is dead, our enemy has eaten Kuoh." They did not think of Kuoh at all. If Who-ah's or Ka-ka's baby had been the victim, the mother would have been thinking of it; but Kuoh had been in their consciousness only when visible, and not always then. She was gone now and immediately she was forgotten. Only in the hour of peril did these people have unity of purpose and will. Only in danger did the least of them become important because a threat against one of them was a threat against the group.

Observing that Ho-wha was no longer furious, Ka-ka drew the infant from her shoulders and looked at it. She wanted to be sure that it was all right. When Kughh made sounds of hunger, Ghoo began to look round her for food. Gah barked at her sister and invited her to play. The four-year-old son of Who-ah climbed a tree and sat perched on a limb, bidding for admiring approval. None of them acted as if only a few minutes ago they had been numbed by dread.

Ho-wha, who had entirely forgotten the serpent, stared in turn at his women; but he was not counting them to learn if one was missing. He was returning to the watchful guardianship of the dominant male. He was doing more than that. The intense excitement had aroused his lust and presently he yelled at Gah, indicating that he wished her to come to him. It was always this way. After being deeply stirred, no matter by what, the women were always more receptive and the men more eager. It was as if their emotions ran in channels not separately but spilled over into one another; and terror or anger, after the danger was removed, poured into the veins of lust.

Gah went to him gladly. Even the ugly old Ghoo would have gone to him. Murah, the immature girl, might have done so. When one of them died, the passion in them stirred toward birth. When one of them was killed, or when one of them was abandoned, mortally wounded or sick, then male and female embraced as if birth and death fought eternally in them for supremacy.

7

THE MOTHERS kept constant watchfulness over the behavior of all the children in the group, but it was not a reasoning vigilance. It was a protective and possessive and sometimes it seemed to be a fiercely jealous guardianship. The sons were their favorites, even so long ago. For their daughters, too, they would have given their lives, but it was on the boys, not the girls, that they looked with the tenderest emotion. Their examination of them was more frequent and more absorbingly curious. For them the penis was a strange and mysterious thing that seemed almost to have a separate life of its own.

The fathers, on the other hand, had no interest in the boys, and little interest in the girls before they were old enough to embrace. When, in playing, the children fought with one another, or when, as was often the case, they curiously inspected one another's bodies, the fathers gave no heed. Sometimes they fondled and excited one another with gentle manipulation. The mothers missed little of that. They did not mind as long as the children seemed playful and happy; but if a boy tried to embrace his sister and she cried out in fear and alarm, then one of the women boxed his ears and drove him away.

One day the children were playing. They liked to swing from limbs of trees or from the network of vine ropes, feeling in swift graceful movement the ecstasy which their ancestors had felt long before. Their ancestors, of course, had lived above ground, and in speed and dexterity had been the peer of all living things. So strongly in their blood was a desire to dip and swing and soar that babies were born with powerful grasping hands and feet. They had lost nearly all of their tails but they had lost little of the rhythms that intoxicated them when swinging from branch to branch or dipping downward in a long curve on the support of a vine.

Today Murah and two of her brothers were playing. The older lad had become, like Murah, too heavy and awkward to swing with much grace and abandon; and the younger one, in consequence, set the enviable pace. He did not have the nimbleness and audacity of his remote cousins who still lived in trees. They could move with the speed and grace of creatures of the air, swinging from limb to limb across the chasms of the forest without ever missing their clutch or pausing a moment in their flight. Who-ah's son would have broken his neck trying to follow them. He did well to bridge twenty feet of space while swinging on a long vine; and when essaying to dip from branch to branch he sometimes missed and fell. When he misjudged the distance or his skill and tumbled to earth, his mother would run to him, not to see if he was hurt but to box his ears for his recklessness.

He fell today. In showing off to his sister and brother

he had ventured much higher than they dared to go. From time to time he sat on a limb and looked down and taunted them. They were swinging clumsily and heavily from the lower branches. The smaller lad had climbed up where tangled vines hung in a downsweeping wall. Because he could have shut his eyes and jumped and closed his hands on a rope, he became increasingly reckless, never suspecting that some of the vines were too insecurely anchored to support his weight. He called to the two below, wishing they would stop their play and give all their attention to him. He yelled over to the group where his mother sat and watched him. When he was sure that everybody was admiring him and waiting for his next feat, he made a very bold leap; and the vine which he clutched stripped its anchor far above him and down he came, head over heels, with a terrified yell that brought Who-ah to her feet. If his plunge had not been broken by the tangled wall he might have struck with enough force to kill him. As it was, he was almost knocked out.

His mother was upon him a moment later and she was a very angry woman. She did not wait for the lad to recover his senses and his breath. Barking with shrill rebuke, she set him on his feet and gave him a blow on the side of his skull that knocked him over. At once she set him up again and slapped the other side of his face. That fetched from him a yell of rage. He moved to run away but Who-ah seized him and bit his neck. When he felt her teeth he howled as if she were murdering him, but she went right ahead with her punishment, slapping and biting him, and chattering at him all the while in a language which he understood. He was a very abashed and crestfallen lad by the time she had finished. What, she was asking in the only gibberish she knew, what did he mean by climbing away up there and then leaping into the air and tumbling down on his head? Did he not realize that such antics would be the death of him? Had he not been a brash and impudent little show-off?

The boy understood her. He crawled away, smarting under the indignity of her hands and teeth and hating her thoroughly. He went on hands and feet into a liana thicket and turned to peer out; and he wrinkled his forehead and thrust his lips at her. If he had been a little more resourceful he would have stuck out his tongue.

Who-ah returned to the spot where she had been sitting. With alert and curious interest, all members of the group had watched the little scene between mother and son. Ho-wha had stared as if bored, Ghoo as if outraged, and Kughh as if convulsed by witless joy. Ka-ka had approved. Wuh looked as if a feeble sense of humor were stirring within him.

A little later he fell to that persistent and careful examination of the body which in all of them was a dominant trait. A thorn had gouged him in the rear of one thigh and left a small wound; and now he was trying to see it. He twisted himself into all possible attitudes; he lifted the leg with both hands and thrust his head down between his legs, striving to lick the wound with his tongue; he put the leg up and across the back of his neck and sat for a little while like a ridiculous fellow, gazing solemnly at his hairy limb. But he was unable to see the wound or to touch it with his mouth. Thereupon he probed at it with a dirty finger and then looked soberly at his finger. He thrust the finger into his mouth and salved the wound with saliva.

After a few minutes he forgot the sore and began to examine his hair and skin. Leaning forward and using both hands, he would part the long hair on his belly or breast and peer for bugs; and when he found one he would clutch it with two fingers and hold it up to rapt and prolonged scrutiny. No matter what kind of pest he found or how repeatedly he found the same kind, he would gaze at it with curious and almost friendly interest before casting it away. Some of the creatures sucked his blood and some merely dwelt in his hair, but he did not distinguish between them.

Small children when finding bugs on themselves often put them into their mouths experimentally to learn if they were good to eat. If the flavor was offensive they made a face and spit the thing out, but if the taste pleased them they swallowed it and searched their bodies for others of its kind. Spiders they spit out with shudders of dislike but a certain species of small grasshopper they found good. When they picked off gnats or mosquitoes bloated with blood, they crushed them and then licked the blood off their fingers.

Wuh never ate any of the creatures. Except for an occasional feast of eggs he was wholly vegetarian by habit and taste; but like an amateur entomologist he would stare with wonder at his captives as if by persistent study of them he might at last discover why they infested him. Sometimes when he found an unusually colorful beetle or a spider with bright markings he worried it to death. One by one he pulled its legs off; and when he had only a torso left he turned that over and over in a palm, searching it for teeth and eyes and genitals.

Today, with painstaking care, he examined every part

of his body which he could see, parting the hair in furrows and spreading it on either side and peering at his brown dirty skin. With a stick he scratched his back. He had learned the use of tools to clean or delight himself. With a sharp stick he reached across a shoulder and down and raked himself vigorously. Then he used two sticks and both hands and prodded up and down his spine. After he had gouged that area and flushed it with tingling pleasure, he examined his feet. Grasping one with both hands and drawing it up against his breast, he stared at it with intense concern. His feet closely resembled his hands. The big toe was far removed from the other toes and was a grasping tool like his thumbs. The other toes were like supple foreshortened fingers. Wuh was not thinking of all that. He peered at his foot as if it were the most remote and least familiar part of him—a part which, in times of reflection, he was astonished to find attached to his leg. It was so tough and calloused that only the strongest and sharpest thorns ever pierced it. The sole of it, like soft dark buckskin, was a pattern of fine wrinkles; and its toes when not in use folded within like his fingers.

With one hand he held the foot against him and with the other he examined it, picking briars out of the hair and flakes of dead skin off the heel. In turn he inspected the toes, drawing small pieces of leaf or twig from under the nails and then straightening and pulling each toe until its joints cracked. After he had cared for one foot, with both hands he set it down as if it were fragile, and then drew the other foot to him.

His own face he had seen but he did not realize that. The first time he ever lay on his belly to drink from a clear pool he had seen it, but he had thought he was looking at a stranger. After staring in bewilderment at the image, he had cautiously reached down to touch it, but his hand broke the water and the face looking at him danced in distortions. That had mystified him. All members of the group were fascinated by the faces which they saw in clear pools, but why or how persons could lie submerged in water and look up at them they did not understand. That was another riddle in their dark and terrible world.

Wuh was curious about his face, and never did he sit to examine himself without prodding over it as if to make out its contours and uses. He thrust fingers into his mouth and gently bit them; he felt his big strong teeth; he shoved a finger into a nostril and sneezed; he softly touched his eyelids and strove to withhold their reflex and touch his open eyes. Sometimes, overcome by wonder of himself, he looked at another person. While feeling over his own face and looking at another's he tried to come to a simple understanding of what a face was. He palmed his ears and pulled the stiff wings forward and over the apertures; he ran exploring fingers across his heavy brow ridges; and he inflated his cheeks and beat on them as if they were drums. They had all learned to make sounds by smiting their distended cheeks or by exhaling through their mouth while with a finger they repeatedly drew their lower lip down as if it were on a spring hinge. In these matters, Wuh was the most versatile artist of them all.

Today, after picking off all the bugs he could find and inspecting every part of his body that he could see, he began to experiment with his lips and cheeks to learn if he could make sounds that he had never made before. Soon he caught the curious attention of the others. They had inflated their cheeks and drummed on them but they had never made such an astonishing lullaby with their lips as Wuh was making now. After fingering his lower lip and creating separate tuneful notes by interrupting a long moaning cry, he blew both lips far out and patted them as he yelled. The effect was so startling that the children came over and sat in a group before him. Eyes watched him with rapt interest. Soon Murah began to imitate him as well as she could. When the sounds did not please her, she stared gravely at Wuh for a few moments and tried again.

Their emulation so delighted Wuh that he astonished even himself with his genius. While experimenting with his lips he quite by chance pinched his nostrils together; and the muted and nasal quality of the sound he made filled him with joy. Realizing that never before had they heard such music, the adults came over and sat with the children, and none looked on with more fascinated interest than Ho-wha. He no longer saw Wuh as a male and a rival. He saw him only as a creature producing strange and mystifying sounds.

Wuh was saying, "Hoo-ooo-ooo," breathing a continuous outpouring of musical syllables, and varying their tone and volume by manipulating his lips and nose. Then he pinched his nose with one hand and drummed on a distended cheek with the other and achieved effects even more astounding. Everyone watched him breathlessly, including the infants clinging to their mothers' backs. When Wuh paused, some of them tried to copy him, but when he resumed, they were eagerly attentive, all of them peering at his nimble hands in an effort to understand what he did. Wuh was intoxicated with joy. Nothing so pleased him or any other person as envious attention, and never before had he commanded the hushed interest of the entire group. There he sat, with all eyes fixed upon him, and if he could have had his wish these persons would have admired him forever.

But he was obscurely aware that their interest was fickle, and that to hold it he would have to put forth greater effort. His eyes in turn studied all of them. If he saw a sign of waning expectancy or hint of boredom, he became almost frantic in the movements of his hands and in the plaintive wooing of his voice. It had occurred to him that in pinching his nostrils together he had an advantage; and when, therefore, the children crouched to look up or stood above him to look down, trying to see what his fingers were doing with his nose, Wuh slyly defeated their gaze and pretended that he was doing many things which he was not doing at all. To mystify them he led them to believe that his sound effects depended chiefly on swift and baffling movements of his hands. He did not let them see that he was pinching his nose.

Murah, closer to him than the others and more attentive, thought at first that he was drumming on his nose with his palms. She tried that but without happy results. She decided next that the hand covering Wuh's nose was experimenting with his upper lip; but again her own efforts produced only a violent sneeze. And all the while Wuh was wondering what else he could do.

Presently nearly all of them began to imitate him and they made a frightening babble of sounds. Ho-wha, and his son Hwah, drummed on their cheeks and roared. Nobody was interested in that. The women, with shriller voices, cried and patted their mouths and sounded tortured. The babies began to scream, not with fear but from a wish to contribute to the hullabaloo. All of them together so completely drowned Wuh's more musical syllables that he gave up in despair, wishing they had sense enough to be silent and listen. When there came an interruption in the bedlam of voices, he fell to again, resolved to be the center of interest or nothing; but almost at once they again overwhelmed and silenced him. Hwah thought he was doing so well that he went away so that he could be alone and listen to himself. Soon Ho-wha and Ghak followed him. Each man went off by himself and made a dreadful racket.

Wuh, left with so many females around him, became excited; and forgetting that he was an inimitable musician, he fixed an ardent gaze on Gah and wondered if he could lure her into the forest. He rose and moved away, still looking at her. When Gah looked at him he beckoned to her to follow him. Perhaps she thought he intended to instruct her in the art of new and unfamiliar music. Certainly she did not suspect what was in his sly mind. She went eagerly when he beckoned but she had gone only a little way when she heard a bellow from Ho-wha. He had been delighting himself with thunderous drumming but he had also been watching his property. He came forward with a threatening rush and a roar. That for Wuh was enough.

With a movement like a shrug he dismissed Gah and turned away, withdrawing again to the margin of this group's life. In sullen despair he sat by the great buttress of a corkwood tree. For all his resourceful genius, the most he could ever get was a few minutes of rapt attention. Then he was a nobody again, an outcast, a lonely and frustrated bachelor. Looking over at Ho-wha and his women, he remembered his little while of triumph. He wanted to be the center of the stage, day and night, with all other persons deferring to his wishes and making room for his will. If he had known that he was squatting on an enormous world, he would have desired to boss it from pole to pole. If he had realized that there was a stupendous universe around him, he might have wished, after conquering the earth, to rule that, too. For such was the egoistic craving of him and his kind.

But he could only sit by a tree, a weaponless and frustrated fellow, darkly unhappy, and lusting furiously to possess and control. Again he thought of Ho-wha and wondered how he could slay him. In his simple mind, thoughts raced along simple channels. In the darkness that engulfed him there was no light, no plan, no future; and there was no joy except the fading memory of himself sitting in a group and delighting them with sounds which they had never heard before.

8

THE PEOPLE of this time were thriftless, and during the colder season they suffered from hunger. Unlike the squirrels and the bees, they had not learned to store supplies against the lean periods or to look beyond the present moment. When food was abundant they ate gluttonously and fattened, and when it was scarce they starved.

Nor had they learned to protect themselves against unfriendly weather. Snow and ice they had never seen, nor even frost, but when during winter months they left the warmth of the jungle floor, searching for juicier plants, they were sometimes chilled to their marrow. Their only protection was their hair. Some of them had a heavy coat of it, but others, like Ghoo, were almost naked. They caught colds during the winter season and sniffled and felt very wretched, but none of them had ever thought of building a shelter. Sometimes they spent a night in a cave or in the great buttressed base of a mora or a corkwood tree, but they did not make these their home. They might have done so if daily moving about had not been with them a precaution against enemies.

The mothers, at least, might have done so. The welfare of their children, and especially of the very young ones, was their chief concern. The fretful sickness of a baby could fill a mother with such anxious and watchful solicitude that other adults were afraid to go near her. Anything that seemed to threaten her child she repelled with terrible violence. The men attacked only what they thought they could frighten or destroy. A mother in defense of her child would leap upon any creature in the world. A man's rage was a dreadful thing, but in comparison with the fury of an aroused mother it was little more than bluster and bluff. When she sprang at an enemy she never paused to consider the danger to herself or to weigh the odds against her. She was ready to sacrifice her life; and when aroused she was, like the lioness, a dozen times more deadly than the male.

In the winter of this year, Ka-ka's baby became ill. She had only very obscure notions of what might be wrong with him but she knew he was not the healthy and lively little fellow that he had been. He was pale and fretful; he whimpered; he refused to eat. As a matter of fact, he had, unobserved by her, devoured a whole litter of poisonous insects. Babies then, as now, often tried to put into their mouths anything they could lay their hands on. They ate spiders and ants and bees. They ate nearly everything that they could chew and swallow; and the mothers, knowing what stupid little gluttons they were, had to watch them constantly. If a wasp came along and settled for a moment in Kooloo's hair, he captured it first if he could and then he promptly thrust it into his mouth. A thousand times he had been slapped for such rashness. He had been shaken and cuffed. He had had his jaws pried open while Ka-ka looked into his mouth and with rough fingers picked from his tongue and teeth the fragments of bugs. He had even tried to chew sticks and stones.

When a baby fell sick, its mother's first thought was of harmful objects which it might have swallowed. That was, indeed, almost her only thought. Sometimes she examined the child from head to feet to see if it had an infested wound or if a blood-sucking parasite had burrowed in its flesh; but such matters never occurred to her until she had peered anxiously and repeatedly into its mouth. If she saw there no sign of gluttonous indiscretion, she was baffled. Ka-ka was baffled now. She held Kooloo up, clutching him around the waist, and stared at him with troubled eyes. For several minutes she would hold him and look at his eyes, and solemnly the child would look at her. She seemed to feel that his eyes might give some hint of his malady.

The second day after he became ill she held him up for a long while and scolded and talked to him. He did not understand her words but he felt her anxiety, and he thrust his lips out, indicating that he wished to caress her. She shook him for his impudence and he whimpered. He understood that in some way he had displeased her. He knew she was scolding him, and because he did not know why he felt resentful and angry. If his gaze wandered, she shook him until he again looked at her, and then he would wrinkle his forehead and pucker his lips and act as if he were about to sneeze. He would distort his whole face as if getting ready to howl, but he knew that howling would do him no good. When his mother was annoyed with him there seemed to be nothing he could do except to look at her and let her look at him until, weary and baffled, she set him down.

And when she set him down he was not surprised to find her peering again into his mouth. With strong hands she would grasp his jaws and open his mouth as wide as it would open. She had done so a hundred times and Kooloo could see no sense in it. Again and again, too, she had thrust a finger into his mouth and scraped along his teeth and tongue and then looked at her finger. He also looked at it but there was nothing to see.

Later, she examined his feces. She spoke a word that sounded like *hoo?*, making a question of it; and Kooloo echoed her. "Hoo?" she said. "Hoo?" said Kooloo. Then curiosity overcame him and he moved toward his excrement, and for that he got a sharp slap on his ear. He gave a howl of dismay but almost at once he forgot the rebuke and curiously watched her. She examined the dung, trying to find in it an explanation of his illness. "Hoo?" she said again and again, addressing the question not to him but to the invisible mysteries around her. Kooloo strove to imitate everything that she did. If for a moment she seemed to lose interest, he lost interest, too; but when, anxiously intent, she bent forward, he did likewise and peered for all he was worth.

The other persons in the group knew that Kooloo was sick. When he lay in his bed, the others came, not together but one by one, to look at him and touch him. Who-ah came and stared at him for several moments. They were all very gentle, including the men. The other children played but less noisily than was their custom. They were careful not to go near Kooloo or disturb him, and if Ka-ka cried angrily at them, they at once fell into abashed silence. Now and then Murah, the most sympathetic one among the children, softly approached Kooloo; and she would crouch by him and pat him or touch her lips to his neck. She would look at him with grave compassion before stealing away.

Almost never for an instant did Ka-ka take her eyes off her son. Instead of allowing him during the day to ride on her shoulders and cling to her hair, she carried him in her arms. But Kooloo had only a bad case of indigestion, and nausea and a little fever. In a few days he was well again, and Ghoo was sick.

She had never been a healthy person. She had a strange organic disease that manifested its symptoms in her sparse hair, yellowish skin, and lackluster eyes. The winter months she found difficult. Then food was scarce and she had to provide not only for herself but also for Kughh, the dwarf; and nearly everything that she could find to eat she gave to him. In starvation she became weaker and the prey of colds.

One morning when the group marched away, Ghoo was too feeble to stir. From her bed she watched them with sick and anxious eyes. Kughh followed the others a little way, but when, in looking round him, he saw that his foster mother was not coming, he set up a cry of alarm. Thereupon they all stopped to learn what the trouble was. Ka-ka came back and went over to Ghoo, who was sitting in her bed. She looked down at her and brown eyes asked what the trouble was, though she had sensed almost at once that Ghoo was ill. Ghoo looked up at her in the meek and apologetic way of one who wanted protection and care but knew that these were not given to sick old people.

Others had come up to stand in a group around Ka-ka and look at Ghoo. The women and children were sympathetic, the men were curious; and Ghak, as if seeing in the woman a portent of his own doom, was frightened and began to clamor for attention. Nobody paid any heed to him. Nor did they give any heed to Kughh who was hopping about and crying like a small child that had lost its mother.

For a long moment Ka-ka looked at Ghoo. Then, as if undecided, she went down on hands and feet to peer more closely. After another searching stare that revealed nothing, she opened Ghoo's mouth and looked into it, seeking a reason why the woman was not able to rise and follow; and finding none there, she examined her for sign of wound or broken bones. Of the invisible maladies of starvation and age she knew nothing. After her examination was done she seemed convinced that Ghoo could rise and follow if she wished to, and she turned away and the group moved with her. Kughh trailed the others until he heard his guardian crying after him.

In turn he looked at the vanishing group or back at Ghoo while his dim mind strove to understand. Then he began to run back and forth. He took a few loping steps in the direction of the group, and stopped short and swung and loped toward Ghoo; and back and forth he went, never pausing for a moment and whimpering all the while. In his simple way he was trying not only to keep them all in sight but also to bring them together. Each time he ran toward the group he went a step or two farther and he did likewise in returning toward Ghoo, and presently he was racing back and forth across a distance of fifty yards. Not once did he hesitate in his frantic efforts or in his plaintive crying like a lost thing. After the group had passed out of sight he stopped, exhausted, trembling, and covered with sweat. He went over and stood by Ghoo and looked at her, his eyes asking what they should do now. Ghoo looked at him and her eyes asked the same question. For several minutes these two persons, the one sick and the other an idiot, looked at one another, knowing that they had been abandoned and were helpless. Their eyes were bright with grief and terror. They listened—but in the wilderness around them there was no sound.

Crying with anxiety and dread, Ghoo began to crawl on hands and feet; and Kughh, overjoyed, ran on ahead, as if feeling that his eager nimbleness would give her strength and speed. He dashed ahead fifty yards or more and stopped to look back and wait. He was impatient and he scolded her and jumped up and down. Ghoo crept slowly like a wounded thing. She was very weak, and only in the dread of being left alone did she find the power to move at all. Overcome by impatience, Kughh rushed back, shrieking at her, and seized one of her arms and tried to drag her. When he pulled at her she sank as if stricken, and for several yards he yanked at her and scolded and asked her in his gibberish to get up and walk. Then in despair he dropped her arm and ran forward again. With eyes and nose he marked the path of the group and shouted with glee as if he had discovered what it had been difficult to find. He yelled back at Ghoo and with wild gestures beckoned to her.

But Ghoo was too sick and weak to move. She was lonely with the loneliness of approaching death, and she was only dimly aware of Kughh's cries or of his attempts a little later to drag her after him. In her tired and starved body she felt him pulling her, and when he had given up she knew he was sitting by her. If she could have made him understand, she would have told him to run on ahead and rejoin the group.

Kughh would not have done that. He was a dwarf and an outcast and he had a feeble mind, but this woman who had cared for him so many years was the only meaning and anchor of his life. He did not realize that she had starved herself almost to death that he might live. He did not know that she was sick. He sat and looked at her and wondered why she did not run ahead with him to find the group. He wondered, too, why she did not find food for him. His exertions had made him hungry, but for so many years he had been babied and cared for that he had little sense of how or where to find food, and little knowledge of what was good to eat and what was not.

An hour later Ghoo had recovered enough strength to sit up and to realize that her ward was hungry. He had been fretting and plucking at her hair. Looking around her, she saw nothing that he would eat. Under her care he had been accustomed to the choicest plants and fruits, and the vegetation here was coarse and tough and bitter. She reached out and stripped leaves from a twig and handed them to him; but Kughh spurned them. He struck them from her hand. He barked at her, trying to express his distaste for all the woody pulp in sight.

Then Ghoo began to crawl about, searching for more succulent plants, and Kughh followed her, angrily observing and sometimes anticipating her moves. At the moment, for instance, when she reached toward some foliage, he gave a bark of rage that told her he would eat none of that. Ghoo filled her mouth with the bitter leaves, as if to teach him that these would sustain life when there was nothing better. Kughh closely watched her. She chewed the bitter mouthful and swallowed it, but Kughh was so dubious that he made signs to her to open her mouth; and when she did so he peered in. Ghoo ate no more of these leaves. They were too bitter. She crawled again, seeking more savory growth, but Kughh would eat nothing that she found and ate. Nevertheless, he watched her as if fascinated and suspicious and baffled, and again and again he looked into her mouth to be sure she was swallowing the stuff.

When night approached he had forgotten that the two of them were alone. Like an infant that feels secure with its mother, he felt safe with her; but Ghoo was anxious and frightened. She crawled to a thicket and sat under it, half-hidden, and Kughh sat by her; and when she caressed him he moved close to her like a child. He looked at her, his eyes asking why there was no food for him, but Ghoo looked at the deepening gloom and was afraid. As clearly as she was able, she wondered what to do, knowing well that old or sick persons, deserted by the clan, were the prey of prowling beasts. If she had not been so weak, she would have tried to climb a tree to spend the night above ground.

After a little while Kughh laid his shoulders across her lap and slept. Ghoo did not sleep. Wide awake, alert, and so terrified she hardly dared breathe, she stared into darkness and listened. Every sound in the deep night made her thin hair rise and her flesh turn cold. She heard invisible wings and the night-crying of birds; and all around her on the soft damp decay of the jungle floor she heard the sound of small feet. These sounds she had heard all her life, and nobody in the security of a group paid any heed to them; but now every sound, no matter how faint or far away or how familiar, seemed ominous and dreadful. For members of a group they were only the sounds that disturbed sleep, but for a sick woman alone with a helpless and overgrown baby they became a part of the unknown and nameless anxieties that haunted her people.

While she listened she also strove to see into the darkness. If a wing passed in heavy flight above her, she looked up, and if a small thing scurried by she leaned forward in an effort to see it; but she knew that the harmless creatures made a lot of noise and the killers came on padded feet. The loudest sounds startled her, but she knew they were nothing to fear. The downward breathing of great wings chilled her, but it was the stealthy movements that made her almost scream. Her ears were sensitively recording all the stir around her and her nose was marking every odor that came on the breeze; but it was her eyes that probed the darkness for another pair of eyes.

The eyes of the great cats she had seen many times. These beasts often approached groups during the night and looked in, but only their eyes, like a pair of green and burning stones, were ever visible in the outer darkness. When Ho-wha roared at them they went away. The eyes went out suddenly and there was only blackness where they had been. It was for the leopard's coming that Ghoo watched and waited during the slow hours of this night. It would come on soft feet that would make no sound at all, and she would not know until she saw a pair of green lights that it was looking at her. She would not be able to see its body. She would not know if it was standing erect and moving its tail or if it was crouching to spring.

And when, after long hours of dread, she saw the two terrible eyes looking at her, she was so choked by terror that she could not scream. The hair rose on her head and over her body; a sensation like that of cold flowing water moved in her flesh. The beating of her heart shook her and trembled in Kughh asleep on her lap, and she could feel the soles of her feet burn as if stung by nettles. But when she tried to move she seemed to be numbed by crushing weight as if not Kughh but a great tree lay across her legs.

For a moment the eyes vanished but almost at once they were looking at her again. As Ghoo stared at them, hypnotized and helpless, she realized that they were approaching, but soundlessly as if floating toward her in the dark. Then she gave a choked cry of despair, an awful strangled moan, and Kughh sat up; and the moment he saw the leopard's eyes he screamed and flung himself, howling and frenzied, to the earth. It was his cry, it was awareness of the threat to him, that aroused Ghoo to furious strength. She leapt to her feet to put herself between Kughh and the beast, and in the same instant the leopard sprang. It struck her with the full force of its weight and knocked her down, and talons and teeth sank deep into her flesh. In the first awful moment of realizing that she was in the beast's grasp she screamed and fought to escape, her hands wildly clutching fur or seeking the throat. She felt no pain. She felt only crushing and smothering embrace, only the utter despair of one alone in darkness with death. The claws gutting at her belly she did not feel, and when open jaws closed on her throat there was no pain then. There was a sense of having her breath choked off. Then there was an inrush of smothering horror as if the black night were pouring into her mind.

When the beast sprang, Kughh shrieked and ran away, plunging blindly and headlong into trees and fighting with them as if they were alive. He knocked himself down and then raced on all fours until spent; whereupon, still howling with terror, he cowered and looked back. He felt around him in the darkness to learn if Ghoo was with him. Too stupid to conceive of her death, he believed that she had deserted him and he began to whimper like a frightened child. He thought that if he waited here she would come.

At the first sign of morning he became a little bolder and moved about, trying to see or smell her. In full daylight he stood up but he was unable to realize at once that he was alone, and it never occurred to him that Ghoo was dead. In searching for her he came to the spot where she had been slain and he could see and smell fresh blood. He did not know that it was her blood. He believed that she was near and perhaps gathering food for him, and he called to her and listened and called again. "Hooo!" he said, but there was no answer of living thing in the quiet dawn.

Again feeling terrified, he began to lope about, crying for her. He would run aimlessly in a direction and give his call and listen. Getting no answer, he would suddenly rush in another direction and repeat his call. After a while he was so frightened that he chased about wildly and without purpose; and when, worn out, baffled, dejected, he paused to listen, he thought he heard her coming to him. Then his dull face awakened with inexpressible relief and joy. With a sound like that of weeping and laughing mingled, he ran forward to meet her, never doubting that she was coming to him and bringing him food. He would run a little way and stop to give his plaintive call and then run again. "Hooo!" he said, but there was no answer in the vast and friendless loneliness around him.

9

Ho-wha and his group quickly forgot Ghoo and her dwarf. Perhaps nobody except Wuh thought of them at all, and he observed only that they were gone. He did not care. Nobody cared much about unfortunate adults who were chronically ill or repulsively malformed. Except in the relations between mothers and their children, strength was not the faithful warden of weakness, nor health of disease.

The well ones and the strong ones had all the problems and worries they could take care of. Even among them, none ever lived into extreme old age or died a natural death. So hazardous was their existence, so constantly surrounded by the forces of destruction, that for life itself and health and a sense of well-being they felt superstitious awe. When for a little while, forgetful of dangers, they felt secure, their egoism was arrogant and despotic, and they behaved as if they were the favored tenants of the planet, chosen to rule and command. Then they were impertinent and overbearing, and each of them was tyrannical toward those weaker than himself. All of them, but more especially the men and boys, liked to order others around and force them to obey and cringe and show deference and fear.

It delighted the lad of nine, for instance, to tyrannize over his brother who was many years younger. He played with him, to be sure, but now and then, if the mothers were not watching, he cuffed him and knocked him down or he snatched food away from him. He did not really covet the food. He felt more important and meaningful if he could force his brother to serve him; and the younger lad, in turn, had a wish to boss Kooloo. This urge to enslave and dominate was in the females, too, but their disposition was to mother rather than to command.

The egoism in any of them was insufferable only when there was no sense of danger. When they felt anxious and afraid, when their attention was drawn from despotic whims to the terrible and inscrutable world around them, then their meekness was as extreme as their presumption or arrogance. In such moments even Ho-wha, or his morose son Hwah, could feel humble and defenseless and lost. Instead of feeling the strength of his muscles and the bold lusting of his hungers, a man then perceived himself, dimly and unhappily, as a friendless creature on a mysterious and unfriendly earth; and his humility or despair was particularly strong if the threat was something that he did not understand at all. Against beasts that moved, that struck with teeth and claw, that behaved in many ways like his own kind, he could assert himself. They were enemies but they were not mysterious. But his emotion was quite different toward such utterly baffling things as thunder and lightning, volcanic eruptions, winds and fire. These were often invisible; and if not invisible they manifested themselves in such dreadful ways that it was impossible to frighten or destroy them.

It was inevitable, therefore, that people should have come to feel not only that the world was unfriendly but that much of it was moved by anger and a wish to kill. If they had been more intelligent, they might have tried to placate the furies around them. No such notion had ever occurred to them. On the one hand they were moved by a vigorous will to conquer and enslave, but on the other they were chastened and rebuked by forces mightier than themselves. Between despotic assertion and humble submission they spent their lives, and each emotion tended to drive the other to greater extremes.

If Ho-wha was lording it over the others when thunder suddenly crashed above him, he behaved as if he had been personally rebuked. Sometimes he whimpered like a child. But sometimes, too, after cowering for a while, humble and abashed, and listening to the invisible voice roaring at him, he felt outraged as if a bluff and a braggart, too cowardly to show his face, had been making a jest of him; and when the danger passed he became a more oppressive bully than was his custom. He howled at his women and he strode wrathfully about, restoring with bluster and abuse his self-respect.

But the other emotion in him also ran to extremes. By nature he was, like all men, a tyrant, and like them he felt most important when others humbly submitted to him. If, when he was roaring manfully, one of the dreadful mysteries spoke to him in rage, his self-esteem collapsed and his majesty sank to the level of any terrified creature. He behaved then as if he felt that he had overplayed his part, as if he had offended some power mightier than himself, and as if to atone for his rashness he had to humble himself.

Of all the devouring angers loose in the world, the most terrible for him and his people was fire. Of what it was or where it came from they had no notion at all. It seemed to be the very substance of anger itself; and as suddenly as it came it vanished, leaving behind it only ruin and the strong smell of its breath. Sometimes they could smell it in the air when there was no other sign of it; and one evening many weeks after Ghoo's death they had eaten and made their beds when Ka-ka uttered a warning and stood sniffing the wind. Observing what she did, the others faced the breeze and smelled of it and talked in the excited way they had when they sensed danger. There was an odor of burning things in the air. Even though night had come, Ka-ka set Kooloo on her shoulders and moved away, and the others fell in behind her; and the group went down the wind. Now and then Ka-ka paused to be sure she was going with the wind and not against it, or to sniff the air for the heat of approaching fire, or to see if all the children had come. Once, unable to tell by looking back, she stepped past Who-ah, who was next in line, and in turn touched all the children as if counting them. She included Gah, who was not a child any longer but a pregnant woman.

They moved across an area that a former fire had devastated but they did not know that their enemy fed on dead growth. Ka-ka did realize after a while that the heat was overtaking them. The smell of it was stronger. The warmth of it was coming down the wind. She turned, scolding at the others, and they all came together in a group around her; but they did not talk. They had no words to express the terror they felt now. In turn they peered into the darkness or looked at one another or pointed to a faint light far away in the sky. Their faces were those of people baffled and terrified. Looking at Ho-wha, Ka-ka gestured to the right of their course and to the left, and Ho-wha, after appearing to consider for a moment, pointed in the direction which he thought they should take.

They resumed the march, swinging leftward, and presently they climbed a hill that offered a view toward the distant fire. On this hill they found another group. The two groups looked at one another, curiously, almost with friendliness, but they did not mingle. Then Ka-ka looked out and across the dark wilderness below.

Far away in the sky she could see the yellow light of the enemy. Rolling away from the light she could see its breath. It was the smoke of a vast encircling fire and it was filling the sky with a darkness deeper than that of the night. Upon the belly of the smoke was the yellow radiance of the flame below.

After a few moments the other group moved away and down the hill, and Ka-ka thought not of them but of the direction they had taken. She looked at the darkness into which they had vanished and then far away at the fire; she turned her face to catch the flow of the wind; and all the while she was trying to tell if the other group had chosen the right way to safety. The other adults, too, were thinking of this matter. They stared at the fire in an effort to decide which direction it was taking. Ghak was running back and forth, his gaze fixed on Ka-ka, and his frightened gibberish telling her that they ought to be going. Ka-ka did not intend to move until she was sure of the safest course. While she waited and watched, the yellow sky turned a pale red and a burst of flame ran up several dead trees and exploded in showers of light. Then a wind caught the torches and waved them like flaming wings, and long tongues leapt into the sky and vanished, and from below there rose a broad crimson sheet. Then the sheet fell out of sight but after a moment it rose again in two tides of flame, with the tree tops like torches between them.

Ghak was frantic. The children began to cry. Who-ah came up to Ka-ka and the two women looked at one another, their eyes asking questions. Who-ah pointed in the direction the other group had taken but Ka-ka scolded her and she withdrew. Ka-ka had lived long enough to learn that this terrible enemy always marched with the wind. She knew that to the right or left of the great anger visible to all of them there was flame low down and hidden, skulking there, like any stealthy killer, and feeling its way. When, three or four hundred yards to the left of the parent fire, there was a sudden gleam in the darkness, Ka-ka thought she knew what the main path of the monster would be; and instead of following the other group she turned down the opposite side of the hill. She went, not with the wind but at a right angle to it, and she moved as fast as she could, paying no attention to gouging limbs or the thrust of thorn and briar. She beat a path for those behind her but after a while she stepped aside and indicated to Who-ah that she was to lead the way. The group traversed several miles and came to and climbed a hill higher than any they had crossed; and there they paused to look around them.

There was no moon or stars visible, but the wilderness before them was faintly alight, as if touched by the afterglow of sunset. Far away the crest of the fire was two or three miles wide; and rolling away from it on the wind were vast clouds of smoke. It was a broad and dreadful anger sweeping through the night. Ka-ka looked the other way and saw higher hills than this on which she stood, each thrust up like a pile of gloom.

Again she led them, going down the hill and into a valley of darkness and climbing another hill. All around her she heard sounds and she knew that other things were fleeing for their lives. Throughout the immense forest there was a frantic emigration of life and all of it seemed to be moving down the wind; but Ka-ka continued to cut across the wind in an effort to outflank it. Living things moved ahead of her. Now and then she could hear or smell them, but they were never visible. She did not know that in the stampede before a fire, no beast ever interrupted its flight to attack another; but if she had known that great cats were cutting across her path almost within reach, she would not have paused.

From hill to hill they went, traveling all night and never stopping for more than a moment until they felt safe. They had come to a mountain, faced with rock, and they climbed from shelf to shelf until they stood on a stone ledge far above the surrounding country. Morning had come. Toward the sun they could see for many miles, and they looked across a broad desolation, fire-swept, blackened, and smoking with death. On the western horizon the fire was a reef of smoke around the sky.

Ka-ka felt that they had had a close escape. She knew that multitudes of living things had perished in that mysterious and devouring anger that had moved through the night. She had seen fires before, and once she had explored a wasteland and found the bones of the dead. Now, after gazing at the ruins below, they turned to look at one another, their eyes eloquent with fear and awe. If they had had words to express their thoughts they might have said: "What is this angry thing and where does it come from?" That was the question in their minds.

Ghak was so exhausted that he fell asleep, but the others stared at a landscape of dead trees, wondering about this engulfing fury that did not kill with hands and teeth but poured in a hot flood. They were so curious about it, now that all danger was past, that the boys went down the mountain to inspect the ruins; and soon the other members of the group followed them. Ghak awoke and descended too. Cautiously, as if the mysterious thing might suddenly rise again, they went to the edge where fire had burned itself out against a ledge of stone. They kicked at the ashes. They gathered ashes in their hands and looked at them, or they examined shrubs that had been green and were now leafless stalks. They talked excitedly to one another, trying to express the wonder they felt.

The older lad entered the devastated area, but when his feet struck a hot ember he yelled with fear and dashed back to Ka-ka. Presently they all ventured out, seeking sticks that were still burning, and marveling when a gray surface, lifted into the wind, became a pulsing red. Intently they looked at it, fascinated by the crimson stain. When they thrust the stick down out of the wind the glow faded to gray but when they held it up again it turned bright. Ho-wha waved the stick about and soon it burst into flame, and the moment flame appeared he dropped the stick and roared at it. They were utterly baffled by this thing that could fasten itself on wood and consume it; for it had no body of its own and no life apart from the things it fed on.

They were so eager and curious that they ventured farther out, forgetting that they were sleepy and hungry and tired. When they came to stricken trees they paused to stare at the smoldering embers in their trunks; and they walked round and round the trees, looking at them and at one another, their eyes asking questions. Apprehensively but resolutely they invaded the desolation. It was the four-year-old lad, running on ahead of the others, who came upon a horrifying sight, and with a yell of terror he rushed back to his mother and tried to climb to her shoulders. He had seen a group of persons who had burned to death.

There had been nine of them and they were all huddled together as if, when there came to them the frenzied realization of doom, they had clung to one another as death closed in. They were only a pile of skeletons now, but in the atmosphere about them there was still an odor of burning flesh. When the living group advanced to look upon the dead, their emotions were so overwhelming that they all set up an outcry. They broke into a sweat of horror, and the children in the extremity of their fear began to defecate; and all of them in chorus uttered their sound of grief. It was a low moaning cry in three syllables, "Haa-ahhh-eahayeh!" that began as a kind of guttural groan and rose to a plaintive wail. Their cry became a chilling lamentation, a dirge, that continued for several minutes without pause; and though their eyes shed no tears they looked stricken with anguish. While lamenting, they all stared at the skeletons, and some of them in grief snatched at the hair on their heads, and others, like Ho-wha, softly drummed on their breasts.

They were uttering more than sounds of woe. Their mournful lament was also a kind of entreaty, a supplication, a prayer to all the unpitying forces in the world that attacked and destroyed. They felt chastened and humbled and defenseless. If they had been a little more imaginative, they might have striven in a spirit of sacrificial giving to placate and appease those terrible enemies, thunder and flame; but they could only cry out of grief and abasement and the superstitious loneliness of their heritage.

If they had gone farther across the miles of desolation they would have found the bones of other creatures, some of whom had been their enemies. They would not have found the king cobra melted to a streak of ashes and stain or the anaconda looped among dead branches like a charred cable, because these did not inhabit the more open woods of the higher hills; but they would have seen the bones of a great tiger that had been encircled and destroyed. The results of ravaging fire the adults had seen before. They had seen anger drop from the sky and sweep over an area and slowly withdraw, leaving a field of the dead. They had no wish to explore farther, and when Ka-ka turned away she headed back for the mountain, talking to herself with low excited cries as if she had gone daft. The others followed; and the sounds they made were mournful astonishment in the women, and rumbling fear and anger in the men. Ho-wha and the sullen Hwah both growled as they waded through the ashes; Ghak chattered with shrill despair; but Wuh, not so deeply affected as the others, was silent. He had lamented with the others while looking at the bones but now he was trailing Murah and thinking of her.

Ka-ka reached the mountain and led the way up until they were again safe but she did not go at once in search of food. She still suffered from grief and shock. Sitting on a stone shelf, with Who-ah and the children around her, she stared out across the burned waste, remembering the dead ones she had seen there. Mother love was a deep and anxious emotion. It was almost the only meaning a woman had. No matter what she did, whether it was sexual embrace, the gathering of food, the making of a bed, or only the calm watching of children at play, her concern and her labor were for her offspring and her life was given to them. In thinking now of the destroying power of flame, she had only the children in mind.

With the men, on the other hand, personal welfare and safety and hunger were uppermost in their thoughts. Ho-wha began to strip leaves and eat. Upon a ledge, Ghak found a smooth pathway of stone and ran back and forth, capering and yelling and disporting in lunatic antics in an effort to fix attention on himself. It was always this way after he had been deeply stirred. In varying degrees it was so with all men. A threat to their existence made them clamorous exhibitionists after the danger had passed—as if by taking the stage they could recover a sense of personal autonomy and worth. Ho-wha and Hwah were feeding but they were also growling angrily and looking at the others to see if they were paying any heed. They acted as if they had suffered an ordeal and had behaved courageously and ought to be singled out for admiration and applause.

In this respect Wuh was no exception, but most of his

hunger for attention he repressed. That was necessary in a group that gave him none and cared little enough what he did. He now fed apart from the others and cast his eye over the landscape, alert, as always, for sign of a wandering female. He wished that Murah would come over his way. If she had done so he would have seized her, never reflecting that she would make an outcry and bring Ho-wha upon him. Of foresight he had, like the others, almost none, and could not plot more than one move ahead or anticipate the consequences of that.

His interest in Gah he had lost, not because she was big with child but because he had sense enough to perceive that she belonged to another. In Murah his interest had grown. She was a vivacious girl with an uncommonly intelligent interest in things about her. But Wuh was interested in her because with one of her brothers she often engaged in erotic play, and she so excited Wuh that he could barely restrain himself. She and the lad explored and patted and stroked one another, rubbed one another's cheeks, clung together, and made the instinctive movements of coitus; and all the while they vocalized their excitement with cries of pleasure. When he saw them behaving thus, Ho-wha stared at them as if puzzled, but the mothers sometimes slapped the youngsters and sent them off alone to mind their business. Their playfulness Wuh watched with lustfully eloquent eyes.

During this day Murah did not come close to him; and after he had eaten a lean meal of bitter leaves and tough shoots, Wuh prepared his bed. He understood that Ka-ka did not intend to leave this mountaintop until she was sure all danger had passed. They were all hungry and thirsty and irritable. Wuh himself was in an ugly mood. After making his bed, he sat in it and looked across distance at the others; and again he wished that he could murder Ho-wha. After a while the others slept and Wuh lay on his bed and looked at the stars.

10

YET THAT is not quite what he did. He could see the stars and the moon because he was above the jungle; but he had no interest in them and he never thought of them. Like all people of his time, he was not interested in anything except the small environment in which he lived. Even the sun, floating every day across the sky, was of no interest to him. In his infancy and childhood it had been there, just as water and trees and food had been around him, and he had grown up accustomed to the presence of these things. His attention was captured only by unusual manifestations of familiar objects. If the moon had pitched out of its course or exploded or come close to the earth, Wuh would have been alarmed and he would have given to it anxious attention; but it was only a light that waxed and waned, that changed its shape, and that alternately appeared and vanished.

The sky was full of stars tonight, and moon and stars flooded the earth with soft radiance. Wuh was used to sleeping in jungle gloom. Now he lay on a summit, with the earth broad and bright around him, but he never thought of that. He was, like the others, imprisoned by a few simple emotions and by an unimaginative mind. He felt no mystery or awe except when things touched his physical welfare. He was not conscious at all of the wide-awake beauty of the night, of its infinite calm and peace, of its fragrance enhanced by moonlight and silence. If there was a faint stirring in his soul, as if he heard soft music far away, it aroused in him no more than angry resentment of Ho-wha.

After a while his keen nose caught a scent that he recognized, and it fetched him bolt upright, sniffing the breeze. It was the strong musk odor of beings like himself, and at once he knew that another group of persons was not far away. Pointing his nose into the wind he sniffed the strong smell of human bodies, and he opened his mouth wide as if to verify the evidence with his throat and tongue. Convinced, he left his bed and went as softly as a cat into the wind. There was no formulated thought in his mind. He went as if an invisible hand had reached out to guide and direct his will. Hunger had made him reckless again. Stealthily he moved down the mountain, guided by the odor in the wind but ready at any moment to turn and flee.

The group he sought was a half mile away, and this distance he covered without snapping a twig or rustling a leaf. Upon approaching close to the strange people he dropped to his hands and went on four feet like a monkey. A shadow moving through the night could have been no more soundless. Soon he could hear their snores, and a few moments later he was able to see several of them, asleep in the moonlight. Wuh sat to study the forms and to consider his next move.

On the far side lay a hulk which Wuh took to be the lord of the group, and such reflection as he was capable of told him that this was so. The guardian would take his position on the windward side where he would be the first to scent the approach of an enemy. The person closest to Wuh seemed to be a young woman, alone in a bed; and on her for a few moments he fixed his impatient and inquiring gaze. As quiet as the moon in the sky he was, sitting there, looking at her, and wondering if she would make an outcry if he touched her.

After deciding that she was the one he wanted, he gave attention to other members of the group, studying their positions and trying to tell if more than one adult male was present. As nearly as he could tell, there was only one. Thought of him, however, made the flesh quiver down Wuh's spine; and each impulse to move forward was restrained by fear of the tyrant who was not more than thirty yards away. Presently he felt so angrily impatient that his teeth clicked a little and saliva fell to his breast. Between the two, the overlord sunk in slumber and the girl almost within reach, he divided his attention, looking in turn from one to the other and struggling between fear and lust. Then his hands reached out, exploring the grass around him by no will of his own. He did not realize that he was seeking a weapon. A former experience was formulating a hint but he had no knowledge of that. On the contrary, he followed his hands and crept forward and came so close to the girl that he could see her clearly. His almost uncontrollable urge was to examine her at once, to turn her over, to draw her to him, to set her up on her hands and feet. The wish to do these things was so strong in him that he began to tremble and sweat, but still he did not touch her and he made no sound.

She was a girl of about ten but large for her age and very hairy. She slept alone. Lying on her side, she presented to him a view of her breasts, and it was on these that Wuh fixed his ardent gaze. They were for him, for all men, the most obvious sign of femaleness; and if he felt a wish to examine them, that was perhaps only to be sure that his eyes were not deceived. Sweating, trembling, and breathing as if half-choked, he crouched above her, his eyes avidly exploring. He looked down her body but the womanliness of her was hidden by thick dark hair.

Then for a long minute Wuh stared at her closed eyes as if by prolonged and ardent contemplation he hoped to make her look at him. If she had awakened to look upon this stranger hovering by her, she might have been hypnotized by the burning hunger of his eyes. His eyes were saying what his tongue had never learned to say—and they were saying it with such intense and unwavering passion that the girl stirred in her sleep. Her movement so excited him that he reached out and touched her. He felt, with the logic of intuition, that he was communicating his wish to her, and that she would soon awaken and look at him. He did not feel that she would yield to him. His fear was too extreme and his awareness of danger was too sharp to allow in him more than a feeble sense of triumph, or to blind him to the fact that he had invaded another's domain.

That the girl was slowly awaking became clear to him. Fear now was stronger in him than lust, and he stopped caressing her and waited. But he continued to look at her with hypnotic eyes, and when, after a few moments, she seemed to sleep soundly again he resumed his gentle attentions. Boldly he moved forward and thrust his tongue against her face. She stirred a little and moved toward him, and in this moment his defenses fell within him like a downrush of blood, and before he could realize what he was doing he had put arms around her and drawn her to him. He was facing her and looking at her when she opened her eyes.

For perhaps a minute they looked into the eyes of one another and did not move. In Wuh's eyes there was only the language of his hunger; in her eyes there was sleep and a question. He thought she was going to yield to him. He thought, indeed, that she had yielded, but when he moved again, intending to set her in a sexual position, she came wide awake and screamed. She leapt up as if not a man but a leopard had crept to her bed. She screamed again, and her cry was wild and ringing in the night. The whole group was instantly aroused. The lord of the family came up from his bed roaring with fury and at once ran to a tree and beat a challenge upon it. The woman and children leapt up, too, and with dramatic suddenness that took Wuh's breath away he found himself on his feet, chilled to his marrow, half paralyzed, and sweating from every pore. The girl had fled from him. And now they all stood there, dark and terrible in the moonlight, looking at him and shrieking with alarm.

He stared across at the lord and the lord stared at him, and thus for a long moment two men looked at one another. Then the lord of this group roared another challenge and rushed forward, and Wuh vanished into a thicket as if thrown by a mighty hand. But he did not go far. He knew that men, in defending their feeding grounds or their family, were content to bluster and shout.

They never pursued an enemy that fled. Wuh, therefore, plunged into hiding and stopped, knowing that he was safe as long as he was invisible. Besides, he was now a very angry man. The passion in him, suddenly stifled, had mixed with rage and fear and turned him sick. He felt dizzy and he acted as if he were drunk. Thought of the tyrant who had driven him off deluged his blood with wrath, and blood surged in him and darkened his senses. On hands and feet he began to crawl away as if he had been flogged. Spiritually he had been. Spiritually he had been debased and outraged. To be denied a female when females were plentiful and to be chased off as if he were only a beast of prey—this was the most humiliating experience that could come to a man. It blighted his self-respect. It so outraged his egoism, his manhood, his conquering and adventurous soul that he could feel only a bewildering urge to kill.

This urge was in him as he crawled away. He went up the mountain to seek his bed and was surprised to find Hwah up and prowling about. They looked at one another, curiously, suspiciously, and without friendliness. The outcry below had aroused this group, but all except Hwah had sunk into slumber again. Hwah had a notion in his mind.

He had grown to be a powerful man almost as large as his father; but he was a thick-witted fellow, habitually sullen and resentful, who moved awkwardly as if his strong young muscles had no mind to guide them. He had become bolder as time fleshed his frame and matured his hungers, and tonight he was ready to dare any man. The screams down the mountain had angered him. He had taken them as a personal challenge and he had been on the point of attacking his father when the cries subsided. So stupid was this young giant that he was unable to distinguish between the enraged voices he had heard and Ho-wha who had done no more than to rise from his bed and look around him. When a battle cry sounded, Hwah felt an urge to attack anything that moved within the range of his vision; and after the yells died away in silence he felt confused and cheated, as if he had been slapped by an invisible and audacious foe. The emotion aroused in him then became a wish to seize and ravish, and this urge was moving him when Wuh unexpectedly appeared.

After staring at Wuh for a moment, Hwah felt an impulse to attack him; and he might have done so without delay if Wuh, sensing the young giant's mood, had not gone quickly and discreetly to his bed. That peaceful gesture left Hwah more baffled than before. He was such an unreasoning blockhead that he could not think of anything as an enemy unless it stood on its legs and faced him. Creatures that took to flight or threw themselves on the earth as if wounded or defeated he could only stare at and dimly wonder about. He looked at Wuh and Wuh slyly watched him. In Hwah's dull mind was the notion that this was the enemy who had roared at him out of the night. But there the enemy lay now as if knocked down and conquered, and he could think of nothing to do about that.

Bewildered, but still angry, he turned to look at Ho-wha who was also supine and peaceful. In turn he stared at one and the other. All the while a thought was entering his mind. The thought said that these two enemies were both defeated or frightened, and that he stood here, by reason of some strength of his own, in possession of this group. As this idea took hold of him with the power of unqualified certainty, the anger in him ebbed and gave way to eagerness; and he turned his gaze from the men to the sleeping women. He seemed to stand there and meditate on the unexpected wealth that had come to him—as if, relieved of all doubts, and chastened to a mood almost philosophic, he wished to savor in full the realization of his triumph and look calmly at his females before choosing one to use.

He now looked in turn at the sleeping females. He made a move toward Gah but stopped short and glanced suspiciously at Wuh. He moved again, and again paused because in him the inhibitions of many years were laying a restraining hand. His emotions were hobbled. He behaved like a man whose bones were too heavy for the muscles that sheathed them. After each awkward advance, he looked over at Wuh or at Ho-wha and seemed to consider the risks.

Wuh all the while was watching him, though he pretended to be asleep. Knowing well what was in Hwah's mind, he eyed him anxiously and wondered if he would fight or slink away when Ho-wha came roaring from his bed. He was also worried about his own part in a struggle that seemed imminent. Sensing that Hwah intended to face the lord and fight it out with him, Wuh began to shake with excitement; and he was so anxious and alarmed that he rose a little from his bed. Hwah saw him move and turned to growl a warning. Thereupon Wuh again sank to his bed and discreetly pretended to be unaware. But he tingled with expectancy and felt the hair rising on his back and crown.

A few moments later he felt angry alarm. Hwah had changed his direction. After approaching and looking down on Gah, he turned toward Murah who lay a few feet away. That, Wuh decided, was more than he could endure without a protest. He had come to feel that Murah was his property. Softly he rose from his bed.

Hwah did not see him. He had dropped to his hands to gaze at Murah with anticipatory delight. When, after a long moment, he moved to possess her, Wuh left his bed and came forward, but he advanced softly and without any notion of what he would do. He approached within a few feet of Hwah. When he saw Hwah clumsily trying to draw Murah to him, his first impulse was to leap upon him; but he restrained that urge, and in the next moment was astonished to realize that he had uttered a ringing cry of defiance. It seemed to him as if another throat had uttered the cry.

Hwah sprang to his feet, and in the same instant Ho-wha sat up. The cry had aroused every sleeper in the group. Murah sat up and looked at Hwah, towering above her; Hwah looked at Wuh and bared his teeth; and Ho-wha rose to his feet and looked at both men. For a tense moment there was silence.

The silence was broken by a bellowing challenge from Ho-wha. At the sound of it, Hwah swung to face his sire. His hour had come. The hour had come that came to every son and father in their struggle over women; and this time Hwah did not intend to cringe and slink away. He bared his big strong teeth. The hair rose straight and stiff on his skull and down his spine. But he did not advance. He was content to wait and to fight only if he must.

It was Ho-wha who advanced. With a cry that roared from mountain to mountain and awoke every sleeping thing within a radius of three or four miles, he, too, bared his teeth and felt his hair rise in anger; and with another bellow he made a savage rush forward. He dashed a few feet, smiting himself, and stopped short to challenge again. They all knew what was coming when Hwah answered the challenge. His voice, as mighty as his father's, was like the crash of thunder. His face was a picture of murderous lust. But he did not advance. He stood his ground and waited, answering challenge with challenge; and when Ho-wha rushed forward again, the women and children moved out of his path. They went off in a group and looked with unhappy astonishment at the two men.

Wuh, meanwhile, had retreated. He wanted Ho-wha and his son to destroy one another; but though he was, in his way, a sly opportunist, he was also a very primitive man, and the challenging cries aroused in him a wish to fight. He stood ten yards behind Hwah and eyed the two warriors, but he was trembling and sweating. He wanted to roar too and beat his breast and leap upon the men.

When Ho-wha rose from his bed he was about forty yards from his son. Each savage dash forward covered only a few feet, but with each advance his fury mounted and his cry became more menacing. His gaping mouth exposed to view nearly every tooth in his jaws. His long upper lip, covered with a very short mustache, was drawn like a tight belt across his upper gum and back into either cheek, with his big nostrils looking like caverns at its edge. Skin was bunched below his eyes and drawn into a deep V between his brows. Hands beat a warning on the broad drum of his breast.

Again he rushed forward as if bent on tearing worlds apart, but he stopped suddenly with theatrical waving of his arms and clutching of his hair. His behavior, in these short advances, was intended to suggest to an enemy his power and ferocity and so frighten him; but Hwah did not budge. In his rage he was a frightful image of his father. In determination he was more than his match. Because it was clear that Ho-wha, for all his fury, weakened a little after each rush, and mixed fear with rage in his bellowing. He had never before faced an enemy that did not give ground—at least no enemy that walked on legs. Each advance was a little shorter than the one that preceded it; and in his voice now there was something plaintive. It was a note of anxiety and alarm—as if, while trying to intimidate his foe, he was asking him to retreat a little, and so allow Ho-wha to pass the whole thing off and save his face.

Perhaps Hwah heard and understood the change in his sire. Perhaps he sensed that the old man was chiefly bluster, and that now, if ever, was the time to attack. From the moment of Ho-wha's first cry he had not moved. But he moved now, and he moved with such unexpected speed that his teeth sank deep into flesh before Ho-wha realized that his foe was upon him. Ho-wha's next cry was one of rage mixed with pain. Hwah's teeth had entered his shoulder, and Hwah's hands, with nails like strong talons, were seeking Ho-wha's eyes and throat.

They were two monstrous men, locked in a death struggle and matched in strength and ferocity; and they fought with an earnestness rarely found among the beasts of the earth. Their fury was that of the lioness; their single-mindedness was that of the stag. Their courage, once they stopped bluffing and closed in, had no equal among any creatures save their own kind. They fought, not to maim or to frighten but to kill; and those who watched them sensed that this struggle would be the death of one of them.

The women, staring at them with fascinated and grief-darkened eyes, began to wail, and the children took up the cry. The two warriors fell to the earth and rolled over and over like cats. They bit into flesh, and the smell and taste of warm blood redoubled their fury. With grasping feet, with rending hands, they strove to tear one another limb from limb, to choke breath off, to gouge eyes from their sockets, to strip cheeks like rotten flesh away from teeth. The most terrible thing was not the sight of them but the sound of their voices. It was a sound that impelled all beasts that heard it to flee for their lives.

If Wuh had not been so fascinated by the struggle, he would have known that his opportunity had come. He would have seized Murah's arm and led her away while there was none to stop him. But his blood was also pouring in a lust for battle, and instead of fixing his attention on the women he moved closer to the men. He ran round them, echoing their cries and seeking a chance to attack either one of them. When, for an instant, Ho-wha broke loose, with blood streaming from his breast, Wuh stepped in, intending to finish the old man off; but in the next moment Hwah leapt upon Wuh and knocked him flat. That so enraged Wuh that his hands clutched about him and one of them closed on a stone; and when he rose to his feet he was grasping a rock the size of a cocoanut. Something awoke and flashed in his mind. Grasping the stone with both hands, he drew his arms up and over his head and hurled it at Hwah. It struck his skull and dropped him and he sprawled, face downward, his whole body shuddering. Ho-wha, almost too weak to move, looked at his fallen enemy and then crouched to peer at him; and Wuh stood back a little with something shining like a dim light in his mind. He did not understand fully all that he had done but he knew that he had felled Hwah with a stone and that the man seemed to be dead. So astounding was this realization that he, too, crouched to look at Hwah; and when he perceived that the skull was crushed and that the man seemed to be dead or dying, he rose to his feet and looked around him as he might have looked if he had conquered a world.

Ho-wha recovered a little of his strength. When he saw Wuh standing near he challenged him and moved to attack; and Wuh, instead of hurling another stone, ran away. The women were lamenting. Ka-ka went over to look at Hwah and above him she set up a mournful chant of grief; and Ho-wha, still puzzled, again bent forward to stare at his foe.

Wuh now perceived that his chance had come. Wasting no more time in foolish anger, he ran to Murah and seized her arm and led her away. When Ho-wha saw them going he began to shout and wave his arms, and the women and children set up a barking outcry; but Wuh did not look back or pause. Leading Murah, he went quickly over a ledge and out of sight. He went downward from ledge to ledge, half-dragging the crying and frightened Murah with him; and he did not stop until he was far from Ho-wha and safe with his woman in a small world of his own.

Part Two

II

If Wuh had stopped to think about it, he would have realized that he was safe from Ho-wha after he had gone a few miles; but he continued his flight as if angry breath were on his back. But there was another reason. He was a man now without a domain of his own, and he knew that. No matter where he went he would be a trespasser. It did not occur to him that if he traveled far enough he might come to an area that he could safely claim; and in consequence he went aimlessly, having no notion of where he was going or of what he would do.

While he journeyed he felt anxious and triumphant, and bewildered by what he had done. He had killed Hwah. He realized that much and he was proud of himself. But he had killed an enemy with a rock, a weapon, with something besides his hands and teeth; and that was such an inexplicable circumstance that he could think of little else while he fled. Memory of it so occupied his thoughts and emotions that Murah, who followed obediently, became a shadowy and secondary object in the twilight of his wonder.

He did not have a mind sufficiently rational to formulate a conclusion. He did not say to himself, "With a weapon you killed a foe mightier than yourself; and now you have a secret, a discovery that is yours alone, and with it you can frighten or destroy all creatures that threaten you. With rocks you can crush the leopards and with clubs you can smite the snakes." No, Wuh did not by any means perceive the matter so clearly. His intelligence did not grasp it at all. His emotions, fed by memory, were obscurely triumphant, but there was no recognition beyond that and no new vision of himself.

After he had gone a few miles and felt beyond danger of attack, he was inclined to swagger and bluster. He threatened the birds that flew above him. When he heard a great touraco drumming in the ceiling overhead, he stopped, but he did not shout a challenge or rush forward. On the contrary, he looked about him for something to seize and hurl. In one moment his impulse was so sharply directed that he looked for a weapon, but in the next he acted as if confusions darkened his intentions. It seemed as if an effort to be deliberate ran into an ambush of capricious whims. It was not foresight, it was the unexpected impulse that flashed with meaning and memory and sent his hand groping. When, a little later, Murah whimpered and with gestures told him she was hungry and tired, he barked at her and then suddenly seized a dead branch and struck her with it. Then, quite as suddenly, the branch dropped from his hand and he looked confused and helpless.

Still later, when Murah cried again, he again seized a stick and struck her. She cowered abjectly and wailed. Wuh stared at her for a moment; but now, instead of dropping the stick, he strode about, growling at the woods and striking at things—as if feeling that he could fix his discovery in memory only by exercising it. He smote trees, and then, experimentally, he fetched the stick in a sharp blow across his own legs. The pain he felt seemed to delight him. Murah, meanwhile, was watching him closely; and because, like all people, she was very imitative, she, too, grasped a club and walked around in mock combat. Presently she was as delighted and excited as he was. When he struck a tree, she ran to it and did likewise; and then suddenly and without warning she approached Wuh and struck him.

Turning on her with a howl of rage, he showered blows on her head and shoulders; and crying with pain she sank before him. Wuh looked down at her and at the stick in his hands, and his eyes winked gravely, darkly, as he thought of himself. He felt an impulse to beat her to death, not because he wished to kill her but only because he was confused by this new power that had come to him. When he raised his stick, Murah looked up and whimpered; and then, instead of striking again, he forgot his club and let it fall from his hands. He seized her arm and began to drag her after him. He did not realize that he had dropped his stick, and he did not remember it. A weapon was still an alien thing that was no part of him. It was hardly more than an unpredictable notion that flashed into his mind and moved him in an urge to kill, or that suddenly vanished from his mind, leaving in him only a bewildering memory.

He would not entirely forget it but neither on the other hand would he be able to keep it in mind. When, after another hour of wandering, he paused to eat, he did not remember his power with a weapon. He was only Wuh again, the sly and cunning and timid one who had no feeding grounds of his own and would have to be a poacher wherever he went. Each lord of a group had, within rough limits, his own domain, and other men invaded at their own risk. Wuh knew that. He realized that even now, while he stuffed his belly, he was an unwelcome stranger in another's field. He fed with both hands and kept an anxious watch. If he had seen an enemy, he would not have thought of grasping a weapon. He would have blustered or fled. It was Murah, the one who would bear children and have need of security, who kept in memory the lesson he had taught her. She had greater need of it, and necessity then, as now, was the mother of progress.

After eating, Wuh wanted to continue his flight. He went off a little way in the gloom and looked back at her; and when she did not follow, he beckoned to her and made movements with his feet to suggest walking. He scolded her in the wordless language he used. When he came over and seized her arm, intending to drag her after him, Murah shook his clutch off and made it plain that she wished to fashion a bed and sleep. She began to make a bed in a bamboo thicket. Wuh looked apprehensively into the gloom around him and listened. He remembered next that Murah was his mate and was alone with him, but his erotic hunger was inhibited by fear. In his mind was a restraining picture of Ho-wha, coming across the earth, bloody and roaring, to recover his woman. He was troubled, too, by the realization that he had entered another's domain. How Murah, in such circumstances, could prepare to sleep he did not understand.

Wuh failed to understand much more than that. He did

not know that he had chosen by far the most intelligent female in Ho-wha's group—and if he had known he could hardly have cared. He did know that Murah felt secure with him because he had killed a man, and had threshed trees and her and everything in his path. She had a dim and happy notion that she, and her children when they came, would be safe with him; and though she felt no love, she did look upon him with an emotion akin to respect and pride. She would make her bed and sleep; and if an enemy came, Wuh would kill him or drive him off. That is what she felt, remembering his show of strength, and that is why, in spite of his anxious gawking about, she made a bed and entered it. She looked at him and wondered why he did not make a bed; but Wuh, a ridiculous fellow whose memory was short, and whose years of bachelorhood had made him apprehensive when there was no cause, stared down at her and wondered what he should do. He talked to her, trying to make her understand his anxiety. "Hooo!" he said, making of the word both a warning and a question. He uttered other syllables, too, that scolded or questioned her; and though Murah understood him she was sleepy. She curled up on her side, laying her head on one arm and drawing her knees up to her belly, and seemed not to hear.

Wuh then decided to make a bed, but while he bent stalks to form a hammock he talked at her, chiding and complaining and disputing like one arguing with himself. And that, in a way, is what he was doing. He was trying, more for himself than for her, to clarify his new position in which he had a mate but no kingdom of his own. Where, he was asking, would they find an area of their own in which they could wander and eat and play and sleep and be unmolested? Did she not know that every man had his own domain from which he drove invaders? Did she not realize that they had made their beds on another's property and might at any moment be set upon and killed or chased out?

No, Murah was not thinking of such matters. The time had not come when the woman looked upon her mate as the one to bring in the food; but she did expect him to drive enemies away and to protect her and her children. That was his job. When the job was too much for him, she sprang forward to assist, but fighting was not her task. Trespassing on another's home was not her worry. And so she fell asleep.

Wuh, still growling like one abused and misunderstood, made his bed and sat in it. Darkness had come, and with it, high in the leafy canopy, was the melancholy music of rain. They were on the edge of lowland jungle where there were months of rain, twilight, and curtains of fog. It was a wet and gloomy and depressing world of parasitic growth where mosquitoes and sand flies and gnats swarmed in fogs of their own, and the cuckoo told over and over its mournful notes. Most people seemed to like this world with its heavy ceiling, its sunless undergrowth, and its smell of centuries of leaf-depth and old trees rotting on the ground; but Wuh preferred open places and friendly light. He was a sad and dispirited fellow at best, and the monotonous language of rain and of huge trees sighing in the winds filled him with anxious and oppressive doubts.

Leaving his bed he went over and sat by Murah and looked at her. Over the side of her exposed to the weather, hair glistened with the jewels of rain, and moisture was a dim light upon her cheek. Her eyelids were closed and wet. Wuh felt so chilled and dejected that he looked round him for a shelter—for a mora or a corkwood tree under whose buttressed roof he could sit; and seeing none he went to a large hagenia tree and stood under its wide branches. Rain did not come down through the ceiling in solitary drops. On the high leaves the drops gathered and coalesced and then came down like a spilled handful of water; and when one of these struck Wuh he shivered. Occasionally, in extremes of wet and cold, people built crude shelters, and with such a project in mind Wuh studied his situation. Looking above him, he saw that two branches formed a downsweeping canopy; and at a little distance away he saw a plant with broad leaves that looked like shadows in the dark. He went over and stripped an armful and laid them upon the two branches. Then he sat under them, feeling that he had done well; but soon the water, gathering on the leaves above, overflowed their basins and poured down upon him. Like a lazy fellow who added to his workmanship only if he had to, Wuh fetched another armful of leaves and spread them above him and sat again. He was experimenting but he did not think of his labor as an experiment. Again and again he gathered leaves and laid them above him across the two limbs. After a while he had a roof that did not leak and he was deeply pleased with himself. He stared up at it as if to understand in what way he had fashioned a miracle. As a matter of fact, he had scattered the broad leaves like shingles, with each overlapping the next; and the water ran from leaf to leaf and spilled from the eaves.

He was so delighted to learn that the water did not touch him that he left his roof and walked around it, trying to understand by what cunning craftsmanship he had protected himself. He stared at it, but the simple mechanical principle he did not grasp. He was, in fact, so dubious that again he sat under his roof to be sure that he had not been deceived; and he gazed solemnly up at it, with both delight and astonishment in his eyes. He shook clinging drops from his body and dusted moisture from his hair; and then he dug into the humus under him, throwing the wet surface out and sitting at last on a dry floor.

He was deeply pleased with himself. For the first time in his life he sat under a rain and was dry and warm because of his own efforts. He knew that he had protected himself but he had only a dim and troubled notion of how he had done it. He was so obsessed by wonder of himself, and doubt that he sat under a roof of his own making, that he resumed his curious peering at his handiwork. With dubious fingers he touched the leaves above him to see if they were dry; he examined the dry earth on which he sat; he thrust his head out to learn if rain was still falling; he listened to the sound of wind and rain in the tree above him and upon the dark wet world around him, and he searched himself for signs of water. When, convinced at last, he drew a long sigh and settled to the luxury of admiring himself, he remembered Murah, lying on a bed out in the storm. He did not care how soaked and distressed she might be. So far as her own welfare was concerned, he would not have cared if she had drowned. But because he was so proud of himself and wanted her to see what he had done, he crawled forth and went over to her. He seized an arm and dragged her out of sleep to her feet and then pulled her after him as if she were a dead thing. She protested and slapped at him; but Wuh was determined to show her how wonderful he was and he took her with him to the roof he had made. He stooped and entered and drew her under it with him; and without waiting for her to see for herself, he began to talk to her, trying to make her understand that he had built this shelter against water and wind. She sat on the dry earth, shivering, sleepy, and not at all interested in his talents; but he continued to talk to her, and presently in his eagerness he left the roof and went into the rain to look again at what he had done. He peered in and scolded her. When she paid no heed he entered and sat by her and looked out at the storm. After a while he felt warm and secure, and he turned to embrace her, but she barked at him angrily and slapped him. Instead of persisting, as Ho-wha might have done, he drew away from her and sulked.

A man's erotic advances were always clumsy and experimental. There were times, he knew, when the female was not approachable; but he did not know why she was not. Neither the man nor the woman had any notion at all of the relationship between copulation and birth. The man was in rut all the time, but the woman was so only for a short while during each moon cycle. Selfish and tyrannical men, like Ho-wha, slapped the women down and made them yield when they had no wish to; but Wuh was not that kind of man. After Murah struck him, he drew away and stared at her and luxuriated in self-pity. During this night he made no attempt to approach her again.

Murah curled up and fell asleep.

Wuh, like a shy and gawky fellow, sat half under the shelter and half in the rain and looked at her. Lulled by the music of wind and water, he dozed, and after a while he sank into sleep and dreamed unhappy dreams. His dreams were simple parables in which he copulated or fled from enemies or starved in bramble patches while others around him fed and grew fat. The climax of each dream aroused him, and then he would bestir himself and listen and scent the odors in the breeze and peer out at the dark world. He would look over at Murah who was curled up like a cat and snoring; whereupon, feeling abused and cheated, he would doze again, with his chin resting on his wet breast.

12

FOR DAYS and for weeks Wuh and his mate wandered through a vast jungle, going without sense of direction or purpose and behaving as if enemies were on their track. The great forest in which they were vagrants was soaked by rains. It was a stupendous wet gloom out of which huge trees a thousand years old lifted their leafy empire to the sun. Titans among them, thrown down by winds or felled by age, lay like rotting monsters in the undergrowth and were so covered by plant parasites that each was a long reef, its trunk hidden and its dead branches clothed with vines. The lush dank wilderness was such a tangle of mosses and creepers and ferns that it was sometimes impenetrable; and under riotous growth that often looked black in the perpetual twilight, invisible streams talked along dark channels or overflowed banks and spread into stagnant pools. Throughout the jungle was the melancholy of sunless life.

The smell of it was the muggy odor of marsh and fen, of sodden and rotted leaf-depth, of decaying boles sheathed with fungus, of swamp-ponds, of plant-rust, of mold and mildew. The breath of the jungle, exuding from mingled rot and growth, was a heavy and saturated atmosphere seldom stirred by a breeze and never cleansed by the sun. Under the oppressive ceiling, drooping and drenched and overladen by its own lush excesses, the air was like the concentrated breath of centuries, keeping all the stench of death and all the fragrance of life, and fertilizing the growth of the living with the decayed pollen of the dead.

Throughout this gloomy wet underworld into which Wuh and his mate had plunged were countless billions of parasites who made it their home. Grasshoppers were there, aglow with moisture and chirping ceaselessly in a realm where there was neither day nor night. Mosquitoes swarmed in ravenous hordes that had little to feed on but darkness. Sometimes they moved in such dense bodies that they were like a dark and agitated cloud of sleeplessness. When they sensed the presence of a moving thing, no matter whether animal or only a released vine, they closed in upon it and sheathed it completely; and if they found it bloodless they rose again in their humming song of hunger. Only creatures protected by feathers or thick hair could live in this underworld that was the paradise of their breeding and the graveyard of their brief and famished lives.

Mosquitoes and sand flies and gnats tortured Wuh and his mate day and night. The pests bothered them little while they were moving, but when they paused to eat or sleep their bodies were so mantled with them that with one slap of a palm they slew scores. The larger ones Wuh sometimes picked off and amputated, tearing legs and wings from the body and then looking curiously at the maimed creature wriggling on his palm. He killed thousands of them but if he had slain millions he could have perceived no thinning in the swarms. His face and hands and feet were pimpled with festered sores where they had sucked his blood. At night he tried to burrow among vines and cover himself with broad-leafed plants, but the blood-hunters found their way in. He would sit up with a roar of anger and scatter his bedding and strike savagely about him; but after a few moments he would become strangely quiet, realizing that he was defenseless.

One evening he hit upon another plan to protect himself. Lying in a sheltered spot with his back to a big tree, he drew Murah against him, intending to use her as a covering while he slept. She did not understand at once what he had in mind and she was obedient to his will until mosquitoes made her frantic; but when she moved to withdraw, Wuh howled at her and drew her against him. She struck him then and leapt up, scolding; and Wuh, as if feeling rather mean and selfish, looked up at her with an expression on his face that resembled a foolish grin.

During these weeks spent in deep jungle they were both driven to experiment, but it was Murah who devised the most adequate protection. Sitting, and drawing her feet under her, she would bend forward, with her face against the earth, and pile leaves around her head; and then she would burrow her hands into the leaf pile and place her palms as a covering over her cheeks. In this cramped position she slept.

Observing what she did, Wuh walked several times around her, studying her position; whereupon he dropped to the earth at her side and copied her way of protection. But he did not sleep. Murah had a heavy growth of hair on her skull; Wuh, in comparison with her, was almost bald. The leeching parasites raised welts on his head and infected him with fever. He became ill. The constant rain and the miasma of the jungle depressed and saddened him, and for many days he was a sick and disconsolate man.

During this time Murah served him faithfully. When not eating, or sleeping from exhaustion, she sat by him under a shelter which she had made and brushed the swarming insects away from him; and while thus engaged she would look at him with grave and motherly concern. Men were restless and fretful, and in sickness they often indulged in self-pitying tantrums, behaving as if convinced that they were the special victims of all the malevolent forces in the world. Or they sulked and despaired as if appointed for death. But patience was part of a woman's heritage. The periodic distress of her menses or of pregnancy, the pain of childbearing, and the watchful care of offspring had taught her to be stoical in the face of illness and to be philosophic about the slow crawl of time.

For Murah, Wuh, during his sickness, was a foolish and petulant child. She did not regard him with ironic amusement; but neither, on the other hand, did she believe he was half as sick as he pretended to be. He had a cold, to be sure, and he sniffled and coughed and moaned. He was alternately flushed and chilled. He refused to eat, or even to try to eat, any but the juiciest things she fetched to him. For the most part his large brown eyes gazed at her with lambent melancholy, as if he wondered whether she knew he was sitting on the threshold of death and was resolved to die without making too much fuss about it.

One day he stared at a huge mosquito that stood as if propped on one of his fingers, its bloated belly a dull red.

He indicated the pest to Murah as if he were too feeble to do more; and at once she slapped it. Then Wuh, with the same owlish despair, looked at the blood stain. He smeared a finger with the blood and touched it to his tongue. Out of his hair he plucked a fragment of mosquito and ate it. Then, as if to avenge himself before dying, he caught several of the creatures and fed them into his mouth. He looked around him and picked up a wandering beetle and a crane fly and ate those too. This perverse industry seemed to brighten his spirits. To his diet, later in the day, he added more mosquitoes, a few moths, and a huge morpho butterfly. Whether he liked the flavor of them, or ate them because he imagined they were trying to devour him, it would be impossible to say. Observing what he did, Murah went away and found a nest and fetched to him three small eggs. Such delicacies as eggs Wuh had eaten before.

He took the eggs one by one as if counting them and laid them by him under the shelter; and then he laid one on a palm and slowly crushed it and licked the juices off his hand, eating shell and all. He ate the other two and added to them some tender vegetable growth which Murah had also brought. He ate all of these things with a sad and melancholy thoroughness, his eyes meanwhile looking at Murah as if to ask what she thought of him.

Murah thought he did very well. She was so delighted that she ran away to find other delicacies, including more eggs and a whole armful of bamboo; but when she returned, Wuh was a most dejected and cheerless fellow. His dinner of vegetables and insects and eggs had been too much for his stomach. He had ejected the whole unsavory mess and was staring gloomily at his vomit.

Murah was excited and annoyed. She brushed his spew away and sat by him, determined that he should eat again. When, after offering him a bamboo shoot, he turned away in disgust, she moved upon him and crushed it against his mouth and tried to shove it down his throat. She broke an egg against his bared teeth and the juices of it spilled down over his breast. With a howl of wrath he moved away and turned to look at her as if she were trying to feed him poison. Their gaze met and for a long moment they looked at one another. In Wuh's eyes were distaste and self-pity and anger. In Murah's was the anxious kindness of a mother who was trying to cure a sick child. Then his attention was caught by the egg juices on his breast and he dipped at them with a finger and licked his finger; but when Murah proffered other edibles he barked and snarled and behaved as if she were wantonly torturing him.

Intuitively wise in the ways of the male, she gave him his time and allowed him to come by the notion that everything done for him he did himself. He cleaned the egg off and ate it, and presently he ate other things and looked round him more cheerfully. Watching her closely, as if he had to be on guard against her destructive whims, he ate a little of the green stuff, paused meditatively to pick off and crush between his teeth a bloated mosquito, and then stared at the rain like one who was trying to decide whether to die or live. And all the while, hovering near, ready to assist, but giving him his way in all things, Murah studied in his face the expressions of delight and disgust and wonder that she saw there. Then she withdrew to lay more leaves on his shelter.

A roof for herself she made a few yards away. Though

only a girl still, she was by far the most intelligent of Ho-wha's children, and a fitting mate for a man as sly and resourceful as Wuh. Her imagination had been stirred by his use of weapons and by his building of a shelter. These had greatly enlarged the periphery of her mental life. They had suggested to her obscure but exciting possibilities of other things that might be done; and as she lay in her bed, fighting off mosquitoes and listening to the rain, she was disturbed by notions, imminent and elusive and beyond reach, as if lights, invisible but certain, had awakened on the margin of her world. They were vague intimations of the shape and purpose of things to come.

Like all other persons, she lived in a small dark prison whose circumference was the boundary of what she could see. Of spaciousness she had no conscious notion; but when nevertheless she stood on a mountaintop, with a broad vista before her, she felt an urge toward release and freedom. She felt the same urge when she stood under a wide and sunlit sky. Then she broke into a gibberish of words, trying to express her delight and wonder in the bigness and mystery of life. When, on the other hand, she moved in the dank and melancholy gloom of the jungle, she felt oppressed and unhappy, small and lost, as one must whose mental world can never transcend his physical view of things. Spaciousness was the fancy's stimulant, and the jungle was its opiate. Her people were dwellers in the great forests, not because the twilit cathedrals were a mirror of their temperament but because they felt safer there.

Lying in her bed, Murah was thinking of the rain and the darkness. What these were she did not know and she was afraid of them. Wuh had shown her how they could protect themselves from rain, but the jungle night, black and saturated with the smells of decay, was a terrible thing that closed in upon her until her own world was less than the size of her own body. It became the size of her mind, and her mind in the steaming opaque depth was only an unhappy question mark. It was little more than an alert and vibrant terror, infinitely small and alone.

Rain was the only sound in the jungle tonight, but she was remembering many sounds; and though she had heard them since the hour of birth she was still frightened by them. During the morning and evening, and often all night when there was no rain, hordes of monkeys swung through the high canopy and made the earth tremble with their awful roaring. When the whole pack howled together, the sound was more dreadful than that of thunder or of the lion. Sometimes one group aroused a second and then a third and then a fourth, and the roof of the world shook as if there had descended upon it a dozen wild thunderstorms.

There were other creatures, too, whose outcries made her anxious and fearful. As night approached, the wood rails gathered in great flocks and uttered piercing screams like things in the clutch of an enemy; the barking of the toucan rang far and wide through the ceiling; and above all other sounds was the ear-splitting whistle of the goldbird. There were many other sounds that disturbed Murah, including the bloodcurdling yells of the macaws and the heavy and monotonous thunder of the bullfrogs.

Tonight there was little to hear except the dripping of rain and the deep breath of the wind across the roof. But

Murah was afraid. It would have taken only a sudden scream to send her fleeing to Wuh's side. She slept little because under her loneliness a faint idea was burning; and when morning came she went to her mate and scolded him and led him away.

13

SHE WAS resolved to leave the wet gloomy lowland and seek higher earth, but Wuh was reluctant to leave the jungle where he felt safe. When he protested or fell behind, Murah chided him or took his arm to urge him forward, or she talked to him, using one-syllable words which for her expressed warnings or entreaties or commands. Her utterances were guttural sounds in which the vowels were little more than heavy breath and the consonants were harsh; and all of her words were verbs. One of them meant *Come!* and another meant *Look!* and a third meant *Listen!* They were quick and exclamatory.

Wuh sensed their meaning. Sometimes he repeated them after her as children do when learning to talk. "Come!" she would say, tugging at his arm; and Wuh would look at her and say "Come?", making of the word a question. His repetition of what she said was more than mere imitation. He was fascinated and delighted by her efforts to talk.

Other people talked in a way. They scolded or fretted

or cried with joy, verbalizing their emotions and thoughts as well as they could. They grunted and chattered, barked and screamed, but spontaneously, improvising expressions of wish and mood, but never giving to them fixed meanings. Murah had gone a step beyond all that. In talking to him day after day, a few sounds were isolated and remembered; and when, for instance, she asked him to listen, she always used the word "Hooo!" This sound had come to mean for her the act of listening, and only that. So it was, too, with a few other words which she used.

After several days Wuh understood what the words meant. He often repeated them after her as if to memorize them—but it was not that. He was delighted with the words because they had come to be so full of meaning for him. With vague but persistent wonder he thought about them and sometimes repeated a word over and over, as if trying to arrive at its complete significance; and after a while he turned the tables on Murah and bade her look or listen when there was nothing unusual to see or hear.

And so, during their weeks of wandering, they learned to share a few simple words that were more explicit than any they had used before. More than anything else since arms had ceased to be legs and hands had ceased to be feet, this discovery of language, of a more communicable bond between emotions and minds, was to be of immeasurable worth in human progress. It would release imagination to new fields. It would encourage and nourish the growth of minds. In Wuh it was like a stimulant that invigorated and sharpened all his senses.

One day he stopped her and said, "Look!" and then, realizing what he had said, he stared round him as if to see what was to be seen. It was as though he had told himself there was something to see and now was eager to learn what it was. Murah came up and they looked around them as if in mock pantomime. "Look?" she said, asking a question. "Look!" said Wuh, infatuated by the word; and again like a very solemn clown he gazed about him.

Murah had learned that he often cried look or listen when there was no reason for it. Then she became impatient with him. He was like a perverse and willful child. He was like one so enraptured by the sound and notion of a word that he had to keep playing with it. And now, as if to hold her attention, he cried "Listen!" At once the word communicated its idea to his mind and he was all ears. He turned his head this way and that and assumed an attitude of intent listening; and Murah, not knowing what he heard, or indeed if he heard anything at all, listened with him. At last she said, "Listen?" "Listen!" Wuh cried, but there was nothing to hear.

He also loved to employ the other three or four words to which her repeated use had given a meaning of their own. "Come!" he would say, and take her arm and lead her off. But presently he would stop as if confused. Then he would remember another word, and the mere act of calling it to mind was for him an exciting thing. "Eat!" he would say, and he would scamper about in search of food even when he was not hungry at all. Each of the words was a command to act, and the moment the word entered his consciousness, he obeyed.

Because they crossed the trails of others, there sometimes was really something to look at when Wuh gave the command. These paths excited both of them. Murah was not afraid, but when Wuh sensed that other persons were near, his impulse was to run and hide, chattering as he went and calling upon her to follow him. He had not been able to realize that he was a man with a mate and was looking for a kingdom of his own. He had forgotten his use of weapons. From day to day he lived in anxious suspense, feeling that in any moment he was likely to be set upon and beaten and driven out.

Murah was pregnant now and suffered his embrace unwillingly or not at all, and Wuh's mind in consequence was turned to thoughts of other females. Neither he nor any other man of this time was promiscuous solely for the vain joy of possessing several women, though it is true that they were very acquisitive, and jealous of any property which they had acquired. But polygamy with them was a pragmatic thing. If Wuh's mate had been available to his desire as often as he wished, he would have been content, and there would have been in him no restless urge to invade other groups. Until Murah advanced far in pregnancy, he had been satisfied.

Now he was an unhappy man with a roving eye. As they emerged from lowland jungle and moved across the domains of nomadic groups, he knew, even though he rarely saw one, that many females were in the area; and in him again was the old struggle between fear and lust. Of this struggle in the male Murah knew nothing, and would have found it inexplicable and senseless if she had known. Erotic hunger for her, for all women, was only a momentary yielding which she did not understand and felt impelled to resist. Before she became pregnant she had found it pleasurable to yield to Wuh—quite as she found it so to have her neck gently bitten or her back scratched. But a pregnant woman was a morose and dispirited woman for whom a persistent and hungry male was an almost intolerable nuisance. For a while she had yielded to Wuh against her will, but more and more her impulse was to slap him and drive him away; and Wuh, understanding nothing of Nature's fumbling experiments and ironic patterns, resented and hated her, and was forced by a design not of his own making to wonder if he could prowl about and capture another female.

Because of this constant and tyrannical hunger in him, which an ironic scheme had mated with lusting in women that was only periodic, he was driven to the solitary perspective of the bachelor; and day by day his vagrant fancies became stronger. When signs told him that other people were near he cried out with delight and ran upon the scent, smelling it and making certain that females had passed this way. If he saw beds where others had slept he examined them eagerly and curiously; and by the odors he could tell which had been used by women and which by men. Those in which women had slept awakened him to wild lusting. On all fours he would crawl over them, sniffing and crying with joy and behaving as if he expected to be able to mate with a lingering presence.

His behavior Murah calmly watched without understanding at all. If she formulated any notions of him, she probably thought he was a little daft and very silly. Realization that others had slept in beds excited her, too, but if she singled out and identified odors they were those of babies. She cared little enough about the adults who were prowling in the forest around her. Her kingdom was one of children.

And so, day after day, these two lived, a man and his mate, separated by the broad difference of biology, the one wishing to seize and impregnate, the other seeking a refuge where she could give birth to a child. Though mates, they were strangers, and the only bond between them was an inexorable purpose which neither understood. Murah wanted peace because the laws of her body impelled her to peace. Wuh wanted to explore and fight and ravish because these were the laws of his being.

In their wandering they moved from a lowland to a highland jungle—from a forest that sweat in gloom and decay to a forest that was a garden of sunlight and good things. It was a bamboo jungle, waist-deep with hemlock and dock and sorrel and blackberry, under a fragrant ceiling of lobelia and senecio and veronia. The balsam, offering green bowers and deep retreats, was festooned and covered over with a wealth of wild flowers whose odors saturated the air. Great hagenia trees, pink of trunk and broad and lacy of foliage, spread wide drooping branches to which clung large moss pads, as if the trees had been upholstered with green velvet. In all directions it was a wonderland that drenched the breath and intoxicated the senses—a strange and deep and holy forest with golden aisles, with dark arbors canopied with orchids and cool mosses and blossoming vines, with high chambers sweet with fragrance and dusk. The vegetation was so succulent that the juices from a crushed handful of it would have filled Murah's cupped palms. From the leafy floors grew appetizing clusters of bamboo shoots. Around gardens of wild celery were a dozen kinds of edible plants. Trees and shrubs drooped under their ripe fruit.

This was the kind of home Murah had been seeking; and as she gathered with both hands the good things and ate, she chattered at Wuh and told him to look at this granary of food and fragrance. Wuh ate, too, but he was silent and fearful. He stuffed his mouth with juicy stalks and blackberries, and he intended, when his meal was done, to set an orchid on his shoulder and strut a little; but he knew that this domain belonged to another man. He expected at any moment to see the enraged fellow dash out of the forest and attack. He fed, therefore, like the guilty poacher he was, his eyes alert and his legs ready for flight. He closed a palm on a cluster of berries and fed them a handful at a time into his mouth, crushing them against his teeth and spilling the juices down his breast. Dark globules of juice hung in his beard and juice dripped from his hands. After he had eaten a gallon of berries he turned to the bamboo, and as his teeth crushed the succulent stems he sounded like one eating celery. Such a feast as this he had not had in a long while. Such a prodigal pantry of tenderness and flavor he had never seen before.

When he had eaten so much that his belly was bloated and taut, and he felt pain from the excess of his gluttony, he went to a drooping wall of orchids and set a lovely flower on his shoulder. Then he walked about, not to attract the attention of Murah, but only for the vain joy of admiring himself. The flower, in a way, was his badge of distinction. He felt that it set him apart and added to his meaning as a living thing. As he strutted, he turned his head in an effort to see the orchid or he gently touched it with a finger. If he had been a little more imaginative he would have made a girdle of flowers and hung it around his waist.

When, suddenly, Murah cried "Listen!" he stiffened so with alarm that his flower fell. He forgot it instantly. A moment ago he had been a regal fellow, surveying himself with immense delight, but now he was only a frightened poacher. He hastened over to Murah and found her in an attitude of listening. "Look!" she cried, but she meant listen. Language for her was still a very uncertain and experimental thing. "Sleep?" asked Wuh, who spoke the only word that came to his mind. Sleep was not what he meant at all. Nevertheless, the word communicated to Murah, and at once she forgot the sound she had heard and turned her thoughts to the making of a bed.

She chose a thicket of bamboo and vines that grew close by a hedge of blossoms. She had no knowledge, nor had anyone, of hoarding food against the lean seasons. If this bamboo patch had been the only food in the area, she would have made a bed of it. Tomorrow was not a concept in her mind. Of time beyond the present she had no notion at all.

After hearing nothing to alarm him Wuh also made a bed, and like his mate he ravaged one of the choicest gardens. Because his belly was full and it seemed to him he would never be hungry again, he plundered a bamboo thicket and a celery patch; and then he stripped armfuls of blossoms and piled them on his bed. When he lay down he sank into a mass of fragrant bloom, and he was so pleased with himself that he went over to see what Murah's bed was like. Thinking he had come to make demands on her, Murah bared her teeth and scolded him; but Wuh was interested only in observing that her bed was not half so luxurious as his own. His enhancement of sensuous delight was so gratifying that he asked her to come with him because he wanted her to see how resourceful he was. But Murah barked angrily and made it plain that he was to go away.

Thereupon Wuh obeyed another impulse and did something that he had never done before. He stripped an armful of bloom and took it over to Murah's bed and threw it upon her. He expected her to admire him, but on the contrary she leapt up and struck him and drove him off. She did not think he was trying to seduce her with flowers. She thought only that he was a pest and a nuisance who interrupted her slumber.

Wuh returned to his bed, a little crestfallen, but the soft and odorous mattress on which he lay soon revived his self-esteem. He sat up in his bed, and like a silly fellow —because there was nobody to look at him—he put flowers on his shoulders and skull; and there he sat, his brown eyes looking round him, and his self-love telling him that he was different from all other things. He deeply wished to be so—and that, too, was part of his heritage.

14

At dawn he awoke to a chorus of bird song, and without leaving his bed he reached around him for bamboo shoots and began to eat. The jubilant caroling of birds he liked, though he himself was a tuneless fellow whose nearest approach to singing was no more than lamentations of grief. Sometimes mothers crooned over their babies, but their monotonous mutterings were more an elegy of loneliness than a song. Human beings had never tried to sing. Their emotions were of sadness and melancholy rather than of joy. The clear recitatives of warbler and wren and lark, ringing in sweet brief lyrics upon the morning, or the antiphonal chorus that answered the querying soloist, stirred in Wuh a vague desire to cry joyfully at the world; but his harsh voice could have harmonized only with that of touraco and cockatoo.

After listening to the choirs and devouring a part of his bed, he felt thirsty, and he set off to find a brook whose gurgling music flowed under the melody of birds. On its bank he sat, not to drink but to make his toilet—because in his personal habits he was unusually clean. With respect to his teeth he was almost fastidious. Morsels of food lodged between them made him unhappy; and now, using a tough briar as a toothpick, he drew his lips back and thrust between his teeth to dislodge blackberry seeds and shreds of bamboo. After this chore was done, he used the briar to remove dirt that was imbedded under his long nails. In this and in all similar matters he was urged not by a desire for cleanliness but for comfort. In turn he drew his feet to his lap and inspected them and dug the dirt from under their nails and pulled some loose calloused hide off his heels. Then he proceeded to scratch his back.

For this task he found and broke off a bramble twig with strong sharp thorns; and with his right hand he reached across his left shoulder and raked up and down his back, and then reached with his left hand across his right shoulder. His face while he curried himself was an image of intense and preoccupied pleasure. His eyes winked gravely; his lips drew back in a kind of ferocious grin. Up and down or across from side to side he plowed his shoulders, and then reached down and behind him to dig at his lower back. While engaged in sensuous gouging at his flesh he espied a large thornbush, and he went over and turned his backside to it and moved up and down against the thorns. This resourcefulness so pleased him that he decided to tear the bush up and take it over to his bed. But first he wrenched off the lower branches, shaping the bush until its trunk was stripped as clean as a club, topped by a thicket of thorns. Grasping the stalk then, he tore it from the earth and broke off the clinging roots and marched back. He was so excited and pleased that he forgot to drink.

When he saw Murah eating, he dropped his formidable club and looked round him for fruit. Above him were clusters of red berries beyond reach, and he called Murah over and indicated by pantomime that she was to bend forward and allow him to stand on her back. Murah said no. Turning the tables on him, she imitated the bent position he had shown her, and the moment he assumed it, she leapt to his back and with both hands fed berries to her mouth. With hands touching the earth, Wuh stood patiently for perhaps a minute, with Murah standing on his back; but then he began to growl at her and try to make her understand that he was hungry. She paid no attention to that. He was only the earth under her, and the berries were luscious. Springing swiftly to one side, he spilled her, but she landed nimbly on her feet and turned upon him, angrily scolding. Her hands and face were stained with juices. With pantomime he again told her that she was to be the ladder while he ate; but when, obediently, she assumed the position, he was taken by another notion. He moved eagerly to embrace her, and with a cry of rage Murah swung and slapped him and ran away.

For a few moments Wuh stood disconsolately under the berries, looking up at them or over at Murah and wondering what to do. Then he found a stick and knocked some of the fruit down, but gathering it out of the deep grass annoyed him and he searched his mind for a better way. He found another stick, with a branch on one end like a hook, and this hook he put over a berry vine and drew the fruit within reach. Soon he prowled about and saw other fruit that looked more appetizing, but it was beyond reach of any stick he could find. He sat in his bed to consider the problem.

While sitting there his gaze fell upon his thornbush. When he seized it, the first, and indeed only, use to which he had put it came uppermost in his mind, and he began to scratch his back with it, lying against the crown and moving his back over the teeth. But this did not please him. He felt, on the contrary, resentful and troubled because obscurely in his mind there had been another notion; and he rose and grasped the club and walked back and forth like one waiting for a former thought to return. When his gaze fell upon the high fruit, two thoughts, unrelated in his mind until this moment, came together and were one.

He did not act at once. He looked up at the berries and then at his club, and during these moments the thought in his mind awoke with the clarity and force of something he had known before and had forgotten. Then he hurled the club at the fruit and berries fell in a shower around him. Instead of looking at them he ran in haste to seize the club and throw it again; and he repeated this act until the bright fruit covered the earth and the branches above him were bare. And still he repeatedly recovered his weapon and hurled it—for he was beside himself with exultant triumph and behaved like one who was determined to knock a forest down. He did not aim at fruit or anything except the ceiling above him. He always grasped and threw the club with both hands. And he began to feel angry as if attacking a foe; he barked in defiant challenge; and he felt more and more invincible as leaves and twigs and sometimes whole branches fluttered and fell.

Presently he threw the club high at arching limbs and it was caught and held; and now Wuh behaved as if the earth had turned to quagmire under his feet. He first looked up at the club and chattered fearfully. If one of his arms had been torn from him and hung on a high branch, he could not have been more astonished and crestfallen. Excited, frustrated, and bewildered, he ran back and forth under the club, crying at it, clutching his hair, and behaving like one who had been mocked and cheated. Around the tree in which his weapon hung he put his arms and strove to shake it. He climbed several feet up the tree and clung to it like a huge insect. Then he came down and ran back and forth, fretting and complaining; and Murah, hearing his tantrum, came over to learn what was wrong.

He barked at her and pointed to his club, dangling thirty feet above him, but what it was or why he was so concerned about it she did not understand. Her attention was drawn to the wealth of fruit on the ground and she pointed at it, and Wuh looked at it too and seemed to consider. He understood that it was there because of his efforts and he continued to talk to her, trying to explain that he had knocked it down. And because he wanted her to see him hurl the club and show off his might he looked for another, but he had such a simple and single-track mind that instead of searching around him for a stick he ran to the brook where the thornbush had grown. He expected to find it still growing there. When he saw only the hole in the earth where it had stood he howled with dismay, as if he had been doubly cheated, and then called to her to come and look. She went over, and he scolded at her and pointed at the spot where the bush had grown and searched her face to see what she made of it. For Murah his behavior was meaningless.

Wuh's gaze now fell on some stones by the brook's edge. After staring at them for a moment he experimentally took one in his hands and turned it over and over, curiously examining it. Another idea was coming to birth. Taking the stone with him, he returned to the spot where he had hurled the club, but the new idea was not communicated to him until he looked up and saw his former weapon hanging in the tree. In turn he looked at it and at the stone in his hands and at Murah. Then he felt an impulse to hurl the stone. He did not feel that he should hurl the stone at the club and try to dislodge it. That thought was too much for him to grasp at once. His urge was merely to throw the stone, and he did so, and when he realized that it had vanished into the jungle he exploded with rage and danced up and down. Behaving like the childish old Ghak, he flew into a furious tantrum and yanked at his hair and howled and beat his breast and slobbered.

Then, suddenly, he was quiet and thoughtful as if ashamed of himself. He looked up at the suspended club, and his eyes became sly and calculating; and he walked about, peering up at it and acting like one who expected to catch it off guard and take it by surprise. He went into the thicket to retrieve the stone he had hurled, and when he was unable to find it he hastened to the brook and returned with several large pebbles, carrying them against his belly and along his forearms. He let them all drop and then stooped to choose one. They so engrossed his interest that he sat and picked up and discarded one after another, all the while grunting to himself like one who plotted mischief but was in no hurry. The pebbles were wet and gleaming. He was fascinated by them.

As a matter of fact, he had again forgotten the club and his wish to possess it. He might never have thought of it if Murah, who had seen him throw the stone, had not come over to look at his armful of pebbles. She seized one and hurled it. That angered Wuh but it also confused him. These stones were his property and it was the loss of one that made him turn on her in rage; but in the next instant her act of throwing recalled to him the club in the tree. He stared up at it; and while he did so, Murah grasped a second pebble and threw it, and a third and a fourth; and Wuh, transfixed by bewilderment and indecision, allowed her to hurl all of them. When he perceived that they were all gone he became angry again, but Murah was pleased and excited, and ran to the stream to gather an armful. Wuh followed her. They both returned with pebbles. Barking with delight, Murah threw hers one by one, tossing them at random. Confused and sullen, he watched her, and he did not protest when, having thrown all her stones, she took those from his hands and pitched them into the thicket. She ran back for more and he went with her; but now, instead of standing by like a bewildered simpleton, he made her understand that he was to do the throwing this time.

Grasping a large pebble with both hands, he drew his arms far back over his head and hurled the stone with all his strength. Murah then threw one, and he howled at her and made her put all her pebbles on the earth with his; whereupon, indicating that she was to get out of his way, he showed off his might. Murah was content to watch him. He threw the stones blindly, awkwardly, and measured his prowess by the number of leaves and twigs he knocked off the trees. If no leaves came down he felt cheated, but if a swarm of them fell he cried with delight and looked at Murah to see if she was watching him.

The next armful she fetched Murah was resolved to hurl, and when he yelled at her, trying to make her understand that all the stones belonged to him, she ran away. She went off a few yards, taking her pebbles with her; and instead of throwing aimlessly she decided to dislodge the club. Wuh paused to watch her and after several moments he understood her purpose. It was such a brilliant notion that he was enthralled. With body tense and mouth agape he stared, his gaze traveling back and forth between her hand and the club and marking the flight of each pebble. He was so enraptured by the bright intelligence of what she was doing that he forgot his stones and stood like one propped and half paralyzed; and when, having thrown all her rocks, she came over to seize his, he did not protest at all.

Not until they fetched a fresh supply did he recover from astonishment. He not only fully understood what she was trying to do; it seemed to him that the idea was his own. As before, therefore, he deposited his rocks on the earth and made her do likewise; and as before he shoved her away from them and made it clear that she was to watch him perform. When, after many trials, a lucky hit dislodged the club and sent it tumbling to the ground, he was so overwhelmed by exultation that he could only hop up and down and scream. Murah ran to the club and fetched it to him, and Wuh seized it as if it were the most priceless thing in the world. For him it was, though its value was bewilderingly uncertain. His first act was to scratch his back with it. His next, an impulse born of wild joy, was to hurl it at a tree; and even while it was in flight he ran with it, crying at it as if it were a live thing. It came tumbling down through the leaves and he grasped and hurled it again. This he continued to do until he was weary and his exulting joy was spent.

But he did not forget it. On the contrary, Wuh identified himself with the club; it was his property but also it was a part of his own meaning. In a way it was himself. When evening came and he prowled in search of food, he took the club with him. He kept it by him when he made his bed and he laid it in his bed before he slept. When he awoke the next morning, the first thing that came to him was memory of it. He raked his back with it a few moments and then leapt up to hurl it and recover it and hurl it again. It had become an extension of his arms, his reach, his strength. It was to make of him the invincible lord of this part of the earth.

15

FOR SEVERAL reasons Wuh and his mate remained in this spot. He was afraid to venture forth, and Murah wished to give birth to her child here because the food was abundant and the climate was refreshingly cool. But the biggest reason of all was the club.

Every day Wuh played with it or tried to put it to new uses. He did not regard it as a weapon or a toy, though obscurely it had for him the qualities of both. Above all else, it was a kind of symbol of his ego. He felt that it was, like himself, a dangerous and unconquerable thing with a life of its own; but it served his will, too, and he used it to scratch his back or to knock fruit down. Sometimes he grasped it and swung it round and round, turning with it until he was dizzy; and again he attacked trees or bushes with it, flailing at them, and howling with joy as the leaves and branches fell. When he went for a drink he took it with him and kept one hand on it. He kept it by him when he ate or slept, and each morning he awoke and turned to it with the delight of fresh discovery. It never occurred to him that if he marched away he could take it with him. Somehow it belonged to this spot where he had found it, and it was Wuh really who stayed with the club and not the club that stayed with him.

Murah, when she felt like it, imitated his antics and procured a cudgel of her own. It was not crowned with stiff spikes but it was a piece of stout thornbush, dead and dry and tough. Like Wuh, she kept it by her at all times, but she did not identify herself with it. It was not a part of herself. For her, indeed, it was a weapon and a tool. She gathered high fruit with it or used it to pull vines down for her bed; and if an enemy had appeared she might have used it to attack.

They had been here a few weeks when, without warning, and as softly as the coming of dusk, the enemy appeared. He was lord of the group whose feeding grounds had been invaded. He was not alone. With him came his family, two women and a child.

At this moment Wuh was sitting by his bed and curiously inspecting his club. He was turning it over, peering at it, biting and smelling it, as if trying to determine what it was. The enemy appeared from the leeward side, and Wuh had not scented him and he did not see him when the big man came into view. It was Murah who saw him first. She cried out and leapt to her feet, with the club in her grasp. Then Wuh sprang up. In the moment of rising he saw the man and the two women and the child. His club lay at his feet.

For a long moment there was no sound. Wuh looked at the stranger and the man looked at him. He was a dull and ferocious giant like Ho-wha. In the shadows where he stood the hair on his skull looked black and tangled. He had bared his teeth in a snarl but he had not uttered a challenge. Behind him stood a young woman, and behind her stood an older female, with a small child riding her back. Both women were peering round their lord at Murah.

It looked at first as if neighbors were calling for a friendly visit. The big fellow was snarling, but something in the scene before him seemed to be of unusual interest. Perhaps it was the club Murah grasped or the one lying at Wuh's feet. On the other hand, perhaps he did not notice these at all. Since he first appeared he had not advanced; but the two women now came forth, one on either side of him. The expression on their faces was one of friendly interest.

Wuh was shaking with fear. Hair had risen on his back and scalp, his lips had drawn back, but he was too paralyzed to attack or flee. Both anger and fear were strong in him but they blocked one another and left him helpless. Though he perceived himself as a poacher who had been caught at last, he did not intend to run unless he had to; and so he snarled and bristled and waited. His club he had completely forgotten.

Murah's behavior was the most remarkable of all. Unless their children were endangered, women never took part in the fights between men or showed much interest in them; but now Murah was angry and she grasped her cudgel like one who intended to use it. She was not incensed in defense of her mate. She was not thinking of him. She was a pregnant woman who did not want to be disturbed and she was ready to fight.

So, too, was the big man. He had been working up a fighting lust, but slowly, as if in such matters he chose to take his time. Vision had communicated two thoughts to his dull brain. He saw here a man who had invaded his domain. He saw a female whom he wished to possess. When he fully sensed these two facts he exploded with rage and smote his breast. Then he made a savage rush forward, his voice roaring and his hands drumming a challenge.

Without realizing what he did, Wuh retreated, leaving his club where it lay. It was Murah who came forward to meet the challenge. Barking with shrill anger and menacing the big man as she came, she ran across half the distance between them. After a dash of four or five steps the stranger paused, and now roared and smote himself and prepared for the next rush. He had not looked at Murah. His gaze was fixed on the frightened Wuh who behaved like one who was ready in any moment to turn heels and flee.

Wuh looked at Murah when she dashed forward and his attention had been caught by the club which she brandished. At once that recognition made a different man of him. He remembered his own club, and there came to him the notion that the stranger was here to seize it. The stranger had rushed toward it and was preparing to rush again; and without hesitating any longer Wuh dashed upon his club and seized it with both hands and whirled it about his head. He began to roar, answering challenge with challenge. Anger became stronger in him than fear, though his voice at the end of each thunderous cry died away in a plaintive whine.

The big man had worked himself into a fighting rage. He clicked his teeth. He smote his breast until the sound made by his palms was a deep drumming through the forest. Hair stood in a shaggy mane upon his head and down his back. If he had not been so lost in fury he might have been fetched up by the amazing fact that his two opponents were menacing him with clubs. But he did not perceive them as clubs. He saw them as arms dancing before him. They whetted his rage, and when he dashed forward again he did not stop until he was almost within striking distance of Wuh.

It was Murah who struck first. When the big fellow halted and began to drum on his breast, she dashed upon him at full speed and brought her cudgel down across his skull. Either astonishment or pain shut his roaring voice off as if a hand had been clapped to his mouth. The blow swung him half around; and before he could move, Wuh leapt in and smote his face with the crown of thorns. Like steel teeth they plowed furrows in his flesh and almost tore off a part of his broad flat nose. Blood spurted and the big fellow found his voice again. He gave a roar that was like the shock of thunder, but in the same instant Wuh laid his club across the man's head. It knocked him stone cold.

Wuh was now frenzied with a lust to destroy, to kill; and he struck again and again until his foe's skull was crushed and the juices of his small brain were mixed like mortar with the pulp of flesh and bone. He smote the giant's shoulders and broke the bones in them. He leapt upon the prostrate body in a crazed dance of triumph. He turned the body over and flogged it, wielding his club with both hands and with such power that he broke the top off and had in his grasp only a thick truncheon.

He had forgotten the women. He became aware of them when they advanced to stare at their fallen lord. Like Murah, who also watched, they looked with astonishment at the broken dead one. Exclaiming, they walked around him—for never before had they seen one man slay another with such thoroughness.

Wuh, meanwhile, had worked himself into such a frenzy of rage and triumph that he had to find an outlet for his emotions or burst. He urinated first. Then he turned to the younger of the strange women and laid hands on her and dragged her toward a thicket. He crushed her under him and copulated with her, moaning all the while as if in pain; and after a few moments he embraced her again. With the tension in him somewhat eased and his mind a little clearer, he returned to the scene, followed by the woman, and recovered his club. He smote the dead man as if unconvinced that he would not rise again and threaten him. And then, suddenly, obeying impulses that shuttled him from notion to notion, he rushed over to a blossoming wall and set flowers on his shoulders and marched about, admiring himself. This whim diverted him for only a few moments. Forgetting the flowers, he seized his club and looked round him for sign of an enemy; and a little later his attention was again fixed on the two strange women.

They had gone off with Murah and were curiously looking at her cudgel. When the younger one moved to grasp it, Murah menaced her with it and scolded her; whereupon, as if to show off, she threw it at a high limb and recovered it and hurled it again. The younger woman, unburdened by a child, and the more intelligent of the two, was quick to imitate her. She searched for a stick of her own and found a piece of rotted stump alive with ants. For a few moments she picked the ants off. Ants crawled over her hands and up her arms and patiently she plucked them out of her hair and cast them away. By the time she had cleaned the stump of its pests she had forgotten what she intended to do. She dropped the stump and began to eat some berries that had been knocked down.

Wuh was still gloating over his conquest. He felt so bold and unconquerable that he would have attacked a lion if one had come into view. But he was also troubled. He had killed a man. He knew that. It was the second time in his life that he had destroyed anything of formidable size, and that recognition alone was enough to fill him with joy. Nevertheless, he was bewildered because it was not clear to him by what means he had triumphed. If he had bitten and choked him and torn at him with hands and feet he would not have been so baffled. He had a confused and haunting memory of having used a club and he now peered at his weapon as if to see if it had teeth. When he let it lie it was a dead thing, but when he seized it then it came to life in his hands and leapt and smote and became a part of him. His attitude toward it was one of wonder not unmixed with awe. If, untouched by his hands, the truncheon had moved about or hurled itself with destructive force, Wuh would hardly have been astonished. It did so when he grasped it, and Wuh did not clearly perceive that he imparted to it his own vigorous will.

This simple mysticism in him, this tendency to anthropomorphize things which he used, made of Wuh an unusual man. The same trait, to be sure, was in all people, but in him it was so strong that it was like an invisible certainty that eluded his senses. A weapon for Murah was no more than that. It was useful when she needed it. It was her property and she was jealous of it, but she did not invest it with mysterious qualities.

At a very simple level, on the other hand, Wuh was a mystic and a dreamer of dreams. It was his kind in the eras ahead of him who would invent gods and people the invisible with the shadows of their fears and desires; who would give totemic magic to inanimate things; who would conceive of sorcery and witchcraft and the black arts; and whose egoistic longings would induce the hypnotic trance of the visionary and insulated soul. All these things Wuh was doing now as well as he could, but his imaginings, his worries, his intensely solemn concern were only vaporous and fickle impulses that kept his emotions in a dance of darkness.

For an hour or two he was absorbed by vague notions. Again and again he peered at his dead enemy or at his inert club, trying to understand in what way the one had slain the other. Again and again he filled his club with life by whirling it about him or throwing it; or he sat, gravely preoccupied, turning it over and over, biting it, rubbing it over his body where he itched, peeling shredded bark off it, or testing with a finger the sharpness of the few thorns that remained. When he struck the invader he had broken his weapon in two, and after a while he came upon the other piece of it and took the two parts and tried to put them together. The club he laid across his lap and the crown he thrust against either end of it. Presently he recognized the end where the two had been severed and he fitted them together in their own dovetailed joint and the crown remained fast without support. He yelled with delight. He grasped the club and whirled it, and the crown fell off. Then he barked with rage and jumped up and down in a tantrum; but his fury passed almost as quickly as it had come, and again he sat, patiently, gravely, and fitted them together again. Countless times he joined them and saw them fall apart. He wore himself out with the dilemma.

He shuttled between fury and patience until evening came and he felt hungry, and he took both parts of the thorn-bush with him when he went to eat.

After supper his attention was divided between his perplexing weapon and his new women. Observing the younger one making a bed near Murah's, he marched over, intending to embrace her; but she barked at him furiously and Murah turned upon him also and the two of them drove him away. Crestfallen, he returned to his bed and to an inexplicable club. He sat in his bed and strove again to make the two parts one.

16

THE STENCH of the dead man drove Wuh and the women to a new spot. Wuh was glad to move. Now that he had a territory of his own, he wished to resume his nomadic habits; but after finding another sheltered place, close by water and abundant food, Murah made it plain that she was not going to follow him in his daily wanderings. She busied herself as if she had settled down for life.

Of Wuh's new mates, Loo, the younger one, was a pubescent girl who was already pregnant when he seized and raped her after the fight. She was healthy, intelligent, and very imitative; and in comparison with most of the women of her time she was quite handsome. The dark brown hair on her forehead was short and of an unusually fine texture, and it grew in a perfect arc above either eye, the two arcs forming in the center a neat triangle above her nose. There were no heavy drooping pouches under her eyes, and there was only a thin fine beard on her cheeks. Her eyes of deep lambent brown were uncommonly large and expressive, and reflected a friendly and inquiring mind. Her height was a little under five feet; her weight was about a hundred and thirty pounds.

From the beginning, Loo established a kind of friendship with Murah. Murah's use of a tool and her constant verbalizing captured Loo's interest and she was quick to copy her. She, too, found a stick she could use, and she chattered responses and questions when Murah talked. She aped Murah's behavior so faithfully that for many days she did only what Murah did. She imitated her in knocking fruit down, in making her bed, and in sitting by a tree and endlessly repeating words. Some of Murah's words she soon understood the meaning of, and her recognition of them gave her deep joy. She learned to distinguish between those that were concepts and those that were only indefinable sounds.

Sometimes she and Murah sat together and talked. Less like two pregnant women than two children enraptured by their own voices, they engaged in voluble duets, one giving a word and the other repeating it, or the two of them crying the word together. "Look!" Murah would exclaim, and Loo, gazing raptly at Murah's mouth, would echo her, or she would make a question of the word and repeat it until Murah answered her. Murah had added three or four other words to her store and now employed about a dozen that had for her definite meanings. Her use of an exclamatory "Ohhh!" was intended to convey a kind of greeting, and with it she always expressed both surprise and joy. "Ohhh!" she would exclaim when she first saw Loo in the morning, or when in feeding she went round a bush and unexpectedly faced her. She had a word for disgust that was harshly consonantal, and she used it when she bit into something distasteful or plucked pests from her hair. "Nghak!" she would cry, and then she would draw her lips back and pull from her mouth a wad of half-chewed food. She always examined the food as if to learn what part of it was bitter or sour. If it was a pest that excited her disgust, she would hold the wriggling thing up and look at it before casting it away.

Another word which she often uttered sounded like "Ahh–ohh–ahh!" This word, denoting distress or aggrieved surprise, she always spoke with plaintive sadness. The first syllable was a low indrawn breath; the second, also indrawn, rose a note or two in pitch; and the third was a mournful exhalation that fell to the depth of her voice. Loo aptly copied her speech but it took her some time to learn the meanings of the few words.

The other woman, several years older, was very different from Loo. She was a dull and phlegmatic and homely creature with yellowish sacs under her eyes, a shaggy mane, a coarse black beard, and a growth of stiff bristles over her big chin. She carried her arms as if they were useless weights that burdened her shoulders. Her posture was more stooped than that of the others, and her head was lower and more forward on her spine. When she moved about, with a yearling son riding her back like an alert and mischievous jockey, she was a gawky and stumbling woman with dangling arms and bowed legs and an unclean hide. When not staring round him, the son often busied himself with the vermin that infested his mother and himself, eating them or curiously pulling them apart. Sometimes he climbed to her shoulders and sat there, with short legs clasping her head, and searched her skull. Much more observant than she, he noted what the others did and strove to imitate them.

One evening while riding her shoulders, he saw Wuh threshing at things with his club. When his mother moved among the berry bushes the lad reached out and broke off a dry limb and smote her such a blow across her skull that he staggered her. That made her furious—and when Koko was furious she had no sense at all. She stripped the youngster off her back and began to flog him with her hands. Then she bit him and he gave such a dreadful yell that the others came running to the scene. Wuh came first and decided that this was no matter for him. Then Murah came, and when she saw a mother abusing her son she looked pained and astonished. The youngster a moment later escaped and began to leap away, hopping like a huge frog; but his mother ran after him and seized one of his legs and held him up, head downward. The child kicked with his free leg and screamed. Loo also came, and now echoed Murah's plaintive remonstrance. Wuh returned to his feeding. If Koko had not punished her child further, the other women would also have gone away; but Koko was in such an insane rage that she began to drub the lad. Still grasping his leg, she yanked him up and down, and each time she lowered him, his head struck the earth. He redoubled his yelps and fought with both hands.

Murah now obeyed an impulse that flushed her with the heat of its anger. She had a long sharp stick in her hands. She thrust it at Koko and it bit the woman like a fang. Then Murah struck her, and the astonished Koko, probably thinking this was an attack on her son, rushed at Murah with teeth bared. At this moment Loo became a participant. She carried a stick, too, and with it she struck Koko such a blow that she stunned her. The lad crawled away, whimpering, and turned to look with amazement at the women.

The din of the battle brought Wuh again to the scene. He was amazed too. Never before had he seen women attack one another. He did not know that this fight had grown out of the magic potency of weapons—first in the hands of the child and then in the hands of Murah. He bellowed at them and beat his breast. He made such a frightful uproar that the women were silenced, and Murah and Loo, abashed and frightened, withdrew. As soon as they did so, Koko rushed to her child and hugged him to her and swung to face her attackers. She was an outraged woman now. She had forgotten that the lad had struck her. It seemed to her only that two women had attacked her son, and henceforth her attitude toward them was to be one of distrust and fear.

Wuh was still bellowing. He had intimidated three persons and he was resolved to make as much racket as he could. He marched about, roaring at them, menacing them, and rushing with howling threat when one of them moved. If he had had his club with him, he might have tried to slay them—because acting in him had become fury, and he, like Murah, was moved in ways unknown to him by the symbol of a weapon. He was not the man, and she was not the woman, that they had been.

The discovery and use of a club was for both of them a powerful stimulus to their mental growth but they were not affected in the same way. To Murah it gave a sense of greater security and peace, and these were qualities of environment which a mother needed. Wuh, on the other hand, who by nature was like all men a hunting animal, was impelled to explore his surroundings. He always took his club with him. Sometimes he went out of sight of his women and did not return for an hour or two. Most of his exploratory wanderings were uneventful, but now and then he came upon an unusual sight.

One day he almost stepped on an enormous python before he saw it. He leapt back with a howl of fear. The hair down his spine stood straight up; his flesh twitched in spasms as if struck with stinging nettles. His impulse was to flee and he would have fled if a second glance had not told him that the monster seemed to be helpless. He cautiously advanced until he had an unobstructed view of the serpent, and this is what he saw.

The python had captured a small deer. It was lying uncoiled to the full length of it, and in its mouth, impaled on fangs, was a part of the beast's head. The deer was still alive. It was so much alive that it stood on its hind feet and knelt on its forelegs, its whole body pulsing as if with intense pain. Its slender muzzle up to the eyes was in the python's mouth.

The serpent saw Wuh but it did not stir. Fascinated, chilled by horror, and emotionally so overcome that he began to sweat and urinate, Wuh stared at the spectacle. Because he was a neurotic man with some power of projecting himself into situations of struggle and pain, he felt both sickened and enraged. The deer was still writhing, but after a few moments its legs gave way and it sank, shuddering, to the earth. The python was as motionless as a fallen tree, but its cold eyes were fixed on Wuh. Wuh had seen great snakes kill and swallow their prey and he knew what would happen. He knew the monster would lie there with buried fangs until the deer was paralyzed or would coil its body around the deer to crush it; and then slowly its throat would distend and it would draw the beast into itself.

For several minutes Wuh stared. The fear in him subsided, the anger became stronger. In his hands was his club. Obscurely, almost frantically, he had been thinking of this long gleaming destroyer and wondering if he dared attack it. He shouted a challenge and raised his club. There was no movement in the serpent. Pale eyes, unblinking and chilling, looked at him. The deer, sunk upon its folded legs, was a quivering thing.

Wuh advanced a little, menacing with his club, and roared again. Then he hurled his weapon. He missed. The python did not stir. He ran around and beyond it and recovered his weapon and threw it again. Again he missed. Because the serpent made no move toward him, he became bolder. With the club in his grasp he approached within ten feet of the creature and looked into the hypnotic eyes. He stooped and peered, curious to learn, if he could, how the deer's head was captured and held. Then he stared at the deer, and from its body his gaze traveled to the hideous upper jaw of the serpent and its soft lip hiding the fangs, and from the jaw his eyes followed the thirty feet of gleaming body stretched out in the grass. There came to Wuh an idea. He ran over to attack the monster's tail.

He looked at it first to be sure it had no teeth or claws and then he smote it such a terrific blow that he almost severed a segment two feet long. The serpent stirred. The whole shining length of it began to writhe and draw up in convulsive coils. With the hair rising on his scalp, Wuh dashed pell-mell into a thicket; and from his place of concealment he looked out. He observed that the jaws had not relaxed. They were still set on the deer's head and did not move. Nevertheless, Wuh was very cautious now and very excited. He was thrilled by the part he was playing. If he had known that this was the first time a man had ever attacked such a monster, except in defense of his life, he would have been overcome by vain joy. As it was, he felt exultant and determined and invincible. He was not done with this fight.

After a few minutes he came out of hiding and considered the matter. There was now no long defenseless tail thrusting out into the deep grass. The mangled thing had been drawn up and under the rope of the body and hidden. Wuh hesitated, hardly knowing what to do, until he observed that the deer's body was still quivering. Then he hurled his club at the massed coils of the body, and when he realized, a moment later, that his weapon lay there on the shining folds, he became frenzied. He ran away, clutching his hair and screaming; but suddenly he stopped his wild outcry and returned and looked at his club and barked at it. He was telling it to come to him. In his way, he was accusing it of treachery and betrayal; for he could have felt no more defenseless if one of his arms had been torn off. He wanted to dash in and grasp it but he did not dare. In the extremity of his grief he dashed around and barked as if out of his mind; but again, as suddenly as before, he became calm and sly. He had another notion and without delay he acted on it.

Running back upon his path he came to a clump of bamboo and broke off a tall stalk and dragged it with him. With this he reached out to the club, trying to capture and draw it to him. With the far end of his pole he could touch the weapon but he could not dislodge it, and instead of retrieving his club frantic maneuvering only shoved it farther from him. Presently it fell out of sight among the coils and Wuh could not see it; and again he clutched his hair and howled with desperate grief. Recovering a little but still babbling like a terrified child, he prodded at the python's body, trying to bring into view the lost part of him; and in this vain industry several minutes passed.

Other persons, meanwhile, had heard his cries and had been moving toward him. His women came, led by Murah; and when they saw their mate engaged with one of their most deadly enemies their astonishment was boundless. They stared at the coiled serpent engulfing its prey and barked at Wuh, but he was too absorbed by the loss of his weapon to pay any heed. He was fretting and talking to himself. If he had been a civilized man he would have been cursing for all he was worth and invoking the help of his gods. He marched over to have a closer view of the python's head but he was not wondering if the creature was helpless. He was fascinated by the monstrous dilation of the throat. The deer seemed to be dead.

Suddenly Murah cried, "Look!" and pointed to the opposite side of the clearing. There, some fifty yards away, was a group of faces. A lord and his family had heard the cries, too, and had come to learn what was going on here. A dozen pairs of eyes peered from anxious faces. Murah continued to sound the warning and Loo echoed her, and Wuh at last became aware of their cries. He looked at Murah and she pointed excitedly at the intruders and Wuh looked at them. When he saw all those faces watching him he turned cold.

He stared at a big man across the clearing. He did not know that the stranger was too astounded to move or grunt. So far as he could tell, here was a spectacle that he had never seen before. Here was a man, like himself, who seemed to be slaying a monstrous snake. It was so incredible that he could only gawk as if hypnotized and feel chills reach to his marrow.

While staring at the strangers Wuh remembered that he had lost his club; and without hesitating or striving any longer to uncover it with the bamboo stick he ran boldly upon the python's body to find it. Such recklessness made the strange man doubt his senses. He saw Wuh leap upon the coiled mass and reach down into it; he saw him almost fall upon it and thrust one arm out of sight as if he were shoving it into the serpent; and he saw him draw forth a club and brandish it, and he heard his triumphant cry. For the stranger the whole scene was a nightmare. It had been all his credulity could support to see Wuh leap upon a live monster. To see him now wave a club and shout a challenge was more incredible still. But it was the scene that followed that ravished the big fellow's dull mind.

Wuh's vanity, his delight in having the club again in his grasp, and the presence of spectators all conspired to make of him a reckless demon. For a few moments he whirled his club and shouted a challenge at the flabbergasted man skulking in the bushes. Then he fell to. He dashed to the head of the python and with both hands he laid his thornbush across the monster's skull. Because the bone of the deer's head was inside the mouth and throat, the blow almost severed the upper jaw. It knocked one cold lidless eye completely out of its socket, and the next blow smashed the other eye. The great coiled body began to writhe and unfold and lash out like a gigantic whip. Wuh did not pause. He rained blow upon blow until he not only demolished the serpent's head but also crushed the skull of the deer. Murah seized a stick and joined him, and Loo followed her, and by the time they finished, the monster's head was only a few ribbons of skin. The jaws, the skull, and the meat of it they pulverized and beat into the earth. Then they stepped back and watched the convulsive writhing of the great body.

Trembling with destroying wrath, Wuh looked round him for other foes to slay. He saw the man across the clearing. Amazement had bulged the big fellow's eyes and dropped his lower jaw. With a cry, Wuh rushed forward to attack him, but the man turned as if a pack of leopards was at his heels. His family swung with him, and like stampeding elephants they plowed through the jungle. They vanished instantly and there was only the sound of them in flight. Nonplussed, Wuh came back and stumbled over the deer and furiously he smote it.

The python had ceased to writhe. Murah was lamenting because the death of anything filled her with sadness. Loo echoed her, but Koko stood back and stared with dull eyes at the python. Wuh was calmer now and curious. He had never had a chance to examine one of these jungle assassins and he walked round it, gingerly touching its cool gleaming body, gazing intently at its iridescent markings, and leaping back if it moved. Once a convulsive twitching enraged him and he smote the carcass until it was quiet.

He led the way to their beds. He was still excited and angry and he cast a hungry glance about him for other creatures to slay; but the jungle was hushed. He marched nobly like the conqueror he was, a proud warrior who had slain his ancient enemy. He did not know that the story would have been different if the serpent's mouth had not been fixed on a deer's skull. For him it had been a fair fight and he was the winner, and he felt that there was no enemy anywhere that could stand up against him now. Growling menacingly, as became one of his might and valor, he broke succulent vegetables and ate. His club lay at his feet.

17

WITH greater care than any woman before her had ever taken, Murah prepared a place for the birth of her child. Though there had been no rain since she had come to this highland jungle, she expected rain, and daily she searched the sky for signs of its coming. To prepare a nest was instinctive with her, but instinct was now guided by memory of the shelters which she and Wuh had built. For many days she was a soberly busy woman.

She chose a large evergreen tree whose lower branches spread far out and drooped; and using the limbs as rafters she hung her materials upon them. These materials were vines and ferns which she broke off or uprooted. She spread them across from limb to limb, forming a ceiling and shaping under the ceiling a dark interior that was cool by day and warm by night. Pausing in her labors, she would enter the shelter to discover how it felt to be inside it, and she would talk happily to herself or to Loo.

The making of a shelter was something Loo had never seen. Murah's resourcefulness delighted her and she strove to assist. She went abroad and gathered all sorts of materials and carried or dragged them to the tree; but most of them were useless, and Murah scolded her and threw them away. Loo brought, for instance, pieces of old dead thornbush, stones, chunks of decaying wood, and velvety moss. The moss Murah was glad to have and with it she floored her house. The other materials she always gravely examined before she cast them away. When she threw an object from her, Loo always stared after it, disappointed and unable to understand why one thing was not as useful as another. Sometimes she recovered the objects and tried to make use of them. She would lay a piece of rotted wood on the roof and stand back to look at it, and she would talk excitedly to Murah, asking her why it was not all right. But Murah would seize it and hurl it back into the forest.

When Loo was thus rebuked, she redoubled her efforts to please and to be of help. She would hurry away to see what else she could find. Now and then she would come with an armful of flowers, and these Murah would take from her and scatter over the floor. But Loo seemed unable to distinguish between the useful and the useless, or perhaps, because vanity impelled her to strive to be the leader, she was interested less in bringing the right things than in bringing everything that Murah seemed to miss.

If Murah brought vines, Loo scorned vines and looked for something different. As likely as not she fetched stones. If Murah gathered flowers, Loo scampered in search of pine needles. She was assisting, but she was engaged in rivalry too. If she had dared, she would have taken possession of the shelter long before it was finished and would have driven Murah out. At first it had been for her a strange, a mysterious, and a very delightful thing. After a while it came to be a wonder that she herself had built. She was no longer content merely to assist. She became arrogantly bossy and scolded Murah and wanted to rearrange the ceiling or the floor. It was not because she believed she could improve them. She was not conscious at all of imperfections or of her own talent for building. Her vain and assertive soul wished to believe that the shelter had been her idea, that she had shaped it, and that it belonged to her.

Koko, who feared and hated both of them, took no part in the work. Her mind was unable to understand what the shelter was or what purpose it was designed to serve. She was so unimaginative that she had the mien of one who lived in a prison of spite. After eating in the morning, she sat all day like the sluggard she was and scowled at the other women or picked parasites out of her hair.

Wuh, on the other hand, was very curious about Murah's house. He often approached to look at it and to express his pleasure. When, urged to assert himself, he ventured to enter the shelter or to make changes in its drooping walls or its soft floor, Murah slapped him and drove him off. If he resisted, Loo joined the attack on him and the two women stung him like big hornets. This was no business of his. His job was to keep enemies away, to march out and slay the snakes and leopards.

After two weeks had passed, the three of them were so set on matching talents and competing with one another that a feud developed. Wuh withdrew so far from the women that the distance was a mark of his resentment; and he resolved to build a house of his own. He did not need a house. He was not going to have a child and he had no use at all for the kind of shelter Murah was making. But he wanted one, nevertheless, and he wanted one because his masculine vanity had been outraged. It was not in his nature, or in the nature of the more intelligent members of his kind, to look with friendliness on rivalry or to admit that they were not inimitable and unique.

He chose a tree and built a shelter much like Murah's. It was a poor copy of hers but he thought it was better and he wanted her to come over and see it. He went to her and pointed at his house and talked to her about it, and in his voice was the pride of a very vain man. Murah looked at it but she was not interested. Wuh grasped her arm and strove to lead her to it. She shook his hand off and scolded him. He marched part way to his house and stopped and made movements with his feet to indicate that she was to walk and follow him. He beckoned to her. When she did not come, he stared at her, perplexed, or he turned to look at his house as if to see if it was in plain view. He hastened over to it and industriously added more vines and moss; he walked solemnly round it, not to note its imperfections or ways by which he could improve it, but to admire it; he entered it and sat and peered out with comical gravity; and again he tried to fetch Murah or Loo over to envy his workmanship.

When they refused, he turned to the phlegmatic Koko. She went obediently, with her son riding her back, and entered the house and took possession of it. She liked the cool and fragrant interior. Her son climbed down and began to turn somersaults on the floor. Wuh stood at the entrance and looked in. When he understood that she had entered not to admire but to possess, he was angry with her, and he went howling in to cuff her and drive her out. He roared at her as if she had tried to defraud him. Koko sullenly went away, and her son ran after her and leapt to her back, his thick bowed legs clasping her waist, his hands clinging to the hair of her shoulders, and his brown eyes looking back at Wuh.

Wuh sat in his house, flushed by the warmth of pride and ownership. He peered gravely at the ceiling overhead and at the walls; and then, obeying a sudden impulse, he hastened out and gathered more materials, striving with prodigal abundance to shame Murah's efforts. He added so much green stuff that at last his shelter resembled a huge and ungainly nest. He had to go down on all fours to crawl into it. When inside, he thrust his head through a wall of vines and looked across at Murah and Loo, who paid no attention to him.

Because the house failed to make the others envious he soon forgot it, and Koko took it over. He did not have, like the women, an instinct for nest-building. As a matter of fact, he did not understand why Murah had built a shelter. When, while feeding or playing, he became conscious of hers, he would remember his own and run over to look at it; but Koko would thrust her head out and bark at him, and like an unhappy man, meanly regarded by his women, he would withdraw.

The feud between Murah and Loo had come to a showdown. Each felt not only that the house was hers but that she alone had built it; and in defense of children or of property relating to their children women were always ready to fight.

When dusk came one evening, Murah entered the shelter to spend the night. Angry and nonplussed, Loo looked in and began to scold her. She set up such an outcry that Koko thrust her head out, and Wuh went over to learn what the trouble was. Standing in the entrance, Loo was screaming at Murah and menacing her; and if she had had words to express her sense of outrage, she would have been abusing and insulting her. Indignity is what she felt. She had built the house and it belonged to her, but there within it sat an impostor who refused to budge.

Wuh came up and thrust his lips out and looked like a clown. This quarrel between two women he did not understand at all. Loo's cries excited him and made him a little angry but he could see nothing to attack. He walked about, grasping his club and staring curiously at Loo's face; and presently he went to the entrance and peered in at Murah. She was sitting calmly with arms lying across her big belly. Wuh stepped back and again fixed his perplexed gaze on the twitching and angry face of Loo.

Loo was in a baffled tantrum. She plucked angrily at her hair and continued to bark and scream but she could think of nothing to do. She might have torn the house down on Murah's head. If Murah had not been so unapproachably calm, Loo might have rushed in to throw her out. As it was, she exhausted herself with rage and confusion, and her voice fell to a plaintive whine. She went around the house, looking at it, crying with low grief, and wondering how she could possess it.

Wuh turned away to seek his bed. Koko's head was withdrawn. Behaving like one heartbroken, Loo went to a clump of vines and made a hammock for the night; but even after she entered her bed she continued to fret and grieve.

The next day she acted like one who had been shamefully treated. She lost her appetite and her zest and moved about as if sick and friendless, or sat alone like one desolate. When she looked at Murah's house her eyes were sad. People, even in this faraway time, loved their property next to themselves. Loo had lost a part of her meaning. No matter how obscurely, she felt as if she had been robbed, as if her sense of personal identity had been maimed and vulgarized. As Wuh loved his club, she loved this house; and if his weapon had been taken from him he could not have been more disconsolate than Loo was now.

Murah, on the other hand, was happy and busy. If a shadow now and then fell across her joy, it was not of Loo but a fear that someone would steal her house. For Loo's grief she was not at all concerned. Her energy was fixed on preparations for birth; and now that she had a nest for it she kept close to the nest. If, when away feeding, she saw anyone approach her house she dashed screaming toward him.

One morning after breakfast was done the stupid Koko confused the two shelters and entered Murah's. Even after she had entered it and let her heavy lazy body sink to the floor she did not realize that she was in the wrong house. Her son knew it and began to explore. He stood on her shoulders and grasped her scalp lock to balance himself. Then he espied a tempting vine in the ceiling and leapt from his perch and clutched it, but the vine did not support him and he came down with a yelp of dismay.

His cry caught Murah's attention. She looked round her and saw Wuh staring raptly at his club and Loo sitting alone by a tree. When she saw no sign of Koko she was suspicious. She was moving toward her house when she observed violent agitation in its walls. Koko's son inside was angry and was trying to avenge himself on the vines. Hastening to the entrance, Murah looked in. Sight of the invaders so astonished her that she was speechless and confused. "Hooo?" she said at last, addressing the gentle question more to herself than to them. She looked over at the other house to be sure that this one was her own; and when she perceived that it was she exploded with rage. She did not stand in the entrance and scold the intruders. She rushed in like a thunderbolt. Her first blow stung Koko; her second missed Koko and hit the lad and knocked him end over end. With a yell of terror, the child plowed into the tangled wall, and his frantic efforts to escape almost destroyed the house. A part of the ceiling fell upon the women.

If she had not heard her son crying, Koko would have fled from the shelter. The cry awoke her somber and sleeping wrath. Her son was entangled in vines now and howling like mad; and because she thought he was being killed, Koko swung in fury on Murah. In this moment the two women were standing with a part of the ceiling upon them. Soon Koko was almost as helpless as her son and fought as if snakes were coiling about her. Her yells were echoed by the terrified cries of her child.

Hearing the racket, Wuh came over, grasping his club with both hands and ready to strike. He had never before seen anything like this. In the ruins of the house three persons were struggling, but none of them was visible to him. The remainder of the ceiling had fallen and he could see only convulsive movements and hear only smothered fury in the depth.

Then Murah's head emerged and she came out clawing like a frightened cat. Koko followed her. The child had so many vines around his neck that he was captured and half-choked but he continued to struggle and to howl with terror. They were all excited by his cries. Loo came over; and Wuh, both afraid and angry, stared at the ruins of the house and wondered what dreadful enemy had the child in its grasp. He was determined but he was cautious. He thought there must be a huge serpent under there with the child and he wanted to see it and learn where its head was before he attacked.

Koko was bolder. She, too, like the others, thought her son was in the clutch of an enemy, but she leapt upon the ruins and began to dig down to him. Murah and Loo encouraged her with shrill cries, and Wuh marched about, barking and peering and waiting for the enemy to come in sight. Koko burrowed in the vines and crawled under them and found her son. She seized him and came plunging out, dragging him after her. The vines around his throat had completely choked off his breath. His eyes bulged from their caves and his face turned purple. Koko seemed to believe the vines were snakes, but Murah knew they were only vines and she tried to tear them away from the child's throat. Then Koko thought she was attacking the boy and she sprang upon her and the two women fought. They bit one another and clutched hair and screamed. Presently Murah laid hands on a stick and smote Koko with it and drove her away. Koko fled to her own shelter and crawled into it, trembling with rage and fear.

When Murah remembered the child and turned again to it, Koko's son was dead.

18

MURAH sat and took the dead youngster to her lap and tore the vines from his throat. She began to lament over him. Holding him up, she searched him for signs of death or life. His limp body and staring eyes and open mouth were for her evidence of death and evoked her mournful cries; but she also thought she saw signs of life in him. After gazing at him earnestly for a long moment she attempted to revive him. As if he were a baby just out of her womb, she slapped his back and blew breath into his mouth, or gently with a finger she peeled the lids back from his bulging eyes.

Anxiously Loo watched her. She echoed Murah's lamentations and sat by her and slapped the body or leaned forward and blew breath when Murah did so. Again and again she looked at Murah's face, her eyes asking a question. Wuh divided his attention between them and the ruins. He still believed a big serpent was concealed there and he moved cautiously around the fallen house, searching for it. When, after several minutes, he saw no sign of one, he forgot what he was looking for, and a little later he forgot the dead child and went off to feed.

Failing to restore the youngster to life, Murah laid it down and went away from it, and Loo followed her. Evening came before Koko stirred. She found her son and carried him to her shelter. She sat and cradled him and thrust a brown teat into his open mouth; and not until she became aware that the lips were not drawing from her breast did she feel alarm. And her alarm, even then, was not acute. She held the child up and looked at him and offered the other breast. She thrust the nipple into the open mouth and sat there, a dull-witted mother who did not realize until later that her son was dead.

Her realization then was not sharp and certain. It was in her a leaden despair that related itself to no cause. She had laid her child aside and she forgot about him except when her eyes happened to turn his way. Then her sense of loss became a little sharper, and a heavy relaxing sadness filled her like troubled sleep. She realized less that her child was dead than that he was no longer active and playful. After darkness came she felt that he was asleep.

The notion that he slept returned to her when morning came. She did not seem to find it strange that the child did not leap up and fasten clutching hands on her dugs. She did not call to him. Koko never talked or even made vocal sounds except when deeply stirred by anger or fear. Between her dull mind and the alert and inquiring minds of the other three there were centuries of darkness. She left her shelter to eat and during the time of her breakfast she gave no thought to her son. She did not remember him until she entered her house after she had filled her stomach and saw him lying by the vine wall.

If she formulated any notion about him then, it was only the thought that he still slept. All day she sat in her house without stirring, her sad and stupid eyes looking out. Now and then something attracted her momentary interest. It was the flight of a bird or the appearance in the entrance of a colorful insect or the cries of Murah and Loo; but if her eyes brightened a little they soon faded to somber brown. Later in the day she went to a brook and drank but she did not, like the others, drink from cupped palms. She thrust a hand into the water and then licked the drops off her hand. In this way her ancestors had drunk a long time before.

Evening came and she went out to eat but she did not, like the others, use a stick to dislodge the choice fruit growing high up or to pull clusters within reach. She ate what she easily came upon, taking the bitter with the sweet, and chewing tough roots or stalks that the others would have spurned. She never flushed her mouth with cold water or removed morsels of food that lodged between her teeth. She did not strive to keep her body free of parasites. Shc even befouled her own house.

The odor of her own filth and of her dead child was soon a stench in the shelter but Koko did not seem to mind. The others were disgusted by the smell and came over to scold her. Murah looked in and puckered her face comically and in angry tones rather than words told Koko that she was a lazy and unclean woman. Koko growled at her. When Murah moved as if to enter, Koko bared her teeth. She was stupid but she was a mother, and she would have defended her child with her life.

That became clear to the others a day or two later. Disgusted by the odors here, Wuh resolved to move.

Naturally, of course, he wanted all the women to go with him. He could count to about ten, and if he had had ten females, he would have known by counting them when they were all present. If he had had twenty females he would have been baffled by any attempt to count them, and he would not have missed one if she had run away. Counting the three he had was easy, and when he was ready to march he perceived that only two were with him. He began to search for the third.

He found Koko squatting in her house and indicated that she was to come with him. He sniffed the awful odors and looked at the decomposing body of the child. Because he was sickened and disgusted he began to shout at her and to menace her with his club. Murah heard his clamor and came over, trailed by Loo. They talked to Koko. They told her to come but she would not budge. She glared at them and snarled like a trapped beast.

When nonplussed, Wuh always danced up and down in frenzied indecision. He wanted Koko to come, not because he felt any affection for her but because she was his property. After hopping around and yelling like a man gone daft, he went off a few paces and beckoned to her. He indicated by the act of walking that she was to follow him. He motioned with his feet and with his hands and pointed in the direction which he intended to take. Murah and Loo also strove to persuade Koko to leave the house.

Then Wuh marched in and grasped her arm and she bit his hand and he came howling out. There was blood on his hand. He stared at the blood and licked it off and presently he was so busy doctoring his wound that he forgot Koko. He told Murah and Loo to come with him and he marched away.

Koko did not watch them go. She did not realize that she had been abandoned. Even if she had known, she was too sunk in stuporous grief to have cared. Her brain was so small and her perceptions were so dull that she had no clear sense of her position. As a dog will remain by its dead master and starve, so Koko was betrayed by the one instinct in her that was strongest and by her blind devotion to it. Perhaps what she felt was a mood related to this spot of environment, and in this mood was the presence of her child. Nothing that she looked at reminded her of him, but all the things around her were obscurely a part of him; and because she no longer felt his hands on her or saw him playing or heard his voice, she was baffled.

When evening came she left the shelter to feed, and she moved about, as she always had, like one lost in reverie. It was not reverie with her, of course; it was a very shallow consciousness. Wuh and the other women perceived objects as things apart from themselves; but for Koko, grazing like any herbivorous sluggard, the food she ate, the trees she looked at, and the earth she walked on were in a way a part of herself. She was guided solely by pleasure and pain.

When she returned to the shelter the smell of it was too much even for her. She looked in but she did not enter. She went around it and sat by the wall just inside of which her child lay. Here she slept, and here, when not feeding, she sat, keeping a vigil that she did not know she kept.

19

Wuh went about a half mile away, and Murah halted him in a spot where food was abundant, as well as the materials for another house. She built a shelter much like the one which had been torn down and in it she gave birth to a son; and she and Loo devoted themselves to the child. Mothers regarded all children in a group as their own. At first, to be sure, Loo knew that this infant had not come from her own body, and for a few days she was able to understand that it belonged to Murah. She only gazed at it with a mother's tenderness or now and then gently touched it; but after a while she thought it was her child, or at least that the two of them shared it—as, indeed, they did. Most mothers did not allow others to fondle their babies, but Murah was an uncommon woman; she trusted Loo and did not feel alarm when she saw the infant in Loo's arms. Because her own child was soon to come, Loo's breasts were ripe with milk and she also nursed the babe.

Nearly every time Wuh came over to look at the

women he found them both staring at the child and talking to it. If he had had a sense of humor he would have been richly amused. The two women were comically solemn. One of them would hold the babe up and gaze at it for a long moment and then look at the other woman as if to learn what she thought of it. They talked about it, and the tones of one another they understood. Now and then they understood the words. "Look!" Murah said repeatedly as if the infant offered rich reward to prolonged scrutiny. Loo would echo her, or almost in one voice they would say look, and then both of them would stare long and earnestly. Or Murah would turn the child over and over on her lap and repeatedly ask Loo to look, as if every hair and wrinkle deserved searching attention.

They were so delighted by the infant and so deeply stirred by the miracle of its presence that they engaged in a kind of rivalry in calling to one another's notice every trivial detail of its anatomy and color. There was no part of its body that they did not touch and exclaim over. It was the baby's genitals, however, that excited their deepest wonder and awe. Of the procreative use of the male organ they had no notion, and it is impossible to say why it so fascinated them. Perhaps it was because they were without this part, but most likely it was because the male organ seemed to have a life of its own. Early in childhood, and with feelings akin to dismay, they discovered that the bodies of all of them were not in all respects alike; and even as grown women they still inspected themselves or curiously searched one another. After each confirmation of the difference, their eyes met, solemn, perplexed, and questioning.

Probably they felt, darkly and obscurely, a sense of

loss, of incompleteness, but this vague recognition did not trouble them as it was to trouble women in a later time. The source of their wonder and the nature of their emotion was more indefinable than that. There was neither jealousy nor envy in them, nor anything like a conscious wish to be different from what they were. They were perplexed. They were baffled by any part of the body that seemed to have, apart from the body's own life, a life of its own.

When Wuh now appeared, Murah beckoned to him to come close, and after he had done so she began to inspect him. For a few moments he stood like a clown and let her have her will; but when her exploring hands began to excite him he growled at her, knowing well she would not accept his embrace because she was nursing a child. Nevertheless, he did no more for a little while than to rumble in his throat and look down at her as if suspicious of her intent; but when the lust in him became a consuming hunger he roared as if tortured and moved to grasp Loo. At once both women turned on him and scolded him and drove him away.

He went to his bed and stood there, looking back at them, a furious and stricken man. When sexual hunger was deeply stirred and then denied, the male felt inwardly convulsed and a little sick and very vengeful; and if Wuh had been able to espy an enemy anywhere he would have attacked. Erotic passion and a lust to kill were related hungers, and either, when driven in upon itself, could find release in the other. Wuh wanted to attack the women but he only stared at them until, unexpectedly, he gave a thunderous challenge. The sound of defiance ringing in his ears seemed to release him from indecision.

Grasping his club, he set off into the jungle, going with no notion of what he intended to do, but driven by emotions that had overwhelmed him and were ready to spill.

After he had threshed about him for a while, and shouted defiance at any ears within range, he felt calmer and paused to think. It was the way of women to build nests and mother their babies; it was the way of men to explore and hunt. Wuh did not, of course, understand that. In this moment he understood nothing except that he stood in a forest and heard far away a trumpet call that gurgled and ended in a shrill squeal. It was the cry of an elephant. Wuh answered it; and when no answer came he proceeded into the jungle and came to a patch of succulent celery. He broke some stalks off and pulled them between his teeth, stripping them of their green bark and leaves until the clear white inner part looked like a peeled willow. This he threw away. He ate for a little while but he was not hungry and presently he resumed his wanderings. Lovely birds hopped from limb to limb above him and scolded him as the women had done; and Wuh barked at them and menaced them with his club. If he could have done so he would have slain them all. He was resolved to kill anything that crossed his path, and this emotion flushed and directed him until he entered a small clearing strewn with stones.

It was only minute creatures that he saw now, but they caught his interest and he went down on all fours to look at them. They were an army of leaf-cutting ants on the march. Each of them carried a leaf several times his own weight, holding it between his mandibles and supporting it across his back. The hundreds of green leaves looked as if a tiny forest were marching across the clearing.

Wuh picked up one of the leaves and the ant clinging to it and stared at the creature. At first he thought the leaf was alive and moving on legs of its own. He set the ant down and at once it began to march, going rapidly to overtake the columns. He lifted it again and set it on a branch several feet above the earth, and without hesitation the ant, still bearing its burden, marched along the limb and down the trunk.

Fascinated by the creature's persistence and nimbleness and strength, Wuh went to the head of the columns and lay on the ground to watch them approach. Across a breadth of thirty feet, and about fifteen feet in depth, the army marched against him. The ants all seemed to move at the same speed, though some of them had leaves twice as large as those borne by others. When the vanguard came to Wuh it did not hesitate. Up and over him the legions poured, walking along the stiff hairs of his body as nimbly as he might have trod a fallen tree. He was soon covered by this little forest of upright leaves. The ants marched across his closed lips, climbed over his nose, detoured around his blinking eyes, traversed the caverns of his ears, tickled the bare skin of his cheeks and forehead, and descended in a steady and unfaltering tide.

When he was in the center of the columns Wuh stood up, expecting the clinging legions to fall from him in a shower; but not an ant lost its footing. They were startled by this sudden upheaval as if an old tree trunk had risen in their path, and for a moment they seemed to consider. Then, as if a command had been given, they started downward, marching without confusion or alarm, and Wuh's green covering was peeled off him from his crown to his feet. He did not see a single ant drop its leaf, and he wondered if the leaf and the ant were not living parts of one another.

As the columns moved away he again experimented. Picking up several of those in the rear, he set them on branches and watched them march down. Then, impatiently, he plucked a marcher, and while holding the creature with one hand, with the other he pinched the leaf and drew it away from the mandibles. He perceived now that the leaf was only a leaf. Still, that is not quite what he thought. He was dimly formulating the idea that the leaf was for the ant what his club was for him. That was such a tremendous and dramatic notion that for a long moment Wuh stared at the ant. Then he set it down, and at once it scurried about as if frantic. Suspecting that it was searching for its club, he laid the leaf in the ant's path; and when the ant came upon the leaf it showed unmistakable delight. For a moment it seemed to wave arms at the leaf and then it seized the leaf in its mandibles, turned it across its back, and set off on the march again. Wuh crawled after this ant until it overtook the columns.

He was deeply excited. He felt that these creatures were moving upon an enemy and holding their clubs ready to attack. In their behavior he sensed more than that. He went over to the columns to observe them again, and while looking at them he was troubled. What he obscurely felt, but was unable to formulate in a thought, was this: he went forth alone to fight and possess, but these creatures went in a group and stayed close together. This lesson, one of the greatest that human beings were to learn, he could not grasp at this time. He had to look at the thing he was thinking about if the meaning of it were not to elude his mind and go off into darkness; and now, as if to confirm an earlier experiment, he captured an ant and set it on a tree and watched it go down. This he did with other ants for several minutes, trying all the while to understand why the creatures did not go off separately and fight alone.

Insects for Wuh had always been pests, but now he had a lively interest in them; and a few days later, while prowling, he came upon a band of army ants. They were big ferocious fellows a half inch or more in length. He had been standing by a large dead tree from a limb of which hung a wasps' nest. Watching the wasps enter or leave their house, he had been remembering Murah's house. In a house he could see no meaning. Then, suddenly, he saw a dozen army ants marching up the dead tree. They approached the nest and paused. After a few moments they came together in a group and seemed to be scratching one another. Unexpectedly, then, they went down the tree and across the earth. Wuh followed them and saw them join a large army of their fellows and run around among them. Then the whole army began to stir as if excited; it closed its ranks and marched. It moved straight for the dead tree, but upon reaching the foot of it the army halted and a few of the ants ran about while the main body of them waited. A few of them hurried around the tree or climbed up it a little way and came down again; and these formed in a group and seemed to rub one another. Of what they were doing or what they planned to do, Wuh hadn't the faintest notion. He observed that, unlike the other ants he had seen, they did not carry clubs, but he felt that they were going to attack something. Their excited activity he did not relate to the wasps' nest. Even when the army deployed into several lines and began an organized march up the tree, it did not occur to him that they were going to attack the wasps. He did not observe that when marching up the tree a few of them seemed to guide the others and keep them in line, but he did see a resemblance between their behavior and that of him and his kind when in single file they moved through the jungle.

The attack came as a complete surprise to him. The vanguard of the columns rushed upon the nest and with strong mandibles began to tear the cover away. Out of the house to repel the invaders came the furious wasps. They set upon the ants, attacking them with their stingers; and Wuh saw one ant after another curl up convulsively as if in pain and drop from the tree. This preliminary engagement lasted for several minutes, and all the first ants to reach the nest were stung and fell one by one to the earth.

Wuh was excited. This, he clearly perceived, was a deadly battle between two kinds of creature, and he stared at them impartially, wondering which side would win. He could see no reason why they should destroy one another. He understood that the ants had attacked and that the wasps were defending themselves. He saw that the wasps were greatly outnumbered. And he bent closely, trying to see if they attacked with hands and teeth.

Up the trunk in four columns, each five or six abreast, moved the army of ants; and for every one stung and killed a dozen rushed forward to take his place. When a wasp was seized by a leg or wing and pulled down, ants swarmed upon it and tore it limb from limb. There were hundreds of wasps, but there were thousands of ants. The earth around the tree was covered with ants, dead or dying, and among them were fragments of wasps, dismembered and dropped. Ants had poured over the nest and covered it with the black and deadly mass of them. They had gone into the nest and driven the last of the wasps out. They were devouring the fat grubs inside, they were demolishing the nest, and they were still fighting the wasps that buzzed in fury around them.

Wuh was so fascinated that he stood like one in a trance. He watched the ants fight until every wasp was slain, until there was nothing left of their house, until there were only the hordes of ants, still hungry and lusting for battle. When their work of destruction was done, they fell into columns and marched down the tree. At the foot of the tree were hundreds of them that had been slain.

The lesson Wuh learned from this dramatic battle was one that he was never to grasp because it was nothing that he could rationally think about. It was something that entered his emotions and fired his imagination and made him a bigger and more resourceful man; but he did not draw conclusions from it. He lived not by logic but by instinct and intuition. Intuitively he realized that there had been power in numbers and that these creatures had attacked together as one. He sensed that they had been seeking food.

When he turned home he wanted to attack and destroy something, and he wanted his females to attack with him. He blustered and growled on his way to them, and when they were within sight of him he roared a challenge and brandished his club. He was so frightening that Murah and Loo vanished into their house. Wuh went over and looked in and menaced them. He did not know that he wanted them to come out and march with him against an enemy.

The women wanted him to go away and mind his business. They fought not for the joy of it but only in defense of their children, and Wuh's furious lusting when there was no enemy in sight they did not understand at all. They had no patience with it. They did not know that a man's meaning and his way of life were in the fields of threat and danger, where he could slay and feel triumphant and make the things of earth tremble before him. They were born to peace, but a man was born to war.

While Wuh was swinging his club and shouting and looking vainly for an enemy, Murah came out in a tantrum and scolded him and made him go away. She thought he was a stupid fellow to trumpet a war cry when there was nothing in sight to cry at. She did not understand her man, and Wuh did not understand his woman. While she had been nursing an infant, he had watched an army of ants destroy an army of wasps. That was the difference between them, the difference between birth and murder, between peace and war.

20

THERE WAS this difference, too, that a woman's sexual hunger lay quietly in her during the time of pregnancy and lactation, but a man's was constant and was a part of his seeking, his curiosity, his wanderlust. It was a part of his deep and restless urge to alter his environment. A woman's unconscious desire was to be impregnated; and then, with her hunger stilled, she was content. A man's unconscious desire was to impregnate every adult female he could find, and from this blind drive in him he found no rest except in physical exhaustion. Nature gave to the woman the spiritual bond between mother and child; but of man she made a wanderer, restless and homeless, and impelled eternally to seek with no clear understanding of what he sought.

Because he was a simple and primitive man, blighted by no taboos and fenced by no barrier except threats against his life, Wuh could neither repress nor redirect his hunger, but lived day and night with the passion of it consuming him. As fully as he could resent anything he resented the two women. Loo had a child also, and she and Murah gave all their time and interest to their infants. When Wuh approached them they drove him off. Far from suffering his embrace, they did not even scratch his back or examine him for burrowing parasites or give to him any of the little attentions that enhanced his self-love. They would not go with him when he prowled. They paid no attention to him when, after an absence of an hour or two, he returned. They had settled in this spot as if they did not intend ever to leave it; but remaining fixed, like the trees, was not Wuh's nomadic way.

When he moved off and beckoned to them or made walking movements with his feet, they scolded him with angry impatience. Murah sometimes advanced to threaten him with a stick. And so, again and again, he went off alone, a morose head of a family who felt vilely abused and misunderstood. His mood was often so ferocious that he would run screaming toward birds and wave his club at them, or knock the life out of big insects that crossed his path. If a leopard or an elephant had faced him he would have been tempted to attack.

Dimly in his mind was a lusting for organized battle. His first experience with the ants he forgot, but again he came upon them and repeatedly thereafter he sought their hunting grounds and watched them march in orderly columns and slay their enemies. After a while he came to the notion that his women should march with him. He loved property and privileges, and the power of the strong over the weak. If he had been imaginative enough to conceive of it, he would have loved organized and ruthless conquest. The leaf-cutting ants devastated everything in the line of their march. The army ants killed any creature that was too stupid or bold to move out of their way. He saw them swarm upon a snake and completely devour it.

The notion that he should eat what he killed had not come to Wuh yet—but the seed of that notion was germinating in his mind. During these weeks it was sexual hunger that goaded him, and his desire to slay was only an aspect of it. If, when he set out to find a female, he came upon the army ants, he paused to study them; and their doings educated him by enriching his emotions and stimulating his mind. These experiences entered the storehouse of his unconscious. His conscious mind, after a while of absorbed study, turned him to fresh interests and set him again on the quest.

One day in his wanderings he came to the spot where Koko had been abandoned. He found her bones but he did not know that they were her bones. He never suspected that in defense of her dead child she had given her life; but he did vaguely remember that he had once lived in this spot, and he recognized the brook where he had uprooted the thornbush. He looked at the ruins of two shelters and at the bones of Koko and her son. He felt no nostalgia and no sense of loss. On the contrary, he was looking for signs of fresh beds and wondering if females had recently been here.

His lust for a female led him at last across the boundary of his domain. The feeding grounds of groups were bounded by rivers or large creeks or by other natural barriers such as ledges of stone. It was a swift mountain stream that Wuh came to. He was afraid of water but today he ventured in to the depth of his knees and looked across the stream, thinking that he smelled the presence of females in the wilderness beyond. He stared next at the water sucking at his legs and pouring down the channel in white cascading. He returned to the shore. Then, as if consumed by thirst, he knelt and drank from cupped palms. Water for him was a strange and destroying thing. He wondered where it came from and where it went to and why it poured endlessly down the same path. Some of it slept in stagnant pools and inland lakes but some of it cried all the time with sleepless anger. He dipped his hands into the stream and liked the coolness on his flesh. He sat and thrust his tough calloused feet into the water and wiggled his toes. The coolness of it was so delightful that he moved forward little by little until he sat in water to his waist. He began to play in it like a child, slapping it with flat palms and splashing it over him; and presently he felt itching in his immersed skin and dug at it and dislodged flakes of dirt and sweat. Almost at once he perceived that the parts of his body which he scratched clean were more sensitive to the coolness and had a paler color; and he learned too that after drawing a foot up and digging at it he could kick it back into the water and wash a part of the dirt off. Wuh, in fact, was discovering the joy of his first bath. At first he sought only sensuous delight but after a while he understood that from head to feet he was sheathed with dirt. He also realized that he felt better after the dirt was removed. Those parts which he cleaned, like his knees, felt more refreshed and alive; but he was an indolent fellow and he soon tired of scrubbing himself. He wanted his women to come here and scratch his back and splash cool water over him.

When he turned away from the stream he looked a little leprous. Off both knees and parts of his feet and thighs and arms he had removed the filth down to clean live skin. In contrast with the darker areas around them these spots were a light brown in color and were very sensitive to the air and sun. The borders of them itched painfully, but when Wuh stopped to dig at them and peel off more filth he only enlarged by a little the clean spots and set the itching edges farther back. His fingernails were so packed with dirt that they distressed him too. He was an unhappy man who felt as if festering parasites had burrowed in his hide.

When he rejoined his women they saw at once that there was a difference in his appearance. They came over and touched with questioning fingers the strange pale spots. Murah thought he was diseased. She called his attention to his naked knees as if he were unaware of them. The sun was baking his knees and they were tender and Wuh growled when she touched them. He had splashed water on his dirty back and now it itched intolerably, and he went down on hands and knees, hoping they would scratch him; but his knees were so tender to the rough earth that he at once stood up, a comical and bewildered man. He wanted them to go to the stream with him and splash water over his body and cool his pain.

But they soon lost interest in him and went away, carrying their babies, and Wuh sat on his bed to examine himself. Against disease, including hookworm, tapeworm, and other parasitic invasions, the people of this time were defenseless; but they were resourceful in the treatment of wounds. His knees and other sunburned parts which he could reach with his tongue Wuh licked, or he spit on them and used saliva as a salve. He sought plants and rubbed their juices on his sores and he even crushed wild fruits and used them as a lotion. In this as in many other matters he experimented, hoping to find something that would be effective. Each poultice of juices cooled his flesh, and as soon as it lost its potency he hunted about for other medicines; and before long he was smeared from head to feet. His strong natural odor was mixed with the smell of berries and bamboo, of celery and chervil, and of everything else around him that yielded juice when crushed.

When evening came he had no appetite for supper. He had a little fever and felt very dejected and ill-treated. Often he turned his anxious gaze on Murah and Loo, who were feeding, with the infants on their backs, and chattering gaily as if the whole world had no trouble in it. Wuh could hear them crushing succulent things between their teeth, and the sound of their eating made him imagine that he was twice as sick as he was. Their gaiety deepened his gloom. Never, he observed, did they look his way or seem to realize that sitting here, alone and forgotten, was a desperately sick man. He did not think of himself as one slowly dying, but self-pity did make him feel that he was vilely put upon. When women were ill they accepted the loneliness of it and did not expect others to hover around them with anxious faces; but when a man was sick he became a child again. He was unable to understand how the world could be bright and gay without him, or why his family should eat when he had no taste for food. All of life became, indeed, his distempered and melancholy vision of it, and he resented anything in sight that did not harmonize with his mood. Too, he felt helpless and dependent and wanted gentle hands on him, and eyes that would look at him with grave concern until he was well again. A child was the heart of a woman's world, but the heart of a man's world was his self-love.

And so Wuh stared at his women and resented them with the despair of an egoist imprisoned in a sickroom. He was not very ill. He had a fever and his palms and ears were hot. He was constipated and perhaps had caught a little cold from sitting in the water so long. Possibly he had a mild case of sunstroke. But the gaiety of the women and their smacking relish of the juicy things they ate so enhanced his gloom that he thought he was a very sick man. He believed, in fact, that he was too ill to rise and walk, and his sense of helplessness so enraged him that he mixed fury with fever. He barked at Murah and told her to come to him. She paused in her eating to look his way but she felt no motherly concern for him and she did not obey his summons. Thereupon he ranted and menaced her with his club. He worked himself into such a tantrum that he felt sick enough to vomit, but he did not leave his bed. With angry and baffled eyes he stared round him and hated everything in sight.

If Murah had come to his bed and murmured anxiously and let him know that she was alarmed, he would have felt much better. If she had patted him and exclaimed over his sun-baked areas and made him know that she understood how tragic and neglected he was, the dark burden would have lifted from his soul and he would have made a pretense of suffering his ills with fortitude. He could easily have gone over and given her a sound drubbing. Such behavior, however, could have been no part of his unconscious acting, or of that emotional blight which demanded attention from her. To be a worthy object of compassion he had to sit here and convince himself that he was unable to move.

That is what he continued to do. After finishing their supper the women entered the shelter and Wuh could no longer see them; and now he howled as if he had been attacked. If he had been a civilized man he might have written an ode to despair or solitude or duty. As it was, he could only work up a childish tantrum and bark at the night. While he was yelling for attention he looked at his knees; and in the way of a child whose grief or anger is easily hushed he leaned forward to peer at them and touch them with an inquiring finger. Then, impulsively, he decided that they needed fresh poultices and he left his bed. He went in search of fruit but as soon as he came to it he began to eat. He did not suspect that he was remembering the gluttonous feasting of the women.

After stuffing his paunch with good things he realized with a pang of dismay that he was sick, and he walked like a sick man to his bed, looking slyly about, meanwhile, to see if anybody watched him. If he had seen his women staring at him, he might have collapsed where he was. He quite certainly would have begun to act with all the cunning he had. Because Wuh, like all persons then and since, was an egoist; he was the core of all things perceived by his senses; and more than food, more than anything else in the world, he wanted sympathy and admiration and applause. Because he had no understanding of the woes that beset him, he magnified them, and felt in his burning skin the imminence of doom.

Reaching his bed he sank to it, his stricken eyes looking over at the shelter. The women were inside, happily nursing their babies. If Wuh could have seen them sitting there, devoting themselves to the infants, he would have howled with fury; but he could neither see nor hear them and he had to sit alone in his bed and suffer and pity himself. He again licked his wounds and tried to cool the fire in his flesh. He stared abjectly at the trees and the night or he distorted his face with anguish, thrusting his big lips out in a slobbering snarl and drawing bushy brows far down on their prominent ridges.

When at last he curled up to sleep, he laid palms over his knees.

21

In a few days both his self-pity and his sunburn were absorbed by time, and Wuh again went forth. He came to the stream, but instead of venturing into it he searched up and down its bank for a way to cross. He found a fallen tree bridging it and walked across on the tree; but as soon as he came to the far side he stopped as if his boldness had frightened him. He knew that he was entering the domain of another and he knew it was jealously guarded. It was not a sense of guilt or shame that made him hesitate: of good and evil, right and wrong, or even of another's privileges he had no notions at all. He paused because he was apprehensive and realized that in thrusting himself upon another's feeding grounds he might have to fight for his life. He carried his club and he was much bolder than he used to be, but he was not a rash man. He preferred to run from trouble rather than face it.

More than any other appetite sexual hunger will drive a male to desperate adventure. The intense lusting of it obsesses not only the emotions but the mind as well, and the mind becomes no more than the plotting servant of the body's hunger. If the erotic ardor in Wuh could have been suddenly appeased, he would have fled back to his home. As it was, he sat on the far end of the tree like a huge meditative insect and sniffed the wind that blew upon him while his eyes searched the jungle for signs of life. Fear had stopped him but it had not turned him from his quest. On the contrary, it enhanced his excitement. It made his heart pound until he could hear the dull blows of it. Fear dilated his nostrils and lifted his hair and brought sweat to his brow. When lust mixed with fear, the former fed on the latter as flame feeds on a wind; because fear, by making him more alert, awoke both body and mind to quivering expectancy. If he had seen a female sexually presenting herself, he could hardly have been more obsessed and desperate.

He left the tree and entered the jungle, and soon he came to beds that were only three or four days old. There were eight beds, and Wuh went to each of them and smelled of it. By the odors he could tell which beds had been occupied by females. A large bed on the windward side had been slept in by the lord of the group and to this bed Wuh gave prolonged attention. He did not see evidence that the bed had been made by a stupid fellow who merely sat down in a clump of vines and reached out to draw them to him. In the expanse of the bed he saw no record of the man's size. Wuh perceived nothing as definite as that.

Two other beds had been slept in by males, and the odors of them made him angry. When he came to the beds that women had occupied, his behavior completely changed. He dropped to his hands and sniffed and barked with delight; and in his face, so dark and scowling a moment ago, there was luminous gentleness. He lay in one of the beds and rolled over in it; and then with the same impulsiveness he rushed to the bed of another female and lay upon it, sniffing the odors and uttering cries of joy.

These doings so ripened his lust that he became frenzied. With the club in his grasp he rushed over to the bed where the big man had slept and shouted at it as if the man himself were there. He menaced this bed and the beds where the other males had lain, but he was only releasing a part of his emotion as a valve lets off steam. After a little while he realized that these were only empty beds and he dashed around them to discover which way the tracks led.

He found the tracks and followed them and came to a second group of beds. He knew that these were fresher. This recognition made him behave with more caution. He stopped his shouting. Moving softly, he examined the beds or the signs of feeding in peeled celery stalks marked by teeth. Then he took the trail and went upon it until he came to a third resting place. These beds had been slept in the night before. Wuh sensed that the group was not far away, and while he was cautiously exploring he heard a sound. It came from the rending of plantain. It was a muffled and crushing sound, like that which might be made by the tearing apart of heads of lettuce.

With prudence now so extreme it was comical, Wuh scouted the enemy's position. He sniffed the air, he listened, he peered. Assuming an attitude, he would stand, tense and expectant, as if listening with his whole body. When silence fell he would relax a little, but the instant he heard fresh rending of plantain he would stiffen, as if from shock, and the hair would rise on his back and scalp. His emotions were alarm, anger, and fear, all mixed in that pattern of excited expectancy which a male feels when he faces combat. His club, stripped of its bark and worn smooth, and almost as hard as stone, was clutched in his right hand.

The several minutes he spent here were given to acting. It was not, of course, deliberate acting, and he was not aware of himself as one playing a part. It was that prelude which most combative males, at least among the mammals, indulge in with ferocious earnestness. It was a kind of tuning-up and rehearsal of a war machine. Part of it was genuine and part was unabashed bluff. The bull pawing and snorting at sight of another bull, or the big cat lashing with his tail and howling as if full of sadness and indecision, was the battle-brother of Wuh, and the acting there had the same ancient meaning as his own.

Wuh knew, for instance, that the male whom he wished to attack was no more than a hundred yards away. He knew that he could remain here as long as he pleased in the privacy of theatrical bluffing. And he sensed that he was being a little ridiculous—because it was the way of the male to put on his act in plain sight of his foe. The act, indeed, lost its value if the enemy could not see it. Its purpose was to frighten the opponent and convince him with violent show of prowess that he had met more than his match.

And so, after a while of elaborate fooling, Wuh began to feel something akin to disgust. He had parted shrubs and peered when he knew there was nothing to see. He had struck bristling attitudes and swung his club and growled and bared his teeth—and there was nothing watching him, not even a bird. The realization of that dampened his ardor. He looked silly. He had no sense of irony, but he was able to perceive the outlines of very gross and obvious incongruities. He understood that mock heroics when no enemy was in sight were, to say the least, beneath the dignity of a conqueror.

He was an uncommonly timid man but he had been tutored by a club and by the organized might of ants. If it had not been for these lessons he probably would have fled home. He did not remember that he had slain a man and beaten the head off a python. Nevertheless, these experiences had become a part of his intuitive knowledge, of the way he felt about himself; and when at last he went forth to place himself in view of his foe, he moved as one whose new boldness was restrained by an old caution. He grasped his club ready to strike, but the hair on his scalp stood straight up.

He went so softly that after coming into view of the feeding group he remained undiscovered for a full minute. During this time he looked at them. The lord of the family was a big shaggy man whose dark brown hair was patched with gray. The long hair on his head and arms hung straight and clean as if it had been combed. He was an old man, but the gray in his hair did not tell Wuh that the man was old. Gray hair had no meaning for him.

After looking at him, Wuh turned his gaze on the women. There were three of them and they marked three generations, the youngest of which carried a child. There were two boys present, both husky lads of about seven or eight. Wuh knew they were males and looked again at the women. The one carrying the child would not be receptive to his embrace, and the oldest one, the grandmother, was gray and feeble. The middle-aged one held his attention. He was staring at her when the vigilant grandmother saw him.

Her first response was a grunt of alarm. Rheumy eyes looked at him; her body, stooped with age, straightened a little. In the moment just before she saw him one hand like a brown claw had reached up and seized a bamboo stalk; and now this hand relaxed and came slowly down and hung at her side. Her next warning, a querulous cry, caught the attention of the others, and they all turned. They all looked at Wuh.

The lord of the group was the first to speak or move but he behaved like the old and weary man that he was. His roar of defiance was hollow and full of bluff. He began to smite himself but not with the ardor of a young man. He rushed forward, but in the tentative and indecisive way of one who had spent his life driving off lusty invaders and was petulantly weary of them. After a short rush he stopped and bellowed again.

Sensing the reluctance of his foe, Wuh felt bolder but he did not move. Intending neither to retreat nor attack he simply stood his ground and waited. He held his weapon ready to strike but he did not threaten with it. The old fellow rushed again but covered only a half-dozen short paces, and in the anger of his cries was an ill-tempered whine. He was afraid because he was old and feeble; and Wuh knew he was afraid.

Not all of the other persons had remained silent. The two boys were barking; the grandmother advanced with her mate and turned on Wuh a murderous grin full of yellow worn teeth. She was the angriest one of them all. If Wuh had been shouting and menacing them, she might have withdrawn, but she had never seen a man stand as he stood without moving a hair. In his hands he clutched something that aroused her distrust.

Wuh had not uttered a sound. Roars were intended, after all, to frighten the foe, and the old man was already so scared that he was sweating and urinating every time he paused. He, too, was baffled by an enemy that stood and waited. Intuitively, Wuh was being directed by the lessons he had learned and by the sharper intelligence of his mind. He was so little intimidated that he shifted his gaze from the blustering old fellow to the woman whom he coveted.

The old man had advanced four times, but each advance had diminished in ferocity and length. Now he stood and drummed on his breast and looked with the eyes of one who felt he was doomed. When the grandmother moved ahead of him, he rushed again, but his three or four steps were hardly more than a shuddering recoil. He was thoroughly bluffed. The distance between him and Wuh was now about a hundred feet.

Knowing that the old fellow was bluffed, Wuh became impatient. He wanted the middle-aged female. He boldly beckoned to her and made movements of walking, indicating that he would go away and she was to follow him. The old man began to growl and sulk, but all the others stared at Wuh with curious and almost friendly interest. The grandmother seemed fascinated by this brash stranger who carried a club and asked a woman to go with him. She advanced. Approaching within a few feet of him, she stopped, a lean and bent old hag whose sad eyes gazed intently at him as if to question his motives. Wuh was tempted to ravish her, but he observed that the other women were approaching. The whole group came up except the old man. He was behaving with the childish fury of one who realized that he faced the life of a solitary outcast. To see his family go willingly to a stranger was a worse bitterness than that of exile. He resolved to fight.

With a choking snort of rage he came forward, swinging his arms and baring his teeth. At this moment Wuh was staring at the middle-aged woman. When he heard the old man's challenge he stiffened and lifted his club. He roared and dashed forward, and at once the old man turned heels and fled. Howling with grief and dismay, he dashed into a thicket, but presently he emerged and shouted at Wuh. He drummed on a tree and danced up and down in fury.

Wuh seized an arm of the middle-aged woman, intending to drag her after him, but she went willingly; and when, after going out of sight into the jungle, he turned upon her, overwhelmed by excitement, she did not resist. All except the old man had followed and now watched him, the women with sad resignation and the boys with envious delight. The older lad felt a wild urge to leap upon Wuh and try to slay him, but he was afraid. Then his attention was caught by the club which Wuh had dropped. He seized it and turned it over and over in his hands. He was baffled by it. He was still inspecting it when Wuh saw the lad and like a madman rushed upon him. With a cry of terror the youngster dropped the club and fled. Grasping his weapon, Wuh looked round for sign of an enemy; and when he saw none, he leapt upon his woman, club in hand, and embraced her again.

A few moments later he set off with his new family,

leading it in single file. He led them to the stream and across the fallen tree, often looking back to see if the women were coming; and as soon as he reached his own feeding grounds he began to show off. He shouted at them and waved his club, and then ran proudly ahead of them like the conqueror he was. By the time he came in sight of Murah and Loo he was insufferably vain. He rushed at the two women, roaring and threatening them as if they were enemies, or marched about as if seeking an encampment for an army. A few moments later he seized the twice-ravished woman and dragged her to his bed.

Murah and Loo withdrew to their house and stared at the strangers. They did not like them and they did not want them here. They especially distrusted the old grandmother who limped around, querulous and fretting, and declared by her behavior that she expected to be, in the way of all old women, the guardian mother of the group.

22

SHE became for Murah an intolerable nuisance. For one thing, she did not understand and she did not like Murah's house. Even when young she had not been very intelligent, and now she was senile and set in her ways. Barking as if she did not like the way things were managed here, she went to the house and began to pluck at it, resolved to tear it down. For her it was only a monstrous wasp nest or anthill. Like a wasp Murah came out of it. She told the old woman to go away, but the grandmother did not understand. Her only language was grunts and lamentations and guttural barks. She was outraged when Murah slapped her and tried to drive her off. For two generations she had been the imperious queen of a group and during that time nobody had opposed her will. She had decided where to feed, where to sleep, where to rest or play; and she had chosen the trails and led the line of march. She had never known a young woman who was bossy and arrogant.

Here where she had lived for weeks Murah was queen.

She had learned to talk a little, to build a house, to fight with weapons. Between her and the quavering old gammer who disputed her right there was a century of progress. The vast difference between the two was manifested a little later when Murah seized a stick and smote the old woman. While the outraged grandmother howled, Murah struck her shoulders and her bony and trembling old hands. She drove the cringing and astonished creature away.

Thereafter when Murah saw the old woman approaching, she would rush upon her and flog her. A grandmother in her last senile years cannot reshape her habits and her life. This poor old hag, feeble and half-blind and shaking with palsy, was brought almost to a nervous collapse; but in her dark little mind her purpose was unwavering. She was resolved to destroy Murah's house, because she thought it was the nest of some gigantic insect. She was determined to be the guardian queen of the family here. She had never spent more than one night in a spot, and her instincts, her caution, her way of life for more than thirty years rebelled against doing so. Each morning after breakfast she prepared to lead the group in a day of wandering.

She would choose a direction and march off, chattering as if to herself and turning to look back; but after the second morning nobody paid any attention to her. She would scream at the other women and stamp her feet like a wound-up mechanism held in restraint. If any of those who had lived under her will looked her way, she would beckon to them and point at the jungle, trying to make them understand that it was time to move. When they did not follow she would retrace her steps and scold them and repeat her pantomime. Like migratory birds heading north or south or fish running up or down streams, she was guided solely by instinct and habit; and when frustrated she was, like them, unable to adapt to new and baffling conditions. Each morning without fail she repeated her act and exhausted herself with angry fretting. Then all day long she would sulk and brood and nod to herself like any old woman for whom the world is off the track.

The middle-aged woman of the three was too chronically ill to bother much with anything. She was infested with hookworm and tapeworm that devoured her energy and gave a yellowish cast to her face; and to Wuh's demands she submitted because she had no strength to resist. When he was not embracing her or urging her to scratch his back or hunt the pests in his hair, she sat apart in the solitude of sickness, her mind bleak and her eyes half asleep.

The youngest of the three was envious of Murah's house and wanted one of her own. She did not know that Murah and Loo had built it. She thought they had come upon it and she spent time hunting for one like it; and when she failed to find one she would sit in her bed and stare at the shelter, her eyes unhappy and covetous. But she never approached it. She had seen Murah flog the old woman and she was afraid.

As a matter of fact, she was awed and frightened by these new people among whom she had come. They did things that she had never seen done before. They did not move from the spot where they lived but went farther afield each day in search of food and sometimes carried a part of the food back to their beds and ate it there. They put sticks to fascinating uses. They not only hurled clubs at the trees, as Wuh often did, for the pure fun of it; they also used sticks and stones to knock fruit down or to draw tall plants within reach. Wuh, in fact, had learned to splice poles, thrusting one end of a bamboo length into the cavity of another, and reaching with his implement high into the ceiling. His club he used to smite all sorts of things, including insects. He would take a bug from his hair and set it on the earth and crush it with a blow that would have knocked a stag down.

It was the boys who were most apt in copying the new modes of life. The use of weapons first frightened and then fascinated them, and after a few days in their new home they strove to imitate everything that Wuh did. They were so zealous that for want of an enemy they attacked one another; and the youngest boy, a lad of four, was right at their heels. The two older boys imitated Wuh, and the youngest of the three emulated his brothers. Their play sometimes became so violent that adults had to interfere.

One morning after he had filled his stomach until it stood out on him, round and taut, the oldest boy found a piece of dead thornbush. He had wanted a club like Wuh's, and discovery of one so elated him that he turned upon his next younger brother. He shouted a challenge to draw the lad's attention, and then, in the manner instinctive with him, he rushed forward, beating his breast with his free hand. At the end of a short rush he paused. He had begun in play, but simulation of a fight aroused his anger and he came on in dead earnest. He fancied himself as a terrible warrior and he was out to kill.

His brother perceived that this was no playful matter.

With a howl of dismay he ran to his mother, the middle-aged woman, and threw himself upon her back to cower behind her. The oldest boy was still coming but he was in no hurry. A male girded for battle always made several intimidating rushes before attacking. These were necessary to work up his wrath. Besides, the older boy, in spite of anger no longer feigned, was hugely enjoying himself. Metaphorically, he had put on long trousers and was showing them off.

Wuh heard the challenge and came up, thinking a stranger had invaded his home; and when he saw the boy threatening his brother, he was possessed by two emotions. One was the urge of the guardian to slap the youngster down and make him behave. The other was the male's response to defiance. The second in Wuh was stronger, and he might have rushed on the boy to flog him if Murah had not come on the scene.

The mother of the boy had been scolding the one with the club, and the grandmother had approached on feeble legs, fretting and chiding. Murah was the queen of the group. In the way of women of her time, she had adopted all the strange children as her own and had kept a watchful eye on their doings. As soon as she heard the youngster's challenge she left her house.

Now she rushed forward, carrying a stick and screaming at him. She did not dramatize the matter, as men did, by dividing the distance into several advances, each more menacing than the one before. She went straight at the young fellow and rapped him across his skull. His anger could not have been more suddenly cooled if she had thrown him into a river. The swaggering fell away from him and left him crestfallen and confused. When Murah struck a second blow, the thornbush fell from his grasp. He retreated, his outraged manhood howling dismally, and Murah ran after him and drove the abashed lad into a thicket where he could think things over.

Her action so bewildered Wuh that he went to his bed. The boy who had been chastised was, it now seemed to him, Murah's child and not a stranger who had come here. In comparison with a mother's attitude toward children, a man's feelings were weak. Women, or an area of land, he regarded as his property, but he did not think of children as belonging to him. He would fight in their defense, especially when they were young, but it was the mothers who bossed and supervised and claimed them.

To the four strange children, Murah and Loo gave the same affectionate interest that they gave to their own. The baby among them clung to its mother, but if she had died or deserted it, either Loo or Murah would have taken it to her breast. Murah particularly would have done so. Maternal hunger varied in its strength. In her it was abnormally developed and would make of her in time a benevolently autocratic grandmother who would try to dominate every member of the group.

But with Wuh, as with all men, children were another matter. A man did not deliver them from his body and nurse them and devote most of his life to them. He did not know that they were part of his own flesh. A woman's ways were blind, but not so blind as his. She knew that the children came from her, and that recognition established between mother and child a bond that the man could never feel. He was an outsider. His presence was tolerated because he could be of service in attacking enemies and driving them away, but his position was not one of dignity and envy.

Neither these reflections nor anything remotely like them was in Wuh's mind, but there was in him the pale emotional color of them, the confusion, the resentment, and a vague sense of being shut out. Nature had endowed him to mate and to fight but circumstances did not fulfill his healthy ego in either of these. Three of his women suckled babies, the fourth was old and unapproachable, and the fifth was sick. On the battlefield his lot was no better. At home there was nothing to attack, and when he wandered afield the wild beasts fled before him.

The hunger in a woman for children was no stronger than the hunger in a man to mate or fight. Wuh was, and during most of his adult life had been, a frustrated male. As a consequence of that, he was a little neurotic. When the deepest egoistic seekings of a creature are denied, the ego's anchors are shaken, its hungers are perverted or distorted, and it becomes a monster among its kind. Wuh was no monster, but neither was he a complete man. Denied the meaning of self that flushed him when he embraced a female or knocked the life out of an enemy, he could only sit, as he sat now, the prey of despairing and unreasoning whims. A lion caged or a wolf trapped must feel the same emotional blight.

He did not know that frustration is the mother of both lunacy and progress. If he could have spent himself on the two lusts of sex and murder, to the end of his virile years he would have been no bigger in mind and soul than he now was. If he had not been frustrated in Ho-wha's group, he would never have discovered the use of a club. If he had not been almost drowned by rain and eaten alive by mosquitoes, he would not have built a shelter. And if he had not had, in this golden summer day, five women who repulsed him, he would have gone on in fat and slothful ease.

He needed a fresh experience to shake him out of himself and lead him to new discoveries. That experience came one morning when the old man presented himself.

23

For several days he had been spying on Wuh's group. When at last he summoned the boldness to show himself, he did not come with angry bluster but stood off at a respectful distance, his gray mane shining in the sun and his eyes asking questions. It was not to seek battle and recover his family that he had come into view. He was old and lonely and wanted companionship.

The instant Wuh saw him he shouted a challenge and advanced, threatening with his club, but a moment later his attention was caught by the two older boys. They echoed his cry and seized weapons and hastened over to place themselves at his side. When he roared again, they shouted too, and when he menaced the old man with his club, they brandished their sticks. When Wuh rushed forward, they rushed with him, and then the three of them made a terrible outcry.

It would be impossible to put Wuh's feelings into words. It would hardly be true to say he understood that three of them were attacking one, or that he was assisted on either flank. He was not remembering the ants and he was not thinking that three of them were stronger than one alone would have been. His recognition was a sense of rather confused triumph, of a greater and more invincible strength in himself. He knew, of course, that the boys were at his side and menacing the invader with sticks; but he perceived, not three separate men going forth to fight, but a mightier Wuh for whom the lads were somehow only additional weapons. Like his own club, they were extensions of himself.

The old man fled. Without answering the challenge at all he vanished, but Wuh continued to march; and with no foe in sight he redoubled the volume of his yells. He went into the jungle, roaring and threshing about him, and the boys did likewise. Organizing and directing Wuh's behavior was unconscious memory of the ants which had moved in columns and destroyed everything in their path. That is what he was trying to do. Soon after the old man disappeared, Wuh forgot him but he was angry and eager. Through the forest he went, with the boys trailing him and copying everything that he did. When he bellowed, they echoed him. If he smote at things in his path, they also struck about them; and when he paused to scent the wind, they came abreast of him and sniffed. Such a formidable destroyer as the three of them this jungle had never seen before.

For an hour or more Wuh stalked but found no enemy worthy of his might. He came upon a big lizard and with one blow flattened the creature's head, and then the boys pounced upon it and beat it into ribbons. He threatened soaring vultures, chattering jays, and a marabou stork that rose gawkily from a pile of carrion. When in soft earth he came upon an elephant's tracks, each a foot deep and a yard wide, he looked round him expectantly. He had the notion that he was invincible, and though it was an idea born of vanity and egoism, it was precious, nevertheless, because only by seeking new and larger adventures could he develop his resourcefulness and his mind.

After he returned to the spot where the women were content to dwell and nurse their babies, he began to show off. The two boys he still regarded as a kind of extension of his own prowess, but he also perceived in them two admiring spectators. They stood gravely by, watching his antics; and if he did only what they had seen him do many times before, they lost interest or scolded him, and their chiding drove him to an effort to excel himself. Nothing that he did aroused their delight until he seized a stone and hurled it at a tree. This feat astonished them. They were so confused by his act that they ran up to him to inspect his hands; for it seemed to them that he had thrown one of his hands away. As a matter of fact, Wuh had almost forgotten his power to hurl things—and he was now as excited as the boys were. He rushed around and seized other stones and threw them, aiming at nothing at all. He behaved like one who, shamed by having forgotten a lesson, was resolved to teach himself again in the shortest time.

The boys were too astonished to imitate him at once. If they had seen him soar like a bird or float like a duck, they would not have looked at him with more awe. Closely observing him, they saw that he grasped things with his hands and flung them away, and presently they did likewise. They shouted with such glee that all the women except the grandmother came over to see what they were doing. When the older lad saw them approach, he hurled a rock at them. He was awkward and his aim was bad, but he persisted, and soon his brother joined in the fun. Then a stone, flung hard and true, struck the middle-aged woman on her breast and almost knocked her down.

That angered Murah. Seizing a stick, she rushed at the boys, and in defense of themselves they hurled rocks at her. They drove her screaming back to her house. They drove the other women into hiding; and by this time they were so beside themselves with elation that they did not realize what they were doing. Espying the grandmother, sitting in melancholy isolation by a tree, they moved to attack. Advancing together, but cautiously now as if stalking an enemy, they threw their rocks and turned and ran back. Wuh stood apart and watched, as if speculating on their doings. He was trying to grasp another idea. He had seen the women run and he knew they ran because objects were hurled at them. Among his confused thoughts was memory of the times when he had knocked fruit from trees. Knocking fruit down and making living creatures run were two different things, and between the two he was able to sense only the vaguest relationship. Just the same, another great discovery was a dim light in his mind. If the women ran, then enemies would run if things were thrown at them. This is the notion which he was trying to formulate.

Meanwhile, the boys, carried to rash extremes by enthusiasm, were pelting their grandmother to death. She was not a woman for them. She was not the queen guardian who had mothered them for years. She was only a target which they were making the most of. At first her cries were low and protesting, but after a stone laid open a gash on her brow she began to scream; and again Murah and Loo came out of their house. They came with stout clubs and struck the lads and drove them off. The boys ran into hiding and peered out as if to learn what Wuh thought of it.

Wuh's intuitions were trying to clarify matters that were too elusive for him. Like one who felt the presence of a new world, and was aware that he stood on its dim and indefinable threshold, he stared at Murah and Loo crying with sympathy over the old woman. But he was not thinking of them. They were only objects that helped him keep in mind the shadowy notions that troubled him. Since leaving Ho-wha he had learned more than could be used in the simple patterns of a simple life. He had become a rich storehouse of experience and the sire of events that were casting their shadow upon the future. He would not be, and could not be, as great as the lessons that had come to him. No man is ever as great as that. Discoveries had so extended his world that he was confused; and all that he could think of doing now, with the brilliance of the last hour shining full upon him, was to find a clump of bamboo and strip the vegetable between his teeth.

24

THE grandmother's wound became infected and she died, and the smell of her forced Murah to abandon her second house. Thinking they were again taking up nomadic ways, Wuh was overjoyed; and on the morning when Murah led off, trailed by the other women, he eagerly fell in, with the two older lads at his heels. But Murah did not go far. As soon as she found a spot that suited her, she began to gather materials for a third shelter.

The next morning, Wuh got ready to march again. He chose a likely direction and moved off, but when he observed that only the boys were going with him he looked back at the women. He called to them and made eager movements of walking. He pointed in the direction he wished to take. He beckoned and shouted and retraced his steps.

Murah ignored him. She had eaten her breakfast and was busy with a shelter, assisted by Loo. The vagrant impulses of the male she did not understand. There was nothing in her instincts or wishes that urged her to wander day after day and year after year; and when Wuh came over to grasp her arm she scolded him. She seized a stick and menaced him.

Wuh turned away, a baffled and unhappy man whose wanderlust was opposed by the kind of anchored life his women had chosen. He wanted to prowl, but they wanted to build nests. He wanted to find and bluff his enemies, but their way was the way of peace. It was his wish to look upon strange lands and new experiences, but they were content within the periphery of a baby-bower and its dooryard. That was the cleavage between them, and in the remote future it was to make strange social patterns of human life.

All day he sulked. In what the women did he could see no meaning and no joy. As industriously as bees, Murah and Loo hung a nest upon the boughs of a tree. If Wuh fixed his attention on their house, it was only in the inattentive and purposeless way that he might have looked at the sun. He watched them tear vines down and drag them to the tree, he heard their chattering industry, he saw them enter the house; but there was nothing in the picture that a man's mind could dwell on with joy. All day he sulked, and the two boys sensed his emotion and shared it. Three churlish and cankered males, they squatted on their haunches and slapped at insects and looked as if they had been doomed to death.

And so for Wuh the days passed until he began to wander again. The older boys usually went with him. They now had stout clubs of their own and they put them to every use which they could think of. Sometimes the three of them came upon pieces of wood where an old tree had fallen and splintered, or upon patches of loose rock, and in both of these they recognized weapons much like their own. They would lay their clubs down and pick up a cudgel or stone and examine it, but always they decided in favor of the tools they were used to.

In their wanderings they seldom had an exciting adventure. Creatures of the jungle fled before them. Occasionally they saw the red-brown flash of a forest deer or the white bands of a vanishing paca or the black fur of a giant weasel. Beasts surprised by streams often took to the water and dived or swam away, and Wuh would stare at them with curious interest; or he would gaze after a tinamou rising like a rocket from the forest floor, or a wood rail screaming across a marsh, or at toucans barking from tree tops. He was accustomed to these and countless other denizens of the jungle; and if he looked at them with fresh interest, it was because his use of a club had placed them in a new perspective. He did not think of them as enemies. They were stimuli, the moving and living things, that made him unconsciously raise his weapon to strike. Though very few creatures threatened him, and almost none dared face him, the world for him, nevertheless, was unfriendly and mysterious, and he trusted nothing in it. Many cries in the jungle made his hair and anger rise because they sounded challenging. Among the sounds of birds, the scream of the wood rail or macaw, the shriek of the parrot, or the barking of the toucan always angered him. The loudest creatures seemed to him the most menacing. The yell of a trumpeter enraged him more than sight of the deadly fer-de-lance slipping noiselessly away. The unexpected croak of a bullfrog could alarm him, but when he saw the vampire bat cross his path like a flying shadow, he did not mind at all.

It was not until late fall that he had an experience that opened another window on the future. The women were content to eat what was around them but Wuh had been going farther afield in search of juicy plants. On this day the boys had wandered off and he went alone. He crossed the tree upon the stream and entered the area where he had stolen a family from the old man. The old man himself he had forgotten long ago.

He went some distance through heavy growth and came to an outcropping of stone. There were several low ledges, lying one above another like enormous steps; and back from these, and down, stood the jungle, leaving here an area of three or four acres open to the sun. The moment Wuh came to the edge of the clearing, a dozen huge flesh-eating birds rose from the topmost ledge; and on looking up he saw many others, soaring round and round in the sky. The presence of these creatures declared to Wuh that among the rocks there was something dying or dead.

He shouted at the birds to frighten them, but they were bold scavengers. They dipped so low that he could feel the air moved by their wings and clearly see their naked legs, their talons, and their long curved beaks. Presently one and then another descended to the ledge and stood there like dirty brown sentinels. Wuh remained at the jungle's edge and screamed at them and waved his club, but those perched on the ledge did not take fright and those in the sky still soared round and round. They were stalking something up there in the ledges. Wuh was not interested in the fate of this thing, whatever it was. In these great hungry birds he felt a threat against his own life, and shouted at them because he wished to frighten them away. When one of them came so low that the air from its wings rushed down upon him, he impulsively hurled his club at it; and then at once, without pausing to consider the hazards, he ran forth to recover his club. The birds perched on the ledge rose in flight. Seeing them go, Wuh believed they were afraid of him and he became bolder.

He retrieved his club and stood in full view, with about two score of the creatures circling above him. He roared at them and beat his breast and worked himself into a terrible fury; and when one of them again came low, he ran after it as a dog will chase birds in flight. He was convinced now that these soaring monsters were afraid of him, and he filled the sky with the thunder of his defiance. In trying to get closer to them to hurl his weapon he went up the hill to the ledges, intending to climb to the summit; but suddenly in amazement he stopped.

Before him at the base of the first ledge was the old man. He was trying to hide and protect himself in a shallow recess in the stone. Wuh did not know that the man was diseased and old and almost too feeble to stand. He did not know that this was the man whose family he had taken. But he did recognize this cringing creature as a male of his own kind, and at once he challenged him and prepared to attack. Forgetting the scavengers above him, he rushed forward a few steps and felt the lust of fear and anger hot in his flesh. He was so intent on his own part that he rushed again, and still again, before observing that his foe had made no move to resist. Then Wuh cooled a little and stared curiously at him.

The old man's rheumy and terrified eyes were fixed on Wuh; but that was all. He was lying back in the recess.

Perhaps he had the strength to stand but he knew that any effort he could make would do him no good. He felt that he was doomed. The utter hopelessness in his eyes said that. The way he lay back and trembled and made no sound told even the enraged Wuh that this man intended to make no fight at all.

Cautiously, then, Wuh advanced until he was close to the old fellow, and he looked down at him, long and earnestly. What he felt it would be impossible to say; his emotions were dark and confused. But he felt no pity, no mercy, no love. He felt no urge to take the old man and lead him back to his group and care for him. But neither, on the other hand, did he feel an impulse to slay him. All that is only a part of what Wuh was feeling. His emotions were as dark as his heritage; but among them, feeble and lost and of no worth in this hour, was the very faint beginning of the notion of fellowship. He did not know that the old man was consumed by parasites within. He did not know that he was old—because Wuh had no conception of age or time. But he did sense that these vultures were waiting for his death.

When at last he looked up, he saw them soaring above him, and he rushed at them, shouting furiously. If he could have laid hands on them, he would have torn them apart. Did he feel an impulse to protect the old man? Perhaps, in the moment when he first turned away, that was the spirit that moved him; because in him, as in all living things, there was intuitive recognition of the two ways in the world, the way of life and the way of death. Out of dread, out of anxious loneliness in self, has come such fellowship as we have, and in running after the scavengers it may be that Wuh came closer to it than any man before him had come. But his interests were fickle, his memory short, and his purposes confused; and presently it seemed to him that he was chasing the creatures because they menaced his own life.

He forgot the old man. He turned away, but at the edge of the jungle he stopped and looked back as if troubled. The birds were still soaring round and round, and several of them again stood on the topmost ledge. Wuh looked at them, but the bright and sudden meaning which they had had for him, a few moments ago, was now lost. Nevertheless, when he took the trail homeward he went like one who had been chastened—like one touched by that loneliness which closes in upon all living things and prepares the way for death.